Life Doesn't Lie

DARLENE CROCKER

Life Doesn't Lie
Copyright © 2018 by Darlene Crocker

All rights reserved. No part of this publication may be reproduced, distributed, or transmitted in any form or by any means, including photocopying, recording, or other electronic or mechanical methods, without the prior written permission of the author, except in the case of brief quotations embodied in critical reviews and certain other non-commercial uses permitted by copyright law.

Tellwell
www.tellwell.ca

ISBN
978-0-2288-0412-3 (Paperback)
978-0-2288-0413-0 (eBook)

Dedicated to John, Kaitlyn and Chelsea
whose lives were fodder for this novel.

Thank you for your inspiration and love.

Some of the events in this story are unbelievably true, while others are just exaggerated.

The rest are outright lies!!

Life Doesn't Lie

JILL DAY 1

Slowly moving towards the balcony's edge, I raised my arm to wave goodbye, but no words would come. I couldn't tell if they were stuck, or if my brain was just numb or lazy. Embarrassed by my choked up response, or lack of one, I attempted to mutter through salted lips, "Please call!"

Looking up with a bewildered smirk on his face, Luke shot back, "I'm only going on a motorbike trip." From his perspective, it all looked so comical. After all, he had gone on many such trips before, and none received such an outpouring of emotion. A grunt and a nod and perhaps a nonchalant, "See ya" thrown in would have been more the routine he was expecting. "Come on Jill, I'll be back in about a week. I'll call you every night, okay?" said Luke with a weak smile, trying to reassure his worried wife.

The summer sun was still hot and sticky, not like the warm comforting sun that would come much later in the day. This was more glaring and intense, making me squirm to get out of the heat. But Luke looked so eager to get underway as he zipped up his black leather jacket and slid his hands into worn, slick, racing gloves. He was going on a biking trip to Sturgis, South Dakota with his buddies; no kids, no wife, no responsibilities required.

"Goodbye Daddy," cried little Molly as she stood on her tip toes to lean over the railing. Perching herself dangerously, she watched her father strap on his motorcycle helmet down below.

"We'll miss you Daddy," blurted Emily in her usual calm and somewhat expressionless face. "Bye!"

Trying to restrain his joy, Luke let out a concealed tweak, hesitated a few moments longer, then with a handful of revs, he was gone. Down the bumpy gravel driveway he bounced along, not looking back, just looking forward to what lay ahead.

Corralling the girls back inside the cabin, "It'll be okay. Daddy will be back," I blurted out in mock confidence, trying to convince myself. Why was I so doubtful? He always came back. He was a wonderful husband and my best friend, and he loved his little "geels" dearly, so why wouldn't he come back? Yet still I had this nagging fear that something was amiss. I couldn't pinpoint anything different about this trip from all the rest. I definitely needed to chill out.

As I moped around our Mayne Island cottage, I suddenly felt so removed from the daily tasks that were calling out to me: make the beds, get dressed, clean up the breakfast dishes and get the girls dressed and ready for the day. I couldn't help but to draw inward and try to figure out my feelings of alarm that were screaming for attention. I had so many questions.

"Mommy, can you brush my hair?" Emily asked, pushing her way onto my lap.

Oh good, I thought, she has such long hair that I'll get some mental space to think things through. But before I knew it, Molly was clamoring to get into my lap as well. Emily then shoved her out and onto the floor, screaming followed, then hits, retaliating pushes and then all out war. No such mental reprieve for me. Oh well, I convinced myself, this is just nuts anyway. What am I fretting myself for? He'll be just fine Jill.

The day went on, taking shape as any other day with a two year old and a five year old. Make snack, clean up, go for walks, make lunch, nap time for Molly, referee more squabbles, etc., etc...... Indeed the mundane had returned to our summer life on Mayne Island. Before I knew it, one day had turned into the next.

LUKE DAY 1

I couldn't escape fast enough! Not that I was eager to leave Jill and the girls, or even Mayne Island, I was just so damn keen to get this motor biking trip underway. I could sense this big stupid grin under my helmet. I made my way to the ferry terminal and got on no problem. That was the great thing about motorcycles; they always had room to squeeze you on, so you needn't worry about reserving a space. I parked my 1100 Kawasaki on the lower car deck, removed my riding gloves and helmet and proceeded to clip my helmet onto my bike. But I thought better of that. Wouldn't want a repeat of what happened in Amsterdam in 1986, no ...I didn't want this trip ruined before it had even got started.

That particular trip began innocently enough, Jill and I on ur old red 800cc BMW. We were on a cross Europe motorcycle trip, which was the adventure of a lifetime for me. We d saved up forever and the day eventually came when we ed our bike in the cargo department of our plane as we cotland. We then traveled through England, France, tzerland, Germany, Belgium, Denmark and were on that fateful day. We had decided to watch an in Vaughn Park in Amsterdam. Parking our le the park, I had clipped my helmet onto the hankfully decided to carry hers into the park e theatre group was quite entertaining and we were fully engrossed in the show, but meanwhile, some thief used a screw driver to carve out the bike's ignition and took off with our Beemer, helmet and all. As we left the park at twilight, I originally thought I had just misplaced the bike – forgot exactly which park entrance I had parked it. Jill and I split up and tore up and down alleys looking. It obviously was not a well thought out plan as I could just imagine Jill confronting some three hundred pound rough looking dude, "Hey you! Stop!! Give me back that bike!!" It hadn't taken long however, to realize what had happened and as luck would have it, a passerby, seeing our plight, offered to drive us to the police station. As we walked in to report the missing bike, a cop was typing up a report at his desk.

Coincidentally, our bike had just been found by an undercover police officer, who upon seeing the carved out ignition and Canadian license plate, realized it was a stolen bike, so he hopped on and rode it to the nearest police station.

The cop, who was almost finished his duty, offered to drive us to that other station, as he lived nearby. Seeing that red BMW was a welcome relief, however the helmet was missing. I should have taken it with me as Jill had done with hers. So we had our bike, but they wouldn't let us ride away without a helmet; like Canada, it was the law there. Seeing that it was quite late and all bike shops were closed, we started to panic. It didn't help matters that the Bed and Breakfast we were staying in was a ways out of town and the last train there had already left the city. To make matters even worse, the B & B hosts were leaving on holidays early the next morning and all our luggage was still there.

Out of desperation, Jill had asked if they had any old lost and found helmets—and as it turned out, they did! It was a dark green full faced helmet with a bright, large marijuana leaf painted on the back. We couldn't stop laughing as I tried to shove this helmet over my large head; it wouldn't fit. However, we had no choice, so everyone pushed and pulled and banged the top until the chin guard covered my nose; that was the best we could do. Thankfully, the cops let us drive off with that, even though there was no way that would meet legal standards. As it turned out I had to wear that stupid thing for two days until we could find a shop with a helmet large enough for my huge head. We sure got a lot of stares as if we were some pot smoking bums, which there were a lot of in Amsterdam...but not riding BMW motorcycles. What a memory!

Standing there now beside my Kawasaki, there was no way I was about to clip my helmet on, so I locked up my bike and then just stood there. I couldn't believe my luck that Jill had released me from family responsibilities—I was actually going on this biking trip with my buddies. Relishing the moment, I again grinned and looked up to see two guys drooling over my bike.

"How many cc's you got on this here puppy?" one of them asked.

"1100," I replied.

"That's a real rice rocket!" the other guy chipped in. He glanced over at his buddy and winked.

"Yeah, it's a sweet ride," I said as I tried to figure out their intentions. After what seemed like a rather long examination of my bike, they finally left. I nodded and waited around for a bit and then left for the stairs myself......with my helmet.

I decided to pass on the children's section on the upper deck of the ferry. No need to listen to screaming kids if I didn't have to. My walk was taking on a bounce, even with all this heavy leather armor I had on. I chose the adult, quiet reading area of the ferry and I drank in the solitude. The waves were drumming out some sort of rock beat and I found myself hammering my thumbs along on my knees. It could have been some Van Morrison tune, or maybe Dire Straits. I think it was actually "Night Train" by Bruce Cockburn. His music always appeared at memorable moments of my life. He is my personal anthem that I just live my life along to. I was lost in the rhythm of the locomotive beat of the song, when before long, we had pulled into Tsawwassen. Gotta like those direct sails that skip Galiano Island altogether.

 I disembarked ahead of the pack, as usual with bikes, and headed for the number ten highway to Chilliwack: our main home out in the country. It was sunny and warm and I found myself singing: "Life is a highway and I'm going to ride it all night long", a classic Cockrane song.

 As I passed other bikers on the road, we gave each other the customary two finger salute. "Shit, this is gonna be fun," I thought to myself still grinning.

 I got to Chilliwack and as I pulled into the driveway, I was reminded of the peeling paint that needed my attention, and the lawn that needed to be cut. Walking into the hollow house, I saw the pile of bills on the floor by the mail slot. This house was one huge and constant reminder of maintenance jobs that infringed upon my play time. Thankfully it was early in the afternoon, with plenty of hours remaining to organize for the trip tomorrow, but best of all, I had the better part of the day to tinker on my bike—gotta get it all tuned and shined up.

 Looking around in the garage, I could see so many half finished jobs: the Ducatti needed new forks, the Beemer had a bent frame, my racing bike still had that last crash written all over it and the pile of dirt bikes....well they were just that—a pile of parts. And what was I going to do with that side car? Yes, I had my projects alright, but they were for another day. I had to focus on getting the Kawi ready. Flicking on the radio, I searched for some tunes to tinker to but instead was assaulted by news of mysterious deaths, missing persons and awful road conditions, none of which I wanted to hear. So instead I decided to give Mike and Rod a quick call to confirm plans for tomorrow and they were just as eager to get this trip on the road—literally. Apparently, Rod's brother, Larry wanted to join the crew. I didn't know him but he had more riding experience than the other two, so it was one less that I'd have to babysit on the road. Not that I minded, I actually took pride in the fact that I had so many riding years under my belt. I would show these guys how motorcycle touring was done.

That night I grilled myself a great big steak and sat on the back deck drinking too much of my home brew wine. I do think my Shiraz is better than store bought, but I have to work on my whites though. I hadn't got two blue ribbons at the Mayne Island Fall Fair for nothing. No, my wine was now award winning. I beamed!

JILL DAY 2

Mayne Island was a place of peace and rest, and I was so grateful to be there. In the midst of a cluster of islands off of Vancouver's west coast, it was small and charming. About a thousand people lived there during the winter, but that number doubled in summer. The once hippy paradise had been slowly taken over by yuppie baby boomers wanting to escape the busy city scene. Historically, even the gold rush diggers, rowing from Victoria would stop for reprieve from the sea, on route to New Westminster. The island would then magically lull all its inhabitants to peaceful sleep, as they listened to the waves of the Salish Sea roll in. It had become our retreat too since we bought our cabin there two years ago. Suffering from postpartum depression after Molly's birth, I focussed on a dream to get me through and since growing up with a summer cottage on one of Manitoba's great lakes was a wonderful childhood memory for me, I wanted to duplicate that for my own children. So our cabin was the fulfillment of that dream. It was, however, my dream—not necessarily Luke's. He would have preferred to travel the world on a motorcycle; that would be his bliss. But, being the generous husband that he was, he went along and committed to buying this piece of paradise.

Perched in the Strait of Georgia, it looked right across to Vancouver. It was magical watching all the city lights reflect upon the sea at night. Our beach was comprised of large sandstone boulders tossed every which way, with leaning Arbutus trees overhead. There were numerous tidal pools to investigate all the sea creatures and Molly and Emily were forever trying to capture the poor little critters and inspect them, dissect them, collect them or perform whatever science experiment they could think of on them. It always amazed me how cruel they could be. Like the time they put a small crab inside their pink plastic Barbie RV and decided to take it for a ride. Realizing what was causing all the splashes, as this bright bubble gum vehicle smashed into some rocks, I hastened to retrieve the poor crab from further torture.

The girls weren't total monsters, however. We once found an abandoned seal down on our beach and I instructed the girls to leave it alone as its mother would soon return for it, but she never did. After several days, Emily was throwing chunks of peanut butter sandwiches at it, which it would feebly sniff. It liked tuna better. Before you knew it, Luke was down there with the girls enthusiastically feeding the seal warm milk from an old syrup bottle. Looking back now, I realize how dangerous that was, letting the girls get so close to a wild creature like that. When we would call the girls in for lunch, the seal would eagerly follow, until Luke would pick it up and recklessly throw it back into the inhabiting sea. It would cry and quickly saunter back onto the flat rocks. Emily wanted it to live in our bathtub! Our one and only bathtub!! She became so protective over it and would often stay crouched down with it on the beach below, and as hungry turkey vultures and menacing eagles swarmed low overhead, she would jump up and furiously scream, waving her arms frantically in the air to ward off these lurking predators. We tried to tell her that these majestic birds would not eat a helpless seal, but we were ignorantly mistaken.

About a hundred feet off our shore there were a couple of rocky, moss covered reefs that, on any given day, and especially in low tide, would be overtaken by at least fifty harbour seals. Soaking up the sun and camouflaged against the sandstone reef, these seals would just bask away the day until the dinner time tide would gradually cover the reefs completely and the overtaken seals would have to swim away.

One warm summer afternoon however, a lone eagle sat on the highest point of the larger reef waiting—just waiting. We could hear all its hungry baby eaglets chirping from their nest high up in a neighboring pine. Sure enough, a young seal pup swam up, or was washed up to this reef, when suddenly the eagle extended its talons and pulled the defenseless seal out of the water. The larger seals that were close by immediately swam off the reef, but others just ignored what was about to happen. The eagle proceeded to strike this little seal with its beak, over and over, until it could grab some flesh and rip it out. Before long, the eagle's white breast was covered in blood as it gorged itself, for several hours, on seal meat. Once it had its fill, it attempted to fly up to its nest, to bring sustenance to its squawking babies. It appeared, however, to struggle to get airborne, as each time it would fly up, it would drop suddenly toward the water, before making its way back to the reef. The eagle tried several times to no avail, until it finally resigned itself and just sat there beside the pile of torn and bloodied flesh, which once was a seal. The eagle didn't consume any more—he just guarded his catch. Finally, many hours later, the eagle was able to successfully fly up to its nest and quiet down his starving brood. Eventually, the tide covered the reef and the seal remnants were washed away but we could trace its whereabouts as swarms of seagulls and turkey vultures grazed on this floating buffet.

Binoculars came in handy to watch all the wildlife around us and one look at this feasting eagle was enough to convince Emily that she couldn't leave her new found seal companion alone on the beach. It became a real problem as Luke had to drag two screaming girls into the cabin at night; they couldn't bear to leave the seal alone. The fact that it cried all night didn't help either. Finally, after about five days, it looked ill; it was listless and weak and its eyes were no longer alive. We called the Vancouver Aquarium and they were willing to rescue the seal and try to restore it to health, but we had to get it to them. We contemplated putting it in a box, loading it into our half ton truck and catching a ferry over to Vancouver, but this was expensive and we weren't sure if the seal would survive the trip. Fortunately, a neighbor was heading back to the city the day after and had agreed to transport the seal to the aquarium. But at five in the morning, Luke had a strange feeling, slid out of bed and lumbered down to the beach to find the seal had grown whitish in color and was laden with insects crawling over its dried and cracked skin; it was dead! Luke slowly picked it up and reluctantly threw it into the frigid sea. He knew the girls would be devastated but what else was he to do? His heavy footsteps revealed his heavy heart. Crawling back into bed, I could see the tears. I didn't say anything.

The girls got over their departed friend much quicker than I thought they would. Besides, they were now trying to befriend one of the many deer that fed in our yard every day. They were everywhere! I loved to garden, but that wasn't really an option on this island, unless I chose to barricade everything I planted with chicken wire. And because hunting deer was illegal on this island and there were no cougars to reduce their numbers, they roamed freely and courageously. They weren't like the deer in Chilliwack, where we lived primarily, who would be so skittish and afraid of any person, noise or movement. No, these deer would just look at you as you walked by, continuing to munch on their greens. They were so calm, you could almost touch them—almost!!

It was outright torture whenever my brother-in-law came over to the island to visit; he loved to hunt deer, but wasn't permitted to here. What I saw to be heaven—the wild animals co-existing harmoniously with man, he only saw as dinner. It made for some very interesting and passionate debates.

Indeed, this was a stimulating environment. The cabin itself inspired me with its tall vaulted ceilings and open spaces. It had large windows, thirty three of them, to take in the evening glow of the sun, as it too fell asleep on the sea. This island A-frame with its huge deck was indeed a gift—a sense of serenity, security and solitude survived here, even thrived. When we did feel like company, we would invite friends over from the mainland. Sure, we did meet some fellow islanders, but they were all weekenders or summer home dwellers like us. The native islanders tended to stick together. The problem was you couldn't count on others being here, it was all a matter of whim, and of course whether you could get a ferry reservation or not, which was a prized commodity when you lived spontaneously. No, this island favored planners!

It was turning out to be a gloriously warm day and so a trek with the girls was in order. Walking to Dinner Bay Park, I was struck by what they had chosen to wear that particular day. Emily donned one of her frilly dresses, berry red with ivy green velvet trim. I think it was a hand me down from one of the cousins. She adored this little girly dress, even if it was a relic of past Christmases. She had chosen to pair this with big pink winter boots—seasonal appropriateness obviously not an issue. Picking up a walking stick to complete her ensemble – one that resembled a princess warrior – Emily marched on.

Molly, though, was a fashion experiment! She strove to dress herself independently, like her older sister, and so often chose to put on whatever happened to be on the floor of her room. It didn't matter that it was filthy with yesterday's spaghetti dinner splashed all over it, or green grass stained, or ill-fitting or not color matched; she just didn't care. On this day, she had chosen navy blue sweat pants, worn inside out, together with an orange doll dress that she somehow managed to get over her head, to wear as a top. It was sleeveless and ripped. She found some black patent dress shoes, but no socks. She would parade down the road with an infectious smile, oblivious to what I, or anyone else thought of her attire. She was passionate about her choices and I lauded her courage and independence.

Being an educator by profession, it meant instilling in your charges self-reliance, since you could never teach a whole class of kids, when each was clamoring for your help, afraid to take a step on their own. Instead you cheered them on, no matter how clumsy their attempts, for you knew that eventually they would improve and become proficient at whatever skill they were attempting to acquire. Since I had been a teacher much longer than a parent, I too cheered on my girls' fumbled independence at dressing or feeding themselves. Sure, friends and relatives shook their heads at me when they saw the explosions of food on Molly's highchair tray, and the wall behind her for out in black leather, his uniform of choice, his exterior looked harder, meaner, more slick. But with his cop cut blond hair tucked into his full face helmet, rather than a black Beanie cap, he looked more like the elementary school teacher that he was, than an American Harley biker type. He was riding a Kawasaki, yet a BMW motorcycle would have suited him more. No doubt about it, Luke had class. It came from his upper middle class upbringing but it shone through no matter how humble of a facade he put on. He was just such an expert chameleon. I remember once someone said about Luke, "Would the real Luke Connor stand up," to which Luke replied, "I don't know who the real Luke Connor is." He became all things to all men, but he did it with charming humor and class.

The truth is, Luke never grew up, which explains his obsession with motorcycles. He just liked to play and have fun – a Peter Pan of sorts. I was content for him to be on this bike trip, this is where Luke came to life. He not only rode bikes, but dissected them, read about them, traded them, collected them and dreamt about future trips on one or the other of them. When we were newly married, Luke spent our wedding gift money on a new bike, not just any bike, but a BMW that he had always wanted but could never afford as a single. Funnily enough, I did not object back then. Fast forward twelve years and many bike trips since, our two kids arrived. Eventually, Luke purchased and rebuilt a two seater side car so that he could take the whole family on bike trips. What a sight it was to see wee Molly with a huge helmet on, peering over the windshield of the sidecar, alongside Emily who was so aloof and nonchalant about it all. She was already a teenager in a five year old's body. Even our Christmas cards depicted us in that one horse open sleigh. Indeed, it gave Luke great joy to include his family with his passion of motorcycling. But this particular trip was different. This was his annual shot of testosterone, riding at racing speed with a bunch of guys, where evenings would be spent discussing spark plugs and tires, racing oil and sore rear ends. No place for the geels or myself. We were grateful to be left behind.

LUKE DAY 2

The next morning was full of anticipation, as I didn't need an alarm clock to get me out of bed; I had jumped out running! After a shit, shower and shave I was off to meet the boys. You would never know that Mike had to bug me for two months, before I would commit to going on this bike trip. I was just so undecided for some reason. A week beforehand, I finally relented and gave myself permission to go and make merry.

Upon entering the Tim Horton's parking lot, I could see a lot of teeth; we were like a bunch of little rotters being let out for recess—just plain giddy!

Mike was riding a Honda Shadow, 900cc. He wore a spankin brand new black leather jacket, black boots and jeans. He was a blond, straight looking guy with short hair and a very trimmed mustache—a relic from the seventies. Computer geek by trade, he was a nice enough guy, I had met him at a neighborhood church. He was a new biker, and since we lived nearby, we often met for rides out to Harrison or Mission or even Sumas. When Rod told him about this trip, he was in.

Rod, was riding a black Harley Davidson and wearing a small black beanie cap and black leathers with plenty of zippers everywhere. He looked slick! This was a far cry from his usual Loomis uniform and truck that he drove by day. The youngest in the group, he had been the instigator. A close friend of Mike's, he planned this excursion, as he had taken this same journey to motorcycle mecca—Sturgis—before. But since he had been riding only a couple of seasons, he was a relative newbie to the sport.

The senior member of our clan was Larry, Rod's older brother. He also rode a Harley and was decked out in black leathers with tassels flying. He too donned a beanie cap for a helmet. As a relic of the sixties, he had many motorcycle tales to tell. He had a long silver pony tail and weathered face which didn't match his profession as a mining engineer. But he was retired now—lucky guy!!

All of us had families to escape. Although Larry's kids were full grown, the rest of us had wives and kids still at home to be accountable to. But this trip wasn't about any of them; it was about us. Just like that crazy movie: Wild Hogs—we were just a bunch of crazy middle aged men seeking some adventure.

That first day, we hit the freeway heading west, crossed the U.S. border at Sumas into Washington State, and then hit the open highway heading south. We were cruising along with Rod and I each vying for the lead position, followed by Mike and then Larry taking the back. It was like a flock of birds flying in V formation alternating the lead to take the wind. When the lead bird tired, he flew to the back of the flock and a new leader emerged to buff the wind. Except in our situation Rod always wanted to lead, after all he had planned this whole trip in the first place. But I naturally took the lead as well. This must have looked rather silly and juvenile to Mike and Larry who gladly brought up the tail end.

Anyways, as we played cat and mouse on the 401, it just happened to be Rod out front when he spotted a dead possum on the road. Luckily he spotted it in time and veered around it. Seeing him swerve, I took note and followed suit. Mike was behind me and unfortunately hadn't noticed the dead chunk of flesh splattered in the middle of the highway, and consequently rode right over the possum, tossing its dead weight into the air with his back tire. Poor Larry hadn't stood a chance. Before he could swerve or even duck, he was wearing this bloody rodent now chopped up into body parts. He had blood and guts hit his chest dead on. His open faced helmet offered no protection from the beheaded animal as it got sandwiched under his visor. As happenstance would have it, Larry had his mouth open in full yawn when he got a spit full of fur. His windshield fairing was covered in yellow, green and red slime that slithered down toward his front tire. Swerving to a stop, Larry, who was now in complete shock, wobbled off to the shoulder of the highway. It took a while, but eventually we realized that Larry wasn't behind us and so we pulled over as well. We made our U turns and slowly came upon this mess of a biker. We didn't know if we should laugh or cry in disbelief. Larry was actually shaking in shock. I quickly dismounted and helped Larry dismount. A few old hankies would not do this clean up job justice—a gas station was definitely needed. Spotting an Arco up ahead, we slowly sauntered in and labored away the hours picking fur balls and bone pieces out of Larry's bike spokes. His leather jacket zipper was encrusted with bloody guts and there was even possum parts stuck up Larry's nostrils. It was all very gross, yet comical at the same time. Usually little boys like things like this: the grosser the better. But this was too much for any of us grown men to take. Trying not to gag, we meticulously cleaned up Larry and his bike as best as could be expected but like curious little rascals, we were enamored with all the crevices that contained recognizable body parts.

"Hey look," Mike pointed out, "there's a claw jammed into Larry's saddlebag." Mike was so proud of his find, holding up this disheveled possum finger high in the air.

Poor Larry just sat there mesmerized still trying to recount what had happened. He wasn't laughing or crying or saying anything. He was still in shock. So we three continued excavating fur, teeth, eyeballs, legs, but mostly unrecognizable chunks of bloodied meat. It was surprising how one small animal could explode into so many pieces and result in such coverage of Larry and his bike. You would have thought he had just hit a moose by all the gore splattered everywhere imaginable. It could have been a lot worse though had Larry lost control of his vehicle but luckily he had his wits about him and maintained control of his bike throughout this ordeal.

Larry wanted to keep riding, oddly enough, I guess to speed up his entry into a well-deserved bathtub. Understandable indeed!! So we hit the highway again at full throttle, watching the road with extra diligence. After about an hour Larry indicated it was time to find a hotel for the night. As luck would have it, all we could find was No Vacancy signs littering the highways. Disheartened, Larry conceded that anything with a bath would do.

"Hey guys, that campground has a hot tub," yelled Mike through his visor. It was better than nothing so we followed Mike down the paved driveway into this KOA commercial enterprise. Nothing like our back to nature provincial parks in Canada, I thought. But poor Larry was the focus now.

We paid our dues and located our camping spot and slowly started to unload. Larry peeled off his sticky jacket and looked around for the hot tub. Stripping off his clothes as he tip toed up to the communal tub, leaving only his underwear on, Larry slowly climbed the stairs leading up to the tub and then gingerly lowered his body into the steaming wash. The tub was full of onlookers, surprisingly most were young and not the usual KOA crowd. We three stood in disbelief as Larry oohed and awwwed.

"Hey Larry, going to rinse all that possum guts off, are you?" Rod shot out, attempting to embarrass his older brother.

"Well I don't see you volunteering to lick it clean, now do I?" Larry yelled back.

With that exchange, the fellow hot tubbers all stared at Larry with disdain and then glanced at each other. They weren't sure what to make of it. Were they kidding? A few grunts and groans could be heard in unison as people started to vacate the hot tub. Shaking their heads and lining up for the exit stairs, each fellow hot tubber left in disgust.

Finally Larry laughed. He laughed and laughed, belting out his holler with glee. I had never seen such a display of delight. It reminded me of a commercial on TV advertising some diarrhea product, where this guy is in the hot tub with a bunch of hot babes and his friends arrive and ask very loudly how the Imodium is working. The looks on the girls' faces was the same: disbelief, disgust, followed by an urgency to leave. But seeing Larry laugh gave us boys the permission to crack up as well—finally. We were waiting to take our cues from him and now he saw how ridiculous this all had been. We all chuckled and snorted, recounting Larry's face as we rode up. Bragging over who found what lodged in where, took up the evening. But no matter, one by one we joined Larry in that hot tub. Many hours and wrinkles later we stumbled out and made our way to our campsite.

It had been a cooking hot day riding in our leathers. I also had kept having problems with my brake light—it stayed on all the time which boiled my battery dry. I had to keep it disconnected but then I couldn't start my bike. Everyone was pretty bagged, so after setting up our two tents, they all crashed. It gave me the chance to rewire my brake light, as I tinkered late into the black evening.

Rummaging through my things in the tent that I shared with Mike, I collected a mitt full of change and headed for a pay phone to call Jill and the girls.

"How's it going momma?" I asked my wife of almost twenty years. I knew Jill hated to be called that but she was such a little mother—to everybody!

"Where are you?" Jill questioned, or should I say interrogated me. She probably had already regretted consenting to this trip.

"Chuckanut Drive—remember this place?" I asked, laughing out loud. How could she forget the time we had camped there, together with our friends Tim and Christine, only to find we had pitched our tents right beside a railway track that we hadn't seen in the dark when we had arrived. Then, in the middle of sleep, an alarmingly loud noise and a bursting bright light awoke us so suddenly that we all screamed and scrambled out of our tents, not sure of whether this was the second coming or what. It had felt like the train was about to go through the middle of the tent. Now that was a rude awakening! Then to add insult to injury, in the morning we found ourselves staring down, with bleary eyes, some pesky crows who had stolen our pancake mix out of our saddle bags and were guarding it up in a tree.

"Yeah, I remember." After a pause and a daydream, "Hey, call earlier tomorrow so Emily and Molly can talk to you. They've already gone to bed," Jill admonished me.

"Well I had better go before the operator comes on telling me to put more coins into this phone—which I don't have. I'll talk to you tomorrow. Bye Jill."

Feeling better now that I had checked in with the boss, I decided it was time for some shut eye. I took a whiz beside the tent and then crawled in for the night.

SIX YEARS EARLIER

Death came calling at the Bancroft household. Fred and Lindsey Bancroft lived six houses down from Luke and Jill Connor on Silver Drive in Chilliwack. The two families hadn't known each other well, but they were neighborly, nonetheless. They would wave and say hello when they passed on the road. They shared the same sidewalk, so would sometimes run into each other and exchange niceties. The Bancrofts had four young, rambunctious boys all close together in age and you would often see them riding their speedy tricycles on the road. In the winter, Fred and his tireless boys would set up their hockey nets, closing the road off temporarily, and have a good Canadian game of hockey. Sometimes other neighbor kids would join them, but mostly it was just their little family playing together. They were close.

One warm summer evening, Fred had just dropped off his oldest son at Karate lessons and was on his way back home. He had decided to stop in at a convenience store for a Coke. He parked his SUV and was getting out, when he noticed a gang of youth squabbling over something.

With four boys, Fred was used to bickering but unfortunately, not this kind. As he reached for the store's door handle, his intuition wrongly directed him to intervene. So instead of going into the 7-eleven, he let the door close on him, and walked toward the group of boys. They were a rather rough looking bunch of teenagers, with a couple possibly being in their early twenties. Fred walked into the middle of them.

"What's the problem here?" he asked with an innocent smile.

"Take off old man!" one of them said, pushing Fred aside.

"You're blocking the door and causing a raucous out here," Fred announced, "and for what?"

"None of your bloody business," the tallest one yelled.

"Hey break it up," Fred said, returning to the middle and pushing the boys apart.

Just then, one of the smaller, scrappy fellows pulled a knife and stabbed Fred in the gut. Falling to the ground, he reached his arm up to them for support. But none was given. The boys quickly split the scene and left Fred in a puddle on the pavement. The night staff, upon seeing the boys flee, knew something was amiss and came running outside. They discovered Fred lying there in agony, with his limp arm holding his bloody jacket over his punctured wound. A call was made to 911, but apparently it was too late; the damage had already been done. Fred died on route to the hospital. He had lost a lot of blood and was in shock and just couldn't pull through.

Lindsey got the fateful call from the police that dreadful night. Throwing her three boys in the car and picking up her eldest at his Karate lesson on the way, they headed for the hospital to identify Fred's body. It was him alright! They were numb and confused. How could this happen? He was just getting himself a drink. He was a kind, gentle father who wouldn't hurt anyone. He was barely forty. The

Bancroft family, or what remained of it, returned home that miserable night and soon the whole street was mourning with them. Six years ago, six houses down, Death had come calling!

JILL DAY 3

The next day came quickly enough as I awoke to screams of "I told you not to touch my things. Now look, you broke it. I'm going to tell mommy on you," ranted Emily, testing her vocal strength.

"Waaaah Waaaah!" was Molly's only recourse. What other defense did she have?

I needed some coffee. This is when I missed Luke the most. The morning coffee routine was full of ritual and tradition and ceremony with Luke at the helm making it. When I made it, it was just coffee. No worshiping of coffee bean aroma at the coffee urn with me. Nope. Any cup will do, any bean will suffice. Just got to get that caffeine pumping through my veins ASAP to deal with all this screaming.

"You that room," I pointed to Molly as I directed her to her bedroom. "And you", I pointed to Emily, "go to my bedroom. And shut the door. Time out!" I yelled. I hate waking up this way. When Luke is here, he's always up before I am and can redirect their little energies before they escalate into THIS! But now I must deal with it. How many days did he say he would be gone? A week at least anyway. What am I going to do to keep these little boxing bunnies de-energized? Maybe I'll call Christine and ask her over for a few days. Between her kids and mine, the fireworks can be very exciting, not to mention an entertaining distraction from what still lingers on my mind.

Finding the cell phone, I fumbled through my old worn address book to find Christine's phone number in Victoria. She must have at least two pages of different numbers and addresses in here, I thought. After twenty years of friendship, life had dealt her some moves. We had met in Red Deer, Alberta where Luke and I both began our teaching careers. Together with her husband at the time, Tim, we became immediate friends. We especially loved to holiday together and that often meant motorcycle trips. Even after we moved to Chilliwack to further our careers, we kept in touch as both Tim and Christine moved to Victoria to complete their university degrees. Unfortunately, as some marriages go, they split, but thankfully our friendship with Christine did not.

"Hi Christine, it's Jill," I enthused into the phone.

"Well, well, well! How are you?" Christine responded full of cheer.

"I'm fine now that I'm talking to you. I'm over on Mayne and Luke has gone off on another one of his bike trips. Was wondering if you and the kiddies could come keep me company for a few days?"

"Let's see," Christine mused as she pondered her crazy and hectic schedule. "I can come actually, but...I don't have the kids this week, they're with Tim," she threw my way.

"Oh!" I muttered, "But you can still come though? That's great! Which ferry will you be on?" I was instantly feeling relieved.

"I'll be there at 5:00 tonight," she said matter of factly. "I'll walk on so you will need to come pick me up if that's okay."

"It would be my pleasure," I quipped.

"See you then," she sang back.

Life Doesn't Lie

"Cheerio," was my favored reply to my friend from the English city of Victoria. Not that either of us had an accent, but we liked to pretend, although she was better at it than me. As I sipped my morning drip I let out a relief call. Then I remembered my two munchkins fuming in their respective rooms. I had better let them out or at least throw them a carrot for breakfast, I deliberated to myself.

After a rather uneventful day, we jumped into the truck and headed for the ferry terminal to pick up Christine. The downhill drive, which took all of five minutes was a roller coaster ride, picking up speed as we went. Driving that big truck, I got airborne even when not deliberate and the squeals in the back seat let me know how much they loved the speed. Just like their father, I thought, shaking my head. As we approached the ferry terminal, it looked busier than usual. There were lines of traffic going in every direction. This was one of the larger terminals, with two berths, so we got ferry transfer traffic here as well. It was quite odd when you thought about it, considering we were such a small island compared to the other gulf islands. But I guess it was due to the fact that we were so central, with Saturna Island right behind us, Galiano just across Active Pass and the Penders right beside us, it made sense to transfer here.

As I waited for Christine's boat to come in I couldn't help but think about the days of yore, before terminals were built. Steam boats would come through Active pass and then just slow down so that the passengers, in their long dresses, together with their animals in tow, could jump over the side of the boat and wade into shore. Picturing the reverse made me laugh even more so, imagining how they would slow down to pick up passengers, waist deep in the freezing ocean, holding a chicken over their head, and just waiting as the steamboat glided into its approach. To think we complained about ferry travel these days!!

Lost in thought, I hadn't seen the ferry coming in to dock. I just heard the shrill voice over the loud speaker announcing their arrival. Peering through the masses, as all the foot passengers disembarked, I noticed color—vivid color. Christine personified! I was so glad! She wasn't called Porta-Party for nothing as her colorful clothes and even more vibrant personality can zap the dullest of days.

"Look at you darling," she snapped at me in her playful English snooty accent.

All I thought was: Yeah-look at me in my dark green shorts and black tank top. I felt so dull next to her. She was decked out in a vibrant red dress with Spanish sayings splashed all over it. Her blond curly hair was done in true Marilyn Munroe fashion. Her funky black hat, gold boots and stone jewelry completed her look, yet I almost needed sunglasses to diffuse her glazing personality. Although I welcomed her sunshine, it reminded me of something, but I forgot what.

Fetching myself from my pensive stare I asked, "How are you darling?" Playing along in less than an English accent, "I'm so glad you came". We gave each other a warm embrace as only long-time friends can give.

I motioned her towards the truck where the seat was reverberating with two bouncing jelly beans for daughters. Swooping them both into her arms at once, I felt their excitement. "Christine, Christine!" they chanted in unison. Emily and Molly were again energized. We drove back from the ferry terminal towards our cabin on the hill all chatting away—happy talk! Let the party begin!

The first order of the evening was food—of course. What shall we stir up for dinner? There's no point preparing a meal before Christine arrives, no—with her, cooking is an event to be shared. Looking through the fridge we mused about the possibilities. Then she pulled out a surprise.

"Look what I brought," she said playfully as she slammed down this cute little brown antique looking suitcase onto the counter. As she opened it up, Molly and Emily craned their necks to see what it could possibly be. Crammed into this case was a culinary treasure: a collection of bottles of assorted spices. Who else would travel, as a foot passenger on a ferry, with a suitcase of spices but Christine? "I have this wonderful recipe for Moroccan rice, for which I'm sure you wouldn't have the spices," she lamented.

It's true, for although this cabin had a fully modernized kitchen, chili powder, oregano, seasoning salt and pepper would have been all that comprised my spice chest. Sorry, no cumin or coriander here. So, that was that! We had Moroccan rice with roasted pistachio nuts and dried cranberries, curried chicken, and salted and oiled eggplant slices, lightly sauteed. I think the French have it: aubergine, rather than eggplant, definitely gives the vegetable credence.

After that sumptuous meal—we have a history of such meals together—we reminisced of motorcycle adventures we shared many lives ago, before divorce was even mentioned in her household. Molly and Emily loved these stories, any stories, and so Christine and I talked the night away, until our voices were quiet and the batteries were removed from our little bunnies. Sleep came over us all. I hadn't even noticed that the phone hadn't rung that evening.

LUKE DAY 3

We got an early start the next day, peeling out of the tent by at least 10:30. I'm sure it had to be noon by the time we cooked up some breakfast on the cook stove and packed up the tents and all. It amazed me how meticulously everything had to be placed into the saddle bags in order to fit it all. Clothing space was limited and therefore had to be worn and re-worn until it stunk...and then maybe worn yet some more. Rolling each item meant less wrinkles and also enabled you to cram more into each side bag. A pillowcase was brought along and then stuffed each night with smelly clothes, which worked great for your pillow. On the back of my bike was a small trunk where I stored my cooking pots and stove, a few metal dishes, cutlery, salt and pepper, a small bottle of dish soap and a dish cloth: a portable kitchen. In the front of my bike, on top of my gas tank, sat my tank bag, which contained my wallet, camera, matches, maps, extra riding gloves and a rain suit. Behind me, on my seat, I had a tent in a bag, a rolled up Therm-a-Rest and my sleeping bag, all held in with several bungee cords. So getting packed up each morning took plenty of time, because if you rushed, it wouldn't all fit. Then you had to start all over, so it paid to be methodical.

Once we were all geared up, Mike, Rod, Larry and I hit some back roads and then onto highway twenty, heading due east. Even though Rod had done this trip before, I seemed to take the lead. We mostly rode in single file as Mike and Rod still tended to take the turns quite wide. My bike just loved to cruise at about one hundred and sixty kilometers per hour, but the boys couldn't keep up, so I slowed to their more comfortable speed of one hundred and ten. It's not that their bikes couldn't get up the clicks, they just preferred a slower ride, being newer riders as they were.

We stopped for a late lunch at some roadside Mexican eatery, before we emerged all belching and farting. Male bonding I liked to call it! We were heading across the state border into Idaho and then that's when we got crazy. Every time we stopped for gas, and that's often when you're riding a Harley with a spit sized gas tank, one of the guys would start talking western. I think the word Idaho just made us laugh after a while.

"So you boys wanna call it a night or yer good fa some more this here ridin?" Mike would ask in his best John Wayne.

""No, I'se a wantin to slap some more leather," Rod would answer strutting around his bike to reach the gas pump.

With hands, ready for the draw, Larry would crack a lazy smile and pretend to blow off his pistol, which was just a gas nozzle in disguise.

Yep, this was downright entertaining, watching these grown men make funny. I joined in by spurring my machine on and slapping her backside, as if my Kawi was some horse and I the cowboy holding the reins. We kept this up for several more hours, until we hit Coeur d'Alene, Idaho. Somehow our country and western talk didn't fit in with this French sounding place. We contemplated speaking French, but that was too much like school. We eventually found a KOA campground and decided to set up for the night.

After a dinner of weenie and beans, I decided I had better find a pay phone and call Jill. I looked through my tank bag, my wallet and jeans' pockets for loose change but couldn't find any. I thought I'd try collect calling. Meandering around the campground, looking for a pay phone, I became disgusted at all the RVs everywhere. This wasn't camping. It reminded me of a Harley Davidson ad I once saw. It had a picture of an oversized armchair with doilies on each arm, a floor lamp and a stereo system set up nearby, all set on a large platform. The slogan was: IF YOU WANT THE COMFORTS OF HOME.... STAY THERE! It was making fun of the Honda Gold Wing crowd no doubt, who traveled with sound systems, heated vests, large padded seats and walkie talkies between rider and passenger helmets.

But here we were surrounded by satellite dishes and bumped out recreational vehicles. There were no people anywhere; everyone was in their abodes microwaving their camp meals and singing along with their karaoke TV sets. Marshmallows were being roasted on propane stoves and cappuccino machines had replaced cowboy coffee brewing over an open pit fire.

I made my way through this maze of fiberglass homes on wheels until I reached a pay phone. Dropping in a quarter, I dialed 0 and then our Mayne Island cell phone number. I was expecting an operator to come on any minute, to whom I would have asked to place a collect call, but instead got a computerized voice which said, "ATT cannot make connection to the cellular network in Canada."

I shook my head and tried again. Same thing. That's weird but oh well, I'll just try again tomorrow, I thought, scratching my head. I wonder what that's all about.

Wandering back to our campsite, I pondered the possibilities.

"Hey guys, any of you able to hook up with your wives?" I asked Mike, Rod and Larry all at once.

"Yeah, no problem," they all seemed to respond in unison.

"Well I couldn't get through to Jill. Just got an automated reply: ATT can't make the connection to the cellular network in Canada. Any of you with Telus?"

"Yeah I'm with Telus," Mike shot back. "But I called my landline back home, not the cell phone number."

"Oh then it must be a problem with ATT then," I speculated.

"I heard something about that at the gas station yesterday," Rod chirped in. "Something about a strike at ATT and so all the management had taken over the operator jobs. I guess they aren't doing a very good job."

We all chuckled. "I guess not!"

I felt relieved and left to relieve myself. When I had returned the fellows were building a campfire, so I turned right back around and headed for the camp store to pick up some beer. You gotta love how you can buy booze on any corner down here in the states, I mused. Funny how I usually drink wine when I'm with Jill, but here with the boys, it's beer all the way. Passing the wine aisles full of bottles of "Bitch" or "Blasted Church", "Frog's Piss" or "Fat Bastard", I settled on a six pack of Coors Light.

We got to feeling pretty good, polishing those brewskies back. Before you knew it, we were all complaining about our jobs. Not that I had a lot to whine about; I liked being an elementary school teacher. You could play. I especially enjoyed running the after school Engine Club, where boys and girls would dissect various two stroke engines and then learn how to reassemble them into workable, and best of all, raceable, go-carts. Although, we had liability issues with the racing aspect of it all, like when one girl flipped her cart or one show-off boy ran right into the brick school, but that was just collateral damage.

As for the classroom behavior management, that was the most stressful part of the job. It was even worse than all the marking that robbed me of my evening tinker time. I think the kids had a hard time taking me seriously when I goofed off so much with them. When it was time to teach, they just didn't want to shut up....or sit down. But who could blame them, they were little boys. Just like us now...here!

Rod complained about driving Loomis trucks all day long and the stress that traffic caused or the tight schedule he was expected to keep. He told us about an incident where someone had tried to rob him. Boy, listening to that, I realized teaching was an easy gig.

Larry talked about retirement and how he missed the stimulation of his former work. He considered retirement to be similar to being laid off; lots of time and no money. I guess he hadn't planned financially as well as he had wished he had.

Mike complained about all the computer viruses and Trojans out there and all the money he kept spending to buy the latest computer gadget. I could not relate to that world. Computers to me were just a tool—not a toy!

It got to be boisterous, bitching with the boys. We got louder and louder until the energy of our words drained and the silences grew. When Larry began to snore we all threw peanuts at his open basket of a mouth, until he would snort, swallow and swivel around on his butt. We thought of keeping score, but then decided against it; we didn't want to choke the old man.

With a few slaps on the backs, we said our good nights and headed off for our tents—Larry and Rod, the two brothers in one and Mike and I shared the other. Trying endlessly to get comfortable, I sighed throughout the night. Mike was talking in his sleep in no time, and boy did he snore. I chuckled to myself listening to the other tent.

"Oh for Pete's sake Larry, go take a crap already. Your farts are stinking up the tent." Rod yelled to his gassy older brother.

With a smile still on my face, I drifted off to dream. That night held the image of my brother Norm racing his go-cart, my dad racing his old Alpha racing car and me on my lime green racing Suzuki motorbike. We were all on the old Westwood racing track in Mission speeding past each other, taking turns playing cat and mouse on the hairpins and cutting each other off. Burning up the track, while peeling rubber all over it, we had the whole place to ourselves. What a blissful sleep I had……..until I crashed!

JILL DAY 4

"These mugs are dreadful," I heard Christine say, awakening my slumber. "And Jill, where do you keep your good beans?"

"Those are our good beans," I joked back. I laughed to myself as Christine pondered which mug to choose: Teacher of the Year, Merry Christmas, Engine Club 2000, or Chilliwack Teachers Association. They were all reminders of our other life back home in Chilliwack, where Luke and I both had comfortable teaching jobs. But Christine wasn't looking for functional, she wanted playful, colorful, artistic. We were these, in diluted form, but she liked concentrate. She wanted expresso. She settled on a chipped, flaky earthenware cup and began the morning coffee ritual while I smiled in bed and waited for the wafts of coffee aroma to beckon me to once again bow to the coffee pot brewing up something from heaven.

Part way through the morning I questioned, "Wonder why Luke hadn't called last night?" Probably having a great time and just forgot, I tried to reason with myself. But since I hadn't asked the question to anyone directly. No one answered.

It was another blazing day and the beach was the order of the day. Our own beach out front favored exploration, but we were after some sandy relaxation where the girls could build sand mansions. We contemplated the various beaches of the island and then settled, without much effort, on Bennet Bay. Christine brought along stick-on tattoos for the girls and they were decorated dolls in no time. We had a great time splashing about and beach combing. It was truly one of the beauty spots on this island, with its expanse of sand and Arbutus trees in abundance. The overlooking homes were all medium bank so as not to disturb our beach privacy. There was plenty of driftwood to make into forts or rafts and the view was mesmerizing, with boats drifting on the blue calm sea and Georgeson Island in the background. I loved introducing visitors to the magic of it all.

It hadn't taken long, before Molly had ditched her bathing diaper and was smothered in mud, sand, clay and seaweed—all thanks to her loving sister, Emily. Before I could admonish her mischievous ways, Christine had retrieved her camera for a laughable keepsake. I almost couldn't recognize Molly as only her white eyeballs were left untouched. She looked like she was from some Zulu tribe, running along the shoreline, involved in some sort of primitive play. Thankfully, the army green wavy water washed over our wailing offspring, restoring her to her former glory. The shallow bay was the perfect playground for an older sister in hot pursuit of terrorizing a toting toddler. It was all so entertaining!

The next order of the day was deciding on what delicious splendors should our taste buds be introduced to during that evening's dinner meal, which took much care and plenty of discussion.

"Let's see. For appetizers I'll make baguette slices with goat cheese, pesto sauce and sun dried tomatoes. They'll be divine once grilled." Christine was thinking aloud but making me drool none the less.

"I'm starving. Let's go," I quipped, jumping up to collect all of our sandy things. Before we knew it, the truck was loaded with everything we brought plus many seaweed creatures covered in slime, pails of broken, yet treasured seashells and buckets of sand, stuck to everything.

As we approached the turn off to Porter Road, adventure struck me. Christine always seemed to draw that side out of me—thankfully. "Hey...let's pick oysters off the beach for dinner tonight!" I enthused.

Luckily Christine is always up for the ride—any ride! "Sure!" she quipped.

So we pulled into David Cove, one of the nicer beaches on Mayne Island that also has a boat launch. After retrieving some screw drivers from under the seat where Luke always had some stashed, together with many other tools that I can't even name, we made our way down to the water. With the tide low, we could see many oysters stuck to the cement ramp of the boat launch. It was remarkable how we had been coming to this island for years and had never dug out oysters before. I had bought some at the Island's True Value store and cooked them up, but never actually picked or dug them up myself. I wasn't about to admit that to Christine, however. With dirty sand pail and screw driver in hand, I bent over to scoop up an oyster—but with no success. Each one was so utterly stuck, it didn't seem to matter how much leverage I applied. Ready to give up, Christine suggested a hammer. Scrummaging through Luke's tool box, I came running back down with the largest and oldest hammer I had ever seen. Together, Christine and I plied an oyster loose by pounding the end of the screw driver with the hammer. I couldn't believe how much effort that took! But we were determined!

As the girls had slowly dragged their sandy playthings back out of the truck, and down to this beach, they were content to continue what they had started earlier at Bennet Bay: the creation of a moat. So Christine and I waded deeper into the cove and worked together to pry more of these suckers loose. We seemed to get a system going and before we knew it, our bucket was full, and feeling victorious, we headed back to shore. As we helped the girls clean up—again, a motor boat pulled into the cove. It became apparent that they were about to take their boat out of the water, so we cleared the boat ramp and watched. One of the men jumped out of the boat and ran up hill to get their truck and trailer, which he then backed down the ramp. As they loaded the boat onto their trailer, I couldn't help but notice all the marine oil or fuel that was surfacing in the water around their boat motor. I hoped the oysters were safe to eat. I knew there were no red tide warnings, which would have prevented us from eating oysters, but I hadn't thought of this pollutant. Yellow lights were flashing within me; proceed with caution. Perhaps they should have been red. But we decided to run the light and take our chances.

Driving up to the cottage, I heard the phone ring. I was glad I had left it on but wondered why I hadn't brought it to the beach with us. It was a cell phone after all.

"Daddy's calling early isn't he?" I said to the girls. "It isn't even suppertime yet." I jumped out of the truck before I was completely parked. I ran inside and picked up the phone. No one was there.

"We have to cook these puppies up," I said as I rolled the barbeque into the center of the deck and confessed the fact that I didn't even know how to turn on the barbeque. Luke had always done that. I became so agitated at myself wondering how I could have let myself become so dependent on someone else. I, who had moved out of the house at seventeen, worked two jobs and put myself through college, who prided herself on being so independent, was now finding herself foolishly dependent. How did I let that happen?

"Well how hard could it be?" Christine asked as she read the instructions on the front of the barbecue on how to light the thing. Before I knew it, she had it burning and we celebrated with a glass of wine.

"Cheers!" as we clunked our glasses together.

Cooking oysters is an interesting thing to watch......NOT! Dropping all nine shells onto the grill, we then closed the lid and waited. Then we waited some more. Finally the shells started to open slightly, signifying that they were ready to eat. Prying them open was now simple. Dipping them into garlic butter and chasing them with swigs of Oyster Bay Chardonnay was simply divine. The girls didn't care for them, but no matter I concluded, in case they were bad, I would not want them sick....or worse! But, as it turned out, my worry was for naught. We were fine.....blissfully fine.

LUKE DAY 4

I woke up in the morning missing my dad. Death took him many years ago but how he used to love to race and how I relished those weekends when I was part of his pit crew. Together with my brother Norm, we three would come home all covered in grease and sweat, running for the showers as we dodged our mom, who understood yet barely tolerated the mess and extra laundry we had created.

I missed mom too, remembering her eccentricities. She had passed away of heart disease after dad had already left us. I can still picture her telling me off after I bought a 600cc BMW motorcycle with the wedding money that she and dad had gifted Jill and me. Or how she would bawl me out for bringing the roasting pan of gravy into the formal dining room to top up our plates. Or the time I showed up for dinner at the Shaughnessy Golf Club wearing a sweater instead of a suit jacket, while Jill had donned dress slacks rather than a dress. I thought she was about to devour us for dinner. Too bad that both parents had left our lives before meeting their grandkids. Mother would have doted on those girls, taking them on shopping trips to Oakridge or Park Royal in West Vancouver once they were older. I'm sure she would die again if she saw how they were usually dressed now; they looked like they should be running around with the artful dodger straight out of a Charles Dickens novel.

I wondered how Emily and Molly were doing.…or Jill? Lying on my sleeping bag and waiting for the guys to get up, I thought of home. They probably have not given me one thought, I'm sure. Jill and the girls have probably gone down to the beach every day and are having a blast…..without me! I miss them.

Hearing the zipper open the other tent, I decided it was time to get up. In no time, everyone was up and stretching their sore bodies and trying to get the kinks out of their necks. We agreed that we needed to get an earlier start if we were going to make any time, so with that we skipped breakfast and raced to see who could pack up the quickest.

Mike would have everything packed and then realized there were still more that had to be crammed in. He would get so frustrated and would tear everything out and start over again. Rod and I were going head to head, meticulously rolling up our sleeping backs and tents, followed by our clothes and pillow cases. We lined up the maps needed for the day's journey and placed them in our tank bags. As for Larry, he couldn't have cared less and didn't even try to compete for lead packer. As it turned out, Rod got that honor as I kept getting distracted by everything and anything possible.

By 9:05 we were on the road, which was our earliest yet. It was overcast that day and I wondered if we would be needing our rain suits. We hadn't rode long before the boys were whining for their coffee, so finding a rundown gas station, we turned in for some stale brew. As I tried to swallow this swill, I noticed the news was on the small TV set hanging in the corner from the ceiling. I walked closer and heard about some huge forest fire in Montana. Oh no, I thought, we're heading that way. Soon Larry, Mike and Rod had gathered around to listen too.

"I wonder if we can ride right through it?" Mike asked.

"Well I don't think we can really ride all the way around it, we'd lose a lot of time," Rod answered.

We decided to take our chances and quickly hit the road again, heading east straight for the Montana state border. Sure enough, what was once lush green forest was now gray haze. Smoke had filled our nostrils and visibility was deteriorating. We could see fires burning up on the hillsides on both sides of us, but thankfully the road snaked right through the middle of it all. There were fire bombers flying overhead and fire trucks everywhere. As we approached police cars, I thought they would make us turn back for sure, but they didn't; they just motioned for us to slow down. We hadn't been going very fast as it was, since it was difficult to see ahead, but we slowed down nonetheless. As we continued on, we marveled at the magnitude of the flames. The heat was immense. We were afraid to stop for pictures or even to pee, lest the fire made its way down to the road and we would then be detoured, or worse, sent back the way we came. So we rode.

But then the unthinkable happened, Larry ran out of gas. I should have figured it would happen with his little Harley gas tank that could hardly hold piss. Seeing that there were no gas stations around, and we weren't sure if we had time to send a runner ahead to buy gas, with fires burning on our tails, we had to get resourceful. Rod suggested we pull one of the cables off one of the bikes and then syphon some gas out of my tank, since I had the largest gas tank and therefore the most gas remaining. I had a better idea. Rummaging through my back kitchen in a trunk, I dug out my camp stove. It ran on different fuels, and thankfully, this time, it had quite a bit of white gas still in it.

"There might just be enough to make it," I said, walking over towards Larry's bike. We drained every last drop into his gas tank, before I reloaded my stove into its trunk on the back of my bike and we took off again. We made it pretty far—but not far enough. Larry ran out of gas again. We were about to try Rod's earlier idea, when Mike spotted a town not too far ahead, and all downhill. We went for it!! With Larry in front, coasting all the way, we followed him into town where he made it to a real gas pump. It wasn't a Chevron, but I thought it might not be the best time to be choosy. We decided we had all better fill up, reserve tanks and all.

The smoke continued and we didn't excite ourselves over the idea of camping in such unbreathable conditions, so a hotel was in order. We were almost at the state border into South Dakota and decided to find a place to stay for the night. We were exhausted! But as we rode, all we could see was No Vacancy signs, so we turned off the main roads. Before long we came across a small, dated motel — two star if we were lucky, probably one. They had one room left. Unfortunately, it only had one queen sized bed, and they were all out of cots, so flipping coins to see which three guys got the bed and which poor soul got the floor, I intercepted and volunteered to take the floor. No way was I going to sleep in a bed with two other guys. No way!! The hard stinking floor wasn't quite so bad since I did have my thermal rest and sleeping bag. But oh, the snoring and the gaseous odors that filled that room that night—it was suffocating. I don't know if the smoke would have been as deplorable. And it was hilarious seeing those grown men not knowing which way to face in bed, as to avoid being too close to each other.

"Hey, stop polluting my pores," Mike shouted into Rod's face, which was way too close for his liking.

"Well get your knees out of my back," Rod yelled at Larry.

"Luke, quit thinking so loud!" And so it went...all night long.

With that awkward evening behind us, we woke, hung over from sleep deprivation. Those three were all pushing each other and mumbling like they were the Three Stooges. I thought better than to rub it in. They had suffered enough.

FIVE YEARS EARLIER

Death came calling on the Frank household. Martha and Rudy Frank lived five houses down from the Connor family on Silver Drive in Chilliwack. They were an older retired couple who pretty much kept to themselves. They did have a horrendous dog however. Martha could often be seen walking her pooch down the street, early each morning. At one neighborhood block party, the neighbors had been speculating over whose dog had been crapping in everyone's yard. Each resident denied it could possibly be their precious pet pooping. However, one particular morning Jill Connor had run out for some milk and was pulling into her driveway when she came upon Martha and her boxer. It was squatting on top of Jill's English ivy and obviously dropping a load. Furious, Jill didn't even stop the car, but proceeded to drive over her front lawn and would have probably run the boxer down had a tree not been in the way. Slamming her gear into park, Jill jumped out, picked up the shitting boxer and threw the dog at Martha. Jill had caught the culprit in the act! A surprised Martha, just huffed off with her hound, leaving an exasperated Jill to clean up.

Word soon spread throughout the neighborhood, as to which dog was leaving the turds around and which neighbor was not being neighborly and picking up after it. Consequently, Martha and her shy husband Rudy stuck to themselves. We all felt sorry for him being married to the likes of her. You could sometimes see him in his well-stocked garage working away at some woodworking project. If the garage door happened to be open and you walked by, he would nod, but never say anything.

Martha and Rudy had grown children, but they lived out of town and were seldom seen. They might have even had one grandson, but that was all rumor.

We had all read it in the local paper one morning; Rudy had died. No one knew why. There was lots of speculation alright, but the autopsy report wasn't conclusive in its findings. The street thought Martha had done it, poisoned him perhaps. But that would have been found in his bloodstream. Some thought he might have fatally injured himself in his workshop, but that surely would have been noted. Most were just hoping that he had died peacefully in his sleep, with no foul play from Martha. Rudy hadn't deserved that! There was an eerie silence on the street following his passing; no blackened rumors were needed. We just all kept our distance.

Five years ago, five houses down, Death had come calling.

JILL DAY 5

"Crepes! Wake up for some crepes!" Christine sang into the morning house. She had woken early, even beating Molly and Emily to the sunrise. Thankfully, she let us sleep till nine before beckoning us to breakfast heaven. She had gone down to the road and gathered some fresh blackberries just as the sun was waking up that day and so, we were being treated to some delicious eats. And of course she had fresh coffee made from her coffee press that she just had to bring along on this trip. She always brought so much stuff. Like the time she was a walk on passenger on the ferry, toting a large old suitcase filled with hand me down clothing from her daughter Tashina, for Emily to wear. And this was in addition to her suitcase for herself. It was overflowing abundance, quite the opposite to motor biking where every inch of space is calculated; where things are weighed. I was always awed by this aspect of Christine's character; since I usually under pack and have room to spare. I marveled and delighted in our differences. That is what made us such enduring and endearing friends.

After that wondrous feast, it was time to prepare for the market excursion that we had planned for that day. A weekly occurrence, the open market was filled with stalls offering tasty eats, home spun jewelry, hand painted greeting cards, sheep skin rugs and goat soaps. There were activists with petitions guarding against proposals for future island developments.

There were booths where you could get a message or cranial adjustment. And if you were lucky, there might even be a busker or two serenading everyone. This place was a carry-over from the seventies hippies with a slightly sophisticated urban, new age feel to it all. It was quite enchanting.

On this particular visit, Christine had brought lovely beaded earrings that her daughter, Tashina had earnestly made, at all of her eight years of age, as well as funky, colorful greeting cards that she had had printed, from some of her five year old son Isaac's quirky drawings. Being the enterprising entrepreneur that she was, and providing her kids with the encouragement to follow suit, she had brought these wares to sell. So we carted an old foldable card table into the back of the truck, together with some plastic lawn chairs, and headed into town for the opening of the public market. As we set up our booth and laid out her wares, we celebrated in all that Mayne Island had to offer.

Young and old, rich and poor, conservative and the more liberally minded all mingled together. Some visitors came to buy; some just came to visit. This was indeed a community meeting place, where gossip was shared and plans were construed, where ideas were inspired and artistic endeavors applauded. We happily parked ourselves down for the next couple of hours, chatting with potential customers and with each other. Emily and Molly were being entertained by face painters and musicians playing harmonica and folk guitars to some of Joni Mitchell's older tunes. Molly soon found a pair of tie dyed socks that she just had to have. With splashes of orange and lemony yellow interspersed with aqua blue—they were full of life. She donned these colorful knee highs that reached almost to her diaper and before you knew it they had worked their magic. Molly was dancing away to "Paved Paradise." In her mind it was the socks that were dancing, she just happened to be in them. It was enough to convince Emily, for she too wanted a pair of magic dancing socks. In no time they were both jumping and prancing around, twirling their bottoms and clapping with their feet. It was a happy sight!

It turned into a relatively hot day, as wafts of sea air blew upon our tanned faces and sea gulls sang overhead.

"I'm thirsty," Emily blurted out.

Realizing that we had consumed all the liquids that we had packed along with us, I took Emily by the hand and strolled the market with her searching for a juice stall. But we couldn't find one, surprisingly. So Emily and I left the market for the short jaunt to the True Value grocery store for some juice, whereupon Emily got an idea.

"Mommy, why can't I have a lemonade stand at the market today? No one else is having one." Emily petitioned me with her big eyes and charming ways. How could I say no to that?

After pondering the idea for a short few moments, I relegated. "You know what Em, I think that would be a great plan."

So we trotted around the grocery aisles, picking up jugs of pink lemonade, plastic cups and the smallest package of crayons I could find to write up a sign. We paid for our items and Emily then had me skipping back to the market, matching steps with her happy feet. Christine cheerfully cleared a spot at the end of her table for Emily to set up her business. We found some paper in the recycling bin at the market and quickly drew up a sign: Lemonade 50 cents. We had line ups in no time, as I helped Emily pour cups of refreshment for her customers and several for herself, of course. Molly was only too pleased to perch herself down beside her big sister to watch all the action, as she twiddled her hair and sucked her thumb. When the paying patrons would smile in gratitude, Emily would giggle in anticipation of her accumulated loot and Molly would grin along, with her thumb still stuck in her mouth. We hadn't thought to purchase any ice but thankfully it was a hot day and the juice was beating the sun—it was getting polished off before it was undrinkably warm.

Way too soon, it was time to pack up, but Christine's kids would be giddy to learn that their crafts had just earned them seventy two dollars....in just three hours. It had been a successful enterprise! As for Emily, she made $14.50. She had never been so rich, although she had absolutely no idea the value of those coins. To her small mind the more coins the merrier, so if someone dropped her a mitt full of pennies, instead of the usual two quarters, she was simply delirious with joy.

We loaded up the truck and headed back to the Connor cabin. We were all desperately ready for some lunch. As we pulled into the driveway, dodging the overhanging arbutus branches and barely missing the tire swing, I could hear the phone ringing so I slammed the truck into park and ran into the house, but I was too late.

LUKE DAY 5

Luckily the hotel served us boys coffee in the lobby, because otherwise we would have spent all morning feeding at the trough of the hotel buffet breakfast. For a two star it didn't smell too bad—the food that is. As for the pee stained carpet and wet dog smell that permeated the entire second floor that we stayed on, that was beyond acceptable.

Caffeined up and ready to go, we jumped on our bikes and anticipated the journey ahead. We were looking forward to reaching our destination later that day: Sturgis, South Dakota. Cruising along, we got a solid three hours of riding in before we had to stop for gas—thanks to Larry. We were just outside of the Custer War Memorial when we spotted a gas station at the bottom of the hill. The roads had become thicker with motor bikes the closer we got to Sturgis, so I shouldn't have been surprised to see the gas station so full. After all, it was the Year 2000 and they were expecting one million bikes to attend this bike rally, celebrating their 60th anniversary of such rallies.

So we waited in line for a pump and decided we had all better fill up. As pumps became available, we each rode up, until we were all dispersed throughout the various lanes of the gas station. Since I had the largest gas tank, it usually meant it took me longer to fill up, on top of that, I occasionally changed my oil as well. I had to keep my bike content—that was my motto. Besides, this particular trip, like all long trips for me, was just a test drive to see how my last mechanical overhaul was measuring up.

Not paying too much attention, as there were bikes and cars, but mostly bikes flying in and out all around me, I looked up, trying to spot one of the guys. But I couldn't see any of them. I screwed my gas cap back on, replaced my tank bag and went in to pay. Coming out of the pay booth I was fully expecting to find Larry, Rod and Mike sitting there together all ready to go and waiting for me...again. But that didn't happen! Instead I came out, and as I was placing my wallet in my pocket, I scanned all the lanes, the roads, the washrooms, everywhere for anything that resembled my crew.

That's odd, I thought, scratching my head. I had wanted to clean the bugs off the face shield of my helmet, but I thought better of it. I guess they were getting impatient waiting for me. I'll just have to race and catch up to them; we all know which way we're heading. So with a handful of revs and popping a wheelie, I tilted my head and booted it out of there. Speeding along the highway, I chuckled thinking that they knew I'd be able to catch them; they knew my love affair with speed. Clocking 160 kms, I zoomed along, cutting a straight path east. I looked at my watch, wondering how long it would take for me to catch up to them. Five minutes max, I thought.

Fifteen minutes later, I realized something was wrong when I hadn't caught up to them yet. Wondering if they had pulled over and were waiting for me, I continued riding slowly, looking down all the side roads, into restaurant parking lots and gas stations.

Then it dawned on me that maybe they were actually behind me. Maybe they hadn't left the gas station ahead of me, but

I was confused by this as I had thoroughly checked for them back there. I decided to pull over and wait. Up ahead was a T in the road which seemed the perfect place to stop and wait, in case they went the wrong way. So I geared down and steered onto the gravel shoulder and shut off my bike and I waited for about fifteen minutes. Growing angrier by the moment, I finally dismounted my bike, took off my helmet and gloves and sat on the roadside for almost another hour....waiting. But they never showed up.

    Confused at this point, I got back on my bike and rode back the way I had just come until I was back at the original gas station. But Mike, Rod or Larry were nowhere to be found. So I turned around and drove east again, very slowly looking everywhere for them, which grew very tiring as there were so many bikes everywhere. I had to especially inspect each parked bike in case they had stopped and gone in somewhere. When I again reached the T in the road, I was fuming.

    "How dare these guys take off on me," I thought aloud. With Mike, Rod and Larry still nowhere in sight, I just kept going. Screw them! I'm just going to ride to Sturgis on my own and possibly meet up with them there. What were they thinking?

JILL DAY 6

The next morning, I again awoke to that wonderful java aroma that Christine concocted. As we lounged, sipping and gazing out the window toward the reef, I recounted to Christine about the neighbor's recent encounter with a pod of orca whales that had quietly swum up, and then in one surprise swoop, devoured their fill of seals off that reef. We would have loved to have seen that spectacle of nature, as we relished the imagery! As it was, we just enjoyed the many hues of the blue sea that morning. Close to the shoreline it was light gray blue, interspersed with frothy white waves. Next, there was a slightly darker shade, followed by a line separating a yet still darker shade of blue. And so it went as you stared out toward the horizon: lines of blue. Where the water met the sky, you could see the darkest blue haze of the mountain range, with white pockets where buildings stood. This view, however, would change daily with the weather and the seasons. On windy days, everything was grey, albeit various shades of grey, with white choppy waves. When the sky was blue, the water followed suit. On foggy mornings, the sea and sky became one fluffy cotton ball. When there was a storm, the turquoise, massive waves would almost reach our lower deck and would blindly rearrange the yielding driftwood on the beach. In early summer, we would enjoy the glorious sunrises and purple skied sunsets; in winter we would get neither. In summer low tides you could wade yourself to the reefs, in winter high tides the reefs disappeared altogether. The summer sun would cast a warm golden hue upon the sea, while the winter sun would cast a cool, crisp glare. You could see the seasons coming as you studied the Salish Sea; sometimes she was your beckoning friend and at other times your menacing foe.

The water was particularly calm this gentle morning however, with ferry boats crossing the strait and a scattering of sail boats, fishing trollers and speed boats cruising by. It was a visual feast for the eyes! The morning also brought many seagulls to poop all over our beach. We called it our beach, but really it belonged to the birds; they marked their territory well. Thankfully, the waves would soon wash over their excrement and prepare the flat sandstones for our lounging. Nonetheless, their squawking was the musical backdrop for our days.

Suddenly I was startled by the ringing phone and I jumped! "Hi Jill, it's Mike. Have you heard from Luke?" He quizzed me seemingly out of breath.

Dumbfounded, I replied, "Well no. Isn't he with you?"

"No. He took off from us and we haven't seen him since," Mike answered in that concerned voice of his, slowing down now to breathe.

Unconvinced as to why Luke would take off, I pushed Mike further. "What do you mean? Where is he? You tell me!!"

Mike breathed in heavily and I knew I was in for an earful. "We were at a gas station yesterday and we were finished filling up before Luke, so we decided to visit this souvenir shop next door. We waved over to Luke and then proceeded across the road. Before we knew it, Luke was gone. We came out of the shop, wondering what was taking him so long and then realized he was no longer at the gas station or anywhere as far as we could see."

"Well Mike, where do you think he is?" I asked beseechingly.

Detecting my fear, Mike paused and then replied, "I'm sure he just raced on ahead to this rally that we were aiming to reach tonight. You know how fast Luke likes to ride. He probably was just getting itchy and decided to beat us all there. We'll catch up to him in Sturgis, I'm sure."

Trying not to overact I said, "Okay, I'm sure he'll call me later tonight." With a false sense of assurance, I hung up the phone.

Mike was one of those kinds of guys you can trust. Serious and rational, he was detail oriented and wouldn't have left anything out. He was also an honest person whom Luke had befriended, so it wouldn't be like him to fabricate his side of the story. I was glad when I heard that Mike was going on this bike trip, he would surely temper my more playful Luke. On the other hand, this was not like Luke to just take off from the group either. He was the most experienced rider of them all and would have felt responsible to show them the ropes of motorcycle touring. He was also very mechanical, so that if any of the guys had bike problems, Luke could trouble shoot. Mike's phone call didn't make any sense to me.

The day blurred on! The kids didn't ask and so I didn't tell them about that telephone conversation. I chose to ignore it in fact. I'm not sure why, but there was a truth to it that rang through me. When Christine inquired, I just brushed it off. Once Emily and Molly were asleep however, I nonchalantly told Christine about the phone call from Mike earlier.

She quickly laughed and said, "Oh remember all those times we got lost from each other, separated on those bike trips, like when we were in San Francisco and blah blah blah................"

I couldn't hear a thing. What if something really was wrong. What if? What if?

"He'll be fine Jill. He's a grown man who has done this lots before. Think of all the stories you'll tell about this someday," Christine reassured me with her wise words.

She's right I thought. This whole thing had a familiar ring. I recounted all the happy endings and told myself this would have one too. With that, the subject was changed, but I was drained. Fumbling to free myself from the wool throw I had been snuggling with, I got up and stumbled toward the bathroom. Peering at the worried weathered woman in the mirror, I didn't like what I was becoming. I completed my evening bathroom routine and called out through the hall, in Christine's direction. "Good night! I need to get some sleep." Then I lumbered to my bed as a zombie.

Christine hadn't really even noticed, as she was lost in a good book. Before long however, the lights went out and all was surreal-very quiet-very dark-no bright sun shining now.

LUKE DAY 6

It was late in the day by the time I had arrived in Sturgis, South Dakota. The streets were alive with parties and hundreds of thousands of bikers had taken over this small sleepy town, that normally only housed about six thousand people. I suppose they were used to this, as the rally was an annual event, but this year they were expecting a million bikers to attend, not the usual ten thousand or so, since it was the 60th anniversary rally. My first order of business was to find a campground. So I rode through the narrow streets and right out of town and all around its perimeter, but every campground was full. "No Vacancy" signs were displayed everywhere. Even yards were taken over by campers with some posting FULL on ripped up pieces of cardboard. I guess the locals figured they might as well cash in on all these arriving tourists. That appeared to be my best bet as well, so I turned around and headed right back into the middle of town.

    I went up to the porch of a small run down house, located next to the town's only church, and knocked on the door. An old geezer answered and spit through yellow teeth, "What do you want?"

    "I was wondering if I could pitch my tent in your back yard....I'll give you twenty bucks." I stepped back cautiously, so he wouldn't feel threatened, as I fumbled to retrieve a twenty from my weathered wallet. I wasn't sure if he would agree as no others were in his yard. He hadn't put up a sign to advertise camping spots, but maybe no one else thought of asking him for one either. I might get lucky.

"Yeah go ahead," he motioned to the back yard, already walking away with his head down. After a few labored steps, he turned around and grabbed my twenty. He looked like he had long ago resigned himself to the fact that the bikers were coming....yet again.

So I pitched my tent right next to the low white picket fence that bordered the church yard. Once I had all my gear unloaded into my tent, I scanned the area, for what had to be the closest graveyard I had ever camped beside. For there, over the fence, were many tombstones, some old with peeling plaster and others new, flat and still shiny, with fresh flowers on top. It seemed strange, the paradox: the life of vibrant flowers next to the colorless grey of death. Why do we do that, I wondered. What makes us associate death with flowers? Everyone sends them after a funeral and we place them on graves; the juxtaposition just makes the deceased appear all the more dead. Are we unconsciously trying to instill new life into the departed? Are we trying to cover the stench of death with the fragrance of flowers? Some of the larger tombs reminded me of a mausoleum, where you could pay homage to the dead in private. Nonetheless, it was a bit creepy looking at all these monuments to death. But I would be next door—a yard away from the dead—and I was just grateful for a place to live for a few days.

I wandered the streets munching a cold hot dog, and looking for Mike, Rod and Larry. But with all the crowds, I couldn't imagine how I would find them. It hadn't taken long though for me to give up searching for the guys and instead I roamed, examining all the bikes. There were rows and rows of them parked diagonally along the curbs on every main road, side roads and alleyways. It reminded me of dominoes; if one were to fall, they all would tumble down. Made me think of a trip to California with Tim and Christine, where once we had reached our destination, Tim parked too close to our bike. It was extremely hot and the black top was soft and spongy. No sooner had Tim placed his bike on the side stand, when the metal sunk right into the road, causing his bike to lean over towards ours. Before Tim or I could jump back and set it aright, it fell on our BMW, which then unfortunately knocked over as well. That was not cool!

But that trip did have some memorable moments: Tim placing a colorful beach ball between himself and Christine to use as a backrest for himself. Riding a Honda Goldwing, the seat was so long, Christine was too far back for him to lean upon. But once we hit the highways, the beach ball would just get blown out by the wind. After chasing down the first two, Tim tried to rig up a bungee cord, so that it held the ball down. This didn't work either. And we were getting tired of looking for Hardware stores so that he could buy yet another beach ball.

Christine, on the back, was also not interested in holding those uncontrollable beach balls down, for she kept her hands busy eating sunflower seeds, or reading a book, or the most hilarious sight yet, knitting. Yes, she would actually attempt to knit on the back of their bike. Eventually, Tim and Christine gave up on the beach balls and Tim would just suffer through nightly back rubs from his wife, to aid his aching lower back.

I wished Jill were here to give me a welcomed back rub, I thought. I should find a pay phone and try to reach her again. So ignoring all those bikes, or trying to anyways, I kept walking down the street until I hit an Arco gas station with a pay phone. I fumbled through my wallet looking for coins, which I never seemed to have, when I saw my BC Telus calling card. Of course, this will work, I enthused! I soon found out however, that it required a pin number which I did not have or could not remember. So I dialed the operator and asked to make a collect call, for surely the ATT strike had been resolved, I hoped. But the operator put me on hold, and then an automated voice came on saying: "ATT cannot make connection to the cellular network in Canada".

I was about to go in to get change when I realized there was no point: ATT was a stupid system that was somehow clashing with Canadian cellular networks. I could remember that futile recording in my sleep. If only we had a land line on Mayne Island, maybe then I could get through to Jill.

I thought of giving Ruth Hamilton, Mike's wife back in Chilliwack, a call in case anyone was looking for me. I could call her land line collect surely, although that would be tacky. No... coins would work to make a pay phone to land line call, I reasoned. But then I laughed, why would Mike or his wife, possibly be looking for me? He's the one who took off on me. I decided to give Jill's mom a call instead; I called her landline collect. I told her I was fine in case Jill was concerned about me. But she hadn't even heard from Jill in over two weeks, so I assumed Jill was not worried about me either. I was going to call our home in Chilliwack and leave a message on the answering machine, but what was the point of that? No one was there and we weren't planning to go back there until later in the summer.

So, since the guys had ditched me and I couldn't reach Jill, and according to her mom, no one seemed to be worried about my whereabouts, I had decided to make the best of it and have myself a good time. And just maybe I'd find the guys tomorrow, in daylight.

That evening, I strolled the buzzing strip of Sturgis, ogling over all the various bikes. There were Honda Shadows, Triumphs, some Gold wings, the odd Norton, but mostly Harleys. I couldn't see one BMW or rice rocket; that crowd would have avoided this scene. There were some side car units, some trikes and even trucks that had pulled in their modified custom bikes on a trailer. I guess they didn't want to ride those trailer queens across the country—too precious for that!

The air was thick with cigarette smoke and pot, guys were drinking in the streets—spilled over from the bars. There were biker chicks too, donned in tight jeans and hard faces with breasts falling out. I had walked by one group of boisterous guys, all hooting at one gal who had just flashed her breasts their way. Jill would flip out if she were here. I hadn't felt like I belonged either. I was a straight laced elementary teacher—I hadn't smoked pot in years—since I was a teenager. Boob flashing wasn't a common form of entertainment in the circles I socialized with either. But here I was in motorcycle mecca; I had that in common with these guys. So as long as I focussed on that, talked about bikes, I just might survive.

In no time I found myself drooling over some custom modifications. It was hard not to, with everyone spit and polishing their babies for the Show and Shine. This was what we were here for. I excitedly made my way through the throngs of people, stopping at many booths. The old guys were the easiest to converse with, they weren't so hard to crack. The truth is, they didn't scare me like some of the guys wearing their bike gang colors; I just avoided those ones. They tended to stare at me too long, dissecting me to pieces.

Before long I had come full circle and was back at the church. I was sleepy despite all the activity around me, and thought I'd get some sleep. Crawling into the tent, I chuckled to think about those three: Rod, Larry and Mike, with only one tent between them. Their loss and my gain I thought. I'd get a good rest with no snoring or shitty farts to contend with. It would be a good night....or it would have been had it not been for the loud heavy rock bellowing from the streets. Sounded like ACDC screaming for someone's soul.

JILL DAY 7

Christine and I yakked away the early morning hours. The days had gone by so quickly, in one respect anyway, but it was now time for Christine to leave. With her roller suitcase packed and her lime green backpack full and slung over one shoulder, she commented, "Well deary, it's time to go...already."

I hated to see her leave. I wasn't ready or willing to face fear in all its ugliness on my own. But the time had come and destiny was pushing me forward.

"Thanks for coming Christine. It's been a blast, as always," I said as I leaned over to hug my friend-my sunshine in an ensuing storm. I squeezed what reassurance I could from her and then we all left the cabin. In a rather mechanical ride to the ferry I felt myself being drawn into a vortex. Another reality was pursuing me. My two sides arguing. Fear or Faith-who would win out? I wonder. I worry. We said our goodbyes at the ferry terminal and then departed ways.

Back at the cabin, the girls and I were painting sand pictures when the phone rang. Boy the calls are coming earlier and earlier each day, I thought. It's not even noon yet. "Hello," I said into the receiver, not sure what to expect.

"Hi Jill, it's Mike again," he said in a very somber voice. "We're at the Sturgis rally now and still can't find Luke. It's almost three o'clock Eastern time and we've looked everywhere

– all the campgrounds, restaurants and miles of booths. We don't know where else to look. What would you like us to do?"

Knowing that they were inexperienced to rallies, I said rather confidently, "Oh just go to the registration table and look for his sign in. If you don't see his name, tell them he's missing." I continued, "Maybe they'll pass on a note to him or something when he does decide finally to show up." That should do it, I confidently said to myself.

"Okay," Mike countered. "We'll do just that", and then he hung up in my ear.

Mike is one of those guys you'd like to hire if you were an employer. He's so dutiful, so sensible, not the most playful of souls, but nonetheless, one great dude. I wonder what his wife, Ruth thinks of him going on this trip. He was kept on a pretty short leash—I'm sure they connected by phone several times each day. His teenaged three kids, however, probably thought it was way cool for their dad to be going on a biking trip to Sturgis; one of the largest, most rough and tumble biker rallies.

Rod, one of the other guys on this trip was a bit more fun loving than Mike. He was relatively new to biking though, so he kept quiet. Lastly, there was Larry, Rod's older brother who, although an experienced biker, didn't know Mike or Luke and was just along for the ride—literally.

Thinking about these guys, I felt better already. I knew they'd see Luke's name at the sign in registration table and all would be well. Oh Luke, I thought, why couldn't you just have ridden with everybody else? Why the need for speed? But knowing Luke the way I do, I smiled. He had been riding for thirty years, he was experienced. He couldn't resist the urge to race either—he grew up at the racetrack after all, watching his dad race. Now his brother was racing too. He was drawn to that world.

I went on with my day, cleaning up the cabin that had become party mecca over the past few days. Foot rub lotion, manicure tools, hair styling accessories, tattoo stickers, the remnants of a girly life, lay strewn everywhere. But what enjoyment we derived, pampering ourselves so. Christine has a real knack for that; I'm more the task master.

"Mommy, can we go to the park?" Emily asked with anticipation. "The other park?"

Realizing that meant the school playground, I said with a sigh, "Oh, I guess so."

Mayne Island School was on the other side of the island but it had an extensive playground, with climbing bars, pulley, swings, etc. Driving through the island we passed the Health clinic, Naan's Hair Styling Boutique, Re-Max Reality, Esso Gas, the video store, the agricultural hall and the museum. The latter was actually the island jail once upon a time, replete with two small cells where the criminals, or gold digging drunks were kept until they sobered up. I couldn't imagine being locked up there, closed in with only your thoughts to further imprison you.

We continued our meandering drive past fields of grazing sheep, under arching arbutus trees, over pot marked roads that desperately needed attention until we reached the busy lumber store. As I parked and exited the truck, the girls didn't even ask why we were there. They knew. Luke always stopped to check the community bulletin board for more used tools, motorcycles, boats, stuff, junk. This was just something he liked to do and I felt closer to him doing the same. The board contained the same old, same old, until I saw: HUSBAND

FOR HIRE. I did not want a husband; I wanted my husband. WILL FIX ANYTHING another ad said. "Oh yeah, try fixing my situation," I heard myself saying. HELP WANTED, to which the cynic in me replied, "Who doesn't want help?" Most of the ads were from the resourceful locals trying to eke out a living from the moneyed weekenders, either by offering their construction services or selling some hand me down, hand me downs. Who could blame them? Once you saw this island paradise, you did whatever you possibly could to stay. But why did Luke have to go?

Once at the playground, Emily and Molly soon met some other playmates and they were off throwing sand at each other. I couldn't help notice the parents. They were a handsome couple, probably the same age as Luke and I. They were friendly too, trying to engage me in conversation.

"So, do you live here?" he asked with restrained curiosity.

"No, but we have a cabin here and spend most of our summers here," I replied, not wanting to appear arrogant, yet wanting to answer his question with something more than a yes or no.

"Oh, lucky for you!" she quickly blurted out, appearing to be happy for me. Not the sarcastic, jealous reply we sometimes get.

But I suddenly didn't feel very lucky. In fact, I felt very unlucky. I was jealous of them together, wishing Luke were here with me and the girls. But he wasn't. Get over it Jill, I kept on saying to myself but the knot in my stomach was creeping up to my throat and was starting to choke me. I could hear this cheerful couple talking to me yet I couldn't answer. My vocal chords were somehow tightened.

After watching life continuing on around me for a while, I wanted to be alone in my little quiet world. I no longer wished to participate, or even spectate, but this friendly couple kept trying to pull me out. It was time to go.

"Come on girls, we need to leave now," I insisted in a firm voice. They ignored me and kept on playing. "I'm going," I stated matter-of-factly. "Look at the rain clouds coming in. We need to go." Without looking back, I adamantly marched out of the playground. The girls soon reluctantly followed with dismay.

Once home, or back at the cabin – this didn't feel like home at the moment, not safe, not a haven of rest, not now – the phone rang.

"Hello," I said out of breath.

"Hello. This is the South Dakota Police Department," an older woman said in a very American accent. "Is this Jill Connor I'm speaking to?"

"Yes it is," I replied slowly, feeling very puzzled.

"We have a Missing Person Report filed on behalf of your husband—a Luke Connor," she said and then waited for my reply. But none would come. "Could you please describe him for me Mam?" she asked in a rather cold, professional voice.

"Ah, oh, he's 45 years old, blond with green hazel eyes. He's six foot one and ....excuse me," I stopped. "Who reported him missing?"

"Let's see," she said looking through her papers. "A Mike Hamilton filed the report."

"Oh," I replied wondering why Mike had gone to the police and not just to the registration table at the rally. That's where I had meant for him to declare Luke missing. Suddenly this was taken to a new level.

"Mam, can you think of any reason why your husband might want to disappear? I mean was there any history of problems with drugs or alcohol? Any marital or financial problems?" she quizzed me.

"Absolutely not!" I shot back. "And he has two little girls waiting here for him. He better not have taken off," I shouted. Tense and trembling, trying to hold back tears, I said, "And you better find him."

"We'll try our best Mam. Have a good day," she quipped before hanging up.

How was I to have a good day after hearing that? What a stupid thing for her to say, I thought. Why had Mike gone to the police? Something more must have transpired since I last spoke with him, I reasoned.

Before long the phone rang again. Oh let it be Luke, please please I begged. "Hello," I quickly said into the phone.

"Hi Jill, Mike here," still speaking in sombre tones, revealing the fact that Luke was still missing.

"Mike, why did you go to the police? Why ..." but I was interrupted.

"Jill, let me explain. Firstly there was no registration table at the rally. There are thousands and thousands of people everywhere. The rally has taken over the whole town. There is no sign in," he informed me, making me feel very naive.

It's true, I thought, I've never been to a rally that big and I suppose things are set up differently. Over the years, Luke and I had gone to BMW rallies, CMA rallies and Gospel Riders' rallies, but they were usually attended by a few hundred bikers, or even several hundred. But this was Sturgis! It usually attracted thousands of people. However, this year was their

Life Doesn't Lie

60th anniversary of their annual romps, and they were expecting a million bikers to gather in Sturgis, South Dakota.

"Anyways," Mike continued, "we filed a Missing Person Report."

"I know," I retorted. "They have already contacted me. So what now?"

"Well the guys and I are going to spend the rest of the day looking in ditches along the roads. Maybe he wiped out and is lying somewhere, unable to move." Mike quipped.

"That's a comforting thought," I said sarcastically, covering my terror.

"We'll let you know if anything turns up Jill," he said in what sounded like a very paternal voice.

"Okay, Bye," I said in a dazed fashion, and hung up my life line.

With my world threatened, the only way I knew how to cope was to try and restore order out of chaos, so I went into cleaning overdrive. I had zero tolerance for any messes that would normally be expected from two little kids. I found myself becoming very short tempered, for my inner world was consuming all my energy, all my patience. I had nothing to offer Emily and Molly and I found myself screaming at them like never before. I wasn't handling things too well and I longed for home and all my supports that are there: family and friends to surround me. The more I drew inward, the more the girls seemed determined to pull me out. I felt like I was losing it.

Molly, for some uncanny reason, chose to trudge around in Luke's size ten black rubber boots. It required much concentration and coordination on her part, just to avoid tripping and falling. But she managed herself well, walking at least a mile in her father's shoes. The sight produced chuckles on my behalf, as the top of the boots rubbed against her diaper. But she was determined! The muddy footprints, however, reminded me of earlier times when Luke would be traipsing through the house after working in the yard, probably pulling out tree roots or something.

As the long day progressed into another never ending night I welcomed the undemanding solitude. Time to think. Time to focus.

B...ring, B...ring—I was startled out of my trance....Oh shit! Now what??

"Hello Mam, this is the South Dakota Police Department," the same lady with the American accent droned. Hopeful for some reassuring news, I listened as she coldly asked, "Could you describe your husband's tent please?" Mike must have mentioned to them that Luke would be camping.

"Well, it's one of those dome shaped three person tents – dark brown with a tan rain cover over it," I described as best I could. I assumed the guys must have described his motorbike because I was glad she didn't ask about that. What would I know—it's black!!

"We will visit all the campgrounds tomorrow in the surrounding area Mam. We have three men on the case. Let's see what we can find," she said in her investigative tone.

Still clinging onto hope, I hung up the phone and looked for something to distract myself from all this misery. It was making me miserable! Just then, I heard water gushing and went to investigate. In the bathroom, the pipe under the sink had sprung a leak and water was splashing unto the floor. I bent down to turn the knob, and stop the flow of water, all the while swearing under my breath, for this was Luke's job.

I could shut this water tap off but I couldn't fix the stupid thing....he could! So now it meant that we no longer would have a workable bathroom sink faucet, until his return. Oh great!! One more reason to need him. I was hating these reminders! I went to sleep.....to escape his memory.

LUKE DAY 7

I awoke in my cozy tent to the chirping of birds. I had to pee urgently, so I frantically crawled out and peered around for a spot to whiz; thankfully there were no alive souls walking around at this ungodly hour, just the corpses next door. Relieving myself under an oak tree, I was somewhat hidden by the neighboring tombstones, out of view from the street out front. Not that any of these bikers would care, as they were peeing openly in the streets. I guess being of a British background however, I still had a sense of decency. But I was not about to knock on the door of the home owner at this hour to use his bathroom, that wasn't an option. He no doubt wouldn't want a stranger waddling through his house either, being as wary as he was already of us biker types. Zipping up my pants, I looked toward his back window. I couldn't see him. It was a good thing, because I didn't want the old geezer coming out of his house and lecturing me about watering his bushes. Who knows? The urine might even bring some of these dead things back to life.

I put on some more clothes and then made my way out to the front street. The town was quiet and still, which seemed odd considering there were bikes overflowing the streets, and even on most lawns. As I shuffled my legs toward the main drag, I heard some action. I witnessed some rough looking dudes sprawled out on a curb, a few others mingling around their parked bikes. But they didn't have coffee cups in their hands, no... they were still slinging back beer; they hadn't gone to sleep yet. I guess that's how it works down here, one day's party just spills over to the next. I kept walking, searching for some place to eat breakfast until I came across this little run down diner with an old Mexican cook who made me one delicious breakfast burrito. He was thrilled to serve me too. He was talkative and friendly and welcomed all the extra business that this rally brought each year, but especially this year. His brother had lost his car manufacturing job and had moved in with him, together with his wife and their four kids, so he had a lot of extra mouths to feed. He needed his business to thrive.

It was a warm, sunny morning as I strode the street stepping over beer cans, cigarette packs, paper napkins and cups, and even what looked like barf. Binge drinking and its common aftermath seemed to be a favorite past time of this crowd; drink till you puke. What a way to measure fun! The streets were starting to fill up, mostly with vendors opening up their shops or setting up their curb side booths. There were posters: "I Survived Sturgis." Or pins with "60th Anniversary" fit onto its tiny head. Bandanas were in abundance, mostly with Harleys pictured or some big breasted biker babe. There were small booths that just sold maps, of the area, the state or of the whole U.S. I decided to check these out for some ideas of where to explore. Seeing one guy that looked more like a grandpa than a hardened biker type, I comfortably sought his advice.

"Good morning!" I let out with a toothy smile.

"Well good morning to you too," he answered warmly back.

"I'm new to the area and was wondering if there were some places nearby worth checking out?" I inquired.

"Well hell yes!" Gramps replied, pulling up his short sleeve to reveal a tattoo. He was a biker after all.

Leaning over the counter to get a closer look, he showed me Mount Rushmore on his bicep. The faces had begun to drool with his sagging skin, but I got the idea. He was so proud of his patriotism.

"Oh is that Mt. Rushmore?" I asked rhetorically. Why I ask questions when I already know the answer bemuses me. My father used to do the same thing. I guess I'm trying to act interested or engage the poor old guy in conversation.

He looked at me like I was stupid. "Of course it's Mt. Rushmore! Why else would I have a bunch of guys' faces tattooed on my arm? You think I'm queer or something?"

This was not going the way I had wanted or even imagined. It was time to get out of there. The fire in Grampa's eyes made me think I had better leave before this escalated into outright hostility. "No, no, I didn't mean it that way. I'll just take the map thanks." I said dropping down a Canadian five dollar bill before I walked away.

"Bloody Canadians!!" I could hear him mutter. "What am I supposed to do with this here funny money? Play Monopoly?"

There was an unpredictability about these biker boys which made me keep my distance. On one side I wanted to pick their brains, especially about their bikes, but on the other hand I didn't want to stir up trouble. They could tell I wasn't one of them for I wore relatively clean jeans, a Nike tee shirt and had short hair; while most of them were covered in black leather pants or at least chaps, sleeveless black Harley tee shirts, big riding boots, long hair—often in a ponytail and they stank. But the most telling feature was their hardened faces with tanned, wrinkled skin and lifeless eyes whereas I was from the West coast's rain forest; I wore white skin that hadn't seen much sunshine. I felt like a target, like they would devour me after toying with me for a while. Kind of like how a mischievous cat will swat a naive mouse back and forth before eating it, knowing full well its intentions from the beginning. But I wanted to enjoy this experience, not just survive it, so I plowed on, to see what other adventures I could fall into. I was feeling reckless!

Before I knew it, I had stumbled onto three sleazy women strewn over some crotch rockets. One was applying lipstick using her Harley's round side mirror, the other had her butt in the air, leaning over her sheep skinned seat, while the third was slinking toward me like a Cheshire cat, grinning wildly.

"Hey, you looking for a good time?" the pussy cat had asked me.

"Are you talking to me?" I innocently asked.

Now walking toward me, these three cougars in pink began to put their arms and hands all over me. They were not what I would call pretty and definitely not cute but they were hot. With their big lips and big hair and big boobs they tried to entice me.

"No thanks ladies," I said shrugging them off and quickly moving on. I was about to look back but then I didn't want to be flashed so I just kept going. Prostitution was right at home here.

Turning the corner I was glad to see a make shift sign that said: Rally Headquarters. It was plastered to an old red brick one story building, resembling an old town hall or something. I was more than relieved to have stumbled upon this place. I skipped up the five steps and through a creaky door and came face to face with what could be called a motorcycle momma. She was an older woman, probably in her late sixties, who seemed to be like a mother to all the younger biker boys.

Everyone seemed to know and love her. She slapped me on the back, as I entered and directed me to the sign in table. Four burley guys sat behind two fold out tables with a big sign behind them: REGISTRATION. I smiled, paid my dues, signed my name and then paused.

"Hey man, move on," one of them motioned me along.

I was trying to scan the sign in sheet for the names of Mike Hamilton, Rod or Larry Peters, but the paper was torn from my hands.

"I just wanted to see if my buddies had arrived yet," I said looking at them, hoping for some answers.

"What do you think? You gonna look through thousands of names?" They laughed at me.

I guess I was expecting some sort of alphabetical ordered list or some semblance of organization. "I guess not!" I rolled my eyes. "But I'm trying to find some guys. We got separated." That was a polite way of saying it.

"Well, see that board over there," one of them shouted in his South Dakota drawl, pointing to a rolling bulletin board across the room, "You can put a note for your pals on that there board."

I nodded and shuffled over, amidst all their penetrating stares. Maybe the guys had beat me here and have already left a note for me as to their whereabouts, I mused. But no luck. The bulletin board was full of ripped up notes, scribbled on every kind of paper: people looking for others, camping spots available, for rent signs, but mostly for sale signs. There were Harleys for sale, a couple of side car units, tires, back rests, even custom seats. I had to laugh at that one as I knew that Harley seats were skinny little things that Jill scoffed at once trying to park her wide rear end on it uncomfortably. It always amazed me the junk people would try to pawn off on suckers like me. But I often found myself with that unfair label, as I loved to buy used remnants of other people's lives. It was my way of recycling and restoring, kind of like what God had done to me; brought wonder and usefulness to what was once, apathy and depression.

This board was also full of things Wanted and I often found self-esteem filling other people's orders, like the time I had spent many hours and lots of bucks restoring an old 57 Chev pick up. I wasn't completely done yet when some eager guy came to our door, all smitten, upon seeing it gleaming in our driveway, and offered me six grand for the thing. Before I knew it, he returned the next day and was driving off with my baby. When Jill saw how despondent I was, she had asked why then had I sold it.

"Because he wanted to buy it!" was all I could say.

"You could have said NO!" Jill shot back in disbelief, shaking her head.

I knew she was right, but what could I say, that was just who I was.

Examining the board now, I could see so many possible bike building projects calling out to me. I was handy and mechanical and I knew I could restore a lot of these bike parts into their former glory. Never mind that I didn't have the time or the money....I could do it! Reality kicked me though and I chose to walk away. I went back to the sign in desk.

"You wouldn't happen to have a pen and paper would you?" I asked, not sure if they were just going to throw it in my face, or tell me to go effin buy some myself. Their black stares continued to tear at my face.

Motorcycle momma happened to be walking past, so one of the guys reluctantly handed me a pencil and ripped off a piece of paper from the bottom of the sign in sheet he was working from.

I humbly accepted and walked back to the bulletin board. Squatting down on the floor I drafted a note:

> MIKE, ROD & LARRY
> I'm camped in the backyard of the old
> house next to the church.
> Luke

That should do it! They obviously haven't come through yet or they would have left a note for me. Now when they come they'll see this and find me.....that is if they want to. I was doubtful considering they had purposely lost me. LOST & FOUND; that's what this board is for, like I was some old discarded jacket or something. I wondered if the guys were interested in recycling and restoring like I was, but at that point I wasn't too keen on restoring our friendship. They needed to be recycled. I was still too miffed. This note however, was my olive leaf. Let's see if they bite.

I gave the pencil back and headed for the outdoors. I decided to take up Gramp's tattoo idea and go visit Mount Rushmore. It was a gloriously sunny afternoon and I made my way back to my tent and geared up for the ride. It baffled me to find my tent's contents intact. I was expecting to be looted daily as I didn't have a lock on my zipped up tent. As far as I could think, why bother. These guys all carried knives and they could slash through this nylon igloo in seconds.

Life Doesn't Lie

It seemed that every other Sturgis biker had the same fabulous idea: to head for the cool mountains on this blazingly hot day. The roads were overtaken by revved up bikes and the usual summer traffic of recreational vehicles must have been traumatized to negotiate the highways with bikes buzzing in and around them. I had Gramp's map visible through my tank bag and it was easy enough to find, on the other hand, I just had to follow the traffic flow. Things started to back up as we approached many parking lots, which were filling up quickly with mostly, but not all bikes since there was the odd car, truck and van parked as well. The trailer traffic was out of luck trying to nose its long rear end into one of those skinny spots. They were charging ten dollars to park, which I was reticent to part with so I decided to park on the shoulder of the highway instead. I dismounted and made my way toward Mt. Rushmore where I could see the faces of different presidents of the U.S. carved into the mountainside. They were massive! As I feebly tried to get closer I was barricaded in by a barbwire fence and realizing that I was supposed to have paid for entrance into this sight, I haphazardly decided to climb the fence, rather than go all the way back down and around to pay at the gate. However, someone spotted me and started shouting at me but it was too late, so I ran for it. Next thing I know this guy is chasing me, and for what? Five bucks, ten bucks? Whatever the cost was to get in this place, it couldn't be worth the chase I mused, laughing. I soon found myself lost in the throngs of people, staring up at the magnificent carved out mountains, as my attendant in pursuit gave up and retreated down the hill. How American I thought, to charge you for everything. In Canada, this would be a provincial park and free for the public to enjoy, but not here, where so much seems to be commercialized. Everyone wants to make a buck!

After I had soaked up this visual wonder, I followed the moving crowds down the paved hill and snuck past the gate, before hopping onto my waiting get away bike. It had a parking ticket on it, which I just nonchalantly threw away into the wind as I sped off carefree. I spent the remainder of the afternoon touring the black hills, poking up at notorious Indian chiefs carved into looming mountains. The weather was perfect and the roads were twisting through the hills. I found myself sometimes riding alone and at other times, smack in the middle of a group, or gang of riders. I didn't wear any colors; I didn't belong to any motorcycle gang, so other bikers weren't threatened by me. We all just gave the two finger salute to each other.

That evening I cruised over to the drag races at the Sturgis drag strip. It was exhilarating watching the youngster crowd pull some wheelies as they shot off the starting line, while the old fogies rode antiquated bikes that wore collector plates. This was very different than the sport racing I engage in back home on my rice rocket, where many cut throat riders race against each other, dragging their metal plated knees around the tight corners. I missed that scene. Since my ominous crash last year, I hadn't gone back. I don't know if that's because I haven't found the nerve to return or just because I haven't put in the money and time to return my sick bike to racing form. My frame is all bent, the fiber glass fairing is half torn off—I'll have to get to that and restore it to its former glory I thought. But at least I wasn't hurt. Jill would have gone nuts had she seen me slide across the track, just missing the next lap of riders coming out of the bend. Had she seen the ambulances drive up and the checkered flags stopping the race, she would have been in tears, no doubt. It is a good thing that she doesn't come out to my races. She claims she couldn't handle it if something were to go wrong—well she couldn't! It was better that she stayed at home. Sure I would like to see her and the girls cheering me on, but I don't want to have to worry about them when I'm careening around the track at two hundred clicks an hour. She would surely flip out if I flipped over. No this was a guy thing! No girls needed!

The sun was falling asleep and I was wanting to as well. So I quietly left the noisy track before the last race was over and rode back to the little backyard beside the church in the middle of town.

I was dead asleep when I woke to footsteps outside my tent. Crawling outside, I peered around to find no one there, just some eerie presence lurking at me as I waved my arm and screeched to scare whatever it was away. Couldn't really make out what sort of creature it was though, so I slumbered back into my cocoon of safety. I dreamt I was being chased… probably the guy at Mr. Rushmore as I escaped payment. Lucky for me I was always one step ahead.

FOUR YEARS EARLIER

Death came calling on the Smith household. Linda and Walter lived amicably together with their motley crew of teenagers, four houses down from the Connor family on Silver Drive in Chilliwack. They both had been married twice before, so they had brought their own kids into this new marriage: a blended family. Walter had two dowdy sons that were very much into the whole Goth thing. They stalked the neighborhood in their black clothing, black hair and ghostly white faces. Emily Connor was particularly afraid of them and would frantically run away from the living room window if she happen to see them glide past.

Linda had two preppy girls and one sport jock of a son. The daughters, Jessica and Stephanie would sometimes babysit for the neighborhood kids, as long as they kept their creepy step brothers at bay. Needless to say, the goths, the preppies and the jock didn't blend very well. There was always gossip circulating about their family friction. Linda and Walter however, were deeply in love and tried to make this family unit work. They could be seen dragging their uncooperating clan out to dinner, or to a sports game in town. It didn't seem to matter what they attended, one or more of them was uncompromising. It was impossible to please them all, so majority ruled, which usually meant the Goths fuming in the back seat.

Linda's jock son had recently taken up hang gliding and so the whole family ventured to be spectators one fateful day. As they sat perched on top of Vedder Mountain watching their son glide, the Goths were mocking the fun. But Walter wanted to show his sons that life could be more pleasant if you only participated in it, instead of always sneering on the sidelines. So with barely one of jock's lessons under his belt, Walter strapped up and proceeded down the training hill. He wasn't doing too badly, when a gust of wind, which came out of nowhere, carried Walter away. With the whole family jumping up aghast, Walter was gliding down the mountain. At first they were all cheering as he seemed to be handling the air pockets, but it was only minutes before the inevitable happened. He wasn't experienced enough to know how to steer his way onto an opening field, and instead got tangled up in the tall pine trees below. He apparently got thrown around, ripped up by branches before being knocked out completely; he had hit the huge Scotch Pine dead on—literally!

Still on top of the foreboding mountain, his anxious family waited patiently, watching the farmer's field where he was to have eventually landed. He never did. After one very long agonizing wait, they all piled into their vehicle and drove recklessly down the mountain to look for Walter. They saw him hanging there, like a string puppet amongst the trees. Search and Rescue had to be called in to detangle him and cut him down.

The preppy daughters, Stephanie and Jessica, together with their jock son no longer were interested in participating in life after that; they had joined the Goths who had always viewed life as a spectator sport. As for Linda, she had become the grieving widow, as she too resigned herself from living.

Four years ago, four houses down, Death had come calling!

JILL DAY 8

The next morning I had resolved in my aching mind that we were going home—back to Chilliwack as I wanted to be with family if or when terrible news were to break. On the other hand, Luke, Mike and the South Dakota Police Department expected to reach me at this number, not my home number. I needed contact. It was imperative. Then I realized, silly me, I'll just bring the cell phone home. I still was not used to a cell phone, we never used it as such. It was always just left on Mayne Island and actually never even left the cabin. It was just a cheaper alternative to a land line phone, for the amount of use it got and we just put more minutes on it as needed.

"Get the phone, get the phone!" I yelled to anyone as it rang while I was on the toilet.

"Hi, Hi," Emily said. I could tell it was someone she knew but not daddy.

"Bring me the phone Emily, bring me the phone," I insisted. Still on the toilet, I heard Mike's voice.

"Jill, we can't find Luke anywhere. I think something's....." Mike's voice was cut off.

"You have three minutes remaining. This is B.C. Telus," the operator intercepted.

"Mike, Mike, are you still there?" worried that I had lost him.

"Yep, still here," he said. "I think something's wrong."

"We'll have to talk fast Mike, I'm running out of minutes. I'll buy another phone card in town here. The police called, they're searching the campgrounds today," I went on to explain.

"Yeah, we already..." Mike was saying when the operator cut in again.

"You have one minute remaining. This is B.C. Telus," the operator just had to remind us.

"I better let you go Mike. Call later. Bye!" I said trying to squeeze in the ending to our call.

Oh shit, I'm out of phone minutes. But then a horrible thought hit me: they don't sell phone cards on this island. I started to panic at the thought of no telephone. That settles it—we're going home.

Throwing the girls into the back seat of the truck, I quickly sped off before I realized I hadn't buckled them into their car seats. I kept driving. Yanking the steering wheel left and right, we were skidding around the corners on the wet pavement. We were fogged in and the drizzle of rain was unrelenting. Pulling into the ferry terminal parking lot, I remembered that we had forgotten to pack up; we had only the clothes on our backs. No matter! Driving up to the pay wicket, I was told that the ferry to the mainland had already left. I had missed it. But I should have known that. There are usually only two ferries per day that left for the mainland: one in the morning and one at night. What was I thinking? I wasn't thinking! When I asked to reserve tickets for the evening ferry, I was told I had to phone them into the system. You have got to be kidding, my expression on my face was yelling. As I didn't have a phone, I pressed down hard on the accelerator without replying to the speaking head and left black skid marks out of the terminal parking lot. I had always wanted to peel rubber.

Luke often did it for fun; I was too sensible...or boring. I did it to make a statement.

Finding a pay phone in town, I tried to phone my way home. "Hello, B.C. Ferries, I'd like to reserve space for a truck, one adult and two kids on tonight's ferry from Mayne Island to the mainland please," I said as I fumbled through my wallet to get my credit card number needed to book a space.

"I'm sorry. Tonight's ferry is full," the stranger at the end of the other line said to my disbelief. "In fact both ferries tomorrow are full as well. You know how it gets after a long weekend. Everyone's trying to get home," she said almost laughing at my predicament. But she didn't know my predicament!!

Realizing there was nothing she could do and knowing from past experience they won't just squeeze you on, I relented and hung up the phone in tears. I needed a phone, I wanted to go home. "I want my mommy!" I found myself saying. Surely B.C. Telus would understand. Digging through my bag for another quarter, I realized I did not have to pay for this call. Just dial 0 for the operator stupid.

"Hello," I said trying to disguise my weeping. "I'm on Mayne Island and I've run out of phone minutes," I explained. I was glad that pay phones weren't calculating minutes on this particular call. "Unfortunately, there is nowhere on this island to buy phone cards so I was wondering if I could buy some minutes from you and just have you put it onto my home phone statement," I asked thinking it would be no problem.

"Is there anyone at your home number to confirm that this would be accepted?" she asked.

"Well no, no one's there," I said in disbelief. "How about putting the amount onto my master card then?" I implored.

"Sorry, we can't do that anymore. Too many fraudulent cases in the past," she explained.

That was it—I cracked. I exploded or rather imploded. With uncontrollable crying, I tried to describe my nightmare. "I have no telephone, I can't buy more minutes, I can't get off the island to go buy more minutes and now you won't sell me more minutes!!" Taking a big breath, I continued, "My husband, who is on vacation, has gone missing. Do you understand? I need more phone minutes. I have been a regular B.C. Telus customer for years. I've always paid my bills on time." I noticed "we" had changed to "I", subconsciously I was already gearing for the worst. "So", I continued, "I expect you to bend the rules and give me some bloody minutes," I sighed after giving her this lengthy rendition.

"I suppose...." she paused, "for compassionate reasons B.C. Telus is prepared to give you ten additional minutes."

"Could I not have any more?" I asked surprised at their stinginess.

"No. I'm afraid not. Ten minutes is all we're prepared to give you," she persisted.

Thankful for anything, I accepted her meager offerings and hung up. Driving carelessly back to the cabin from the pay phone in town, I was preoccupied with trying to plot my remaining phone calls, as the girls were half asleep in the back seat and were unusually quiet. There would be no allowances for Mike, only the South Dakota Police department.....or Luke, of course! I only had ten minutes, which had to last me for at least two days until I could get of this blinkety blinken island. It was becoming my prison.

The telephone hadn't rung the rest of the day. Not that I was expecting it to—that would have meant good news and since no one had any, no one was calling. I could feel it in my pit. It was now overcast and I walked around in a cloud and even my girls' screams didn't faze me. The knot in my stomach was huge. It was a weight, an anchor pulling me down—down. I couldn't get off the couch; my body was dead weight. Emily was pulling me to get up and play with her but I couldn't muster the joy; I couldn't get my bones to cooperate. She finally retreated and then returned with a tray of lotions and face cloths and make up. Bless her little heart – she knew how to cheer her mommy up when she was in the doldrums. She proceeded to pamper me by washing my oily face with a warm face cloth, smothering me with her care. I could handle this as no response was necessary. I didn't have to converse with her, I just had to lay there, play dead, which was only half true. She was the beautician, however to me right then she was the mortician. She over moisturized my face and neck and then attempted to make me over with makeup. With broad blue strokes over my eyelids and round apples for cheeks, Emily tried to model me after Barbie. It seemed fitting as we were both of 1959 stock, however, I looked nothing of Barbie's vintage. It hadn't taken long for Molly to get in on the action.

"I want to do Mommy too!" she blurted, climbing on top of my bloated tummy.

"No!" Emily screamed. "I'm doing Mommy," as she pushed Molly off me.

"No No don't fight!" I interjected placing my arms between their jostling bodies. "Here, Emily you can finish one whole side and then Molly can put makeup on the other half of my face," I quickly said hoping that I succeeded in averting a war.

With pouts and sullenness Emily redid her half of my face. With eyelids extra blue and cheeks now full blown red, her attempt at making me beautiful looked more like a drag queen but she was delighted.

Next it was Molly's turn, however, her idea of makeup had nothing to do with making oneself pretty; she had her own imagination to guide her. National geographic magazines were more her inspiration than Vogue or Chatelaine. Grabbing the black eyeliner she drew squiggly lines around my eyes and then used the darkest eye shadow to fill in around my eyes. She was using a lot of black and brown which should have been my clue as to where she was going with this. No red cheeks or pretty eyes or cherry lips for little Molly; she preferred the raccoon look. When my face was caked with goop and I could stand no more, I insisted that she was now done and I staggered to a mirror. To my horror and then curiosity and then laughter, I saw a combination of a monkey and raccoon looking back at me.

"Ahh!!" was all I could yelp as I scared myself in the mirror.

Little Molly was jumping with glee, so happy with her make over job. She had made her half of my face into an animal, which she thought definitely outdid her sister's attempts of beauty. I hadn't seen this coming, but what could I have expected from a toddler? I decided to run with it.

"I know, this half of my face shall be named Beauty," I said in a high pitched voice with a sickening sweet smile. "And this half of my face....is the Beast!" I roared with a menacing grin as I crouched low hovering over the girls. After they got over their initial fear of their crazy mother, they giggled for the story that was to follow. It was a moment of escape, a reprieve, yet it felt good to connect with my daughters and to hear them giggle.

* * *

That evening a light of hope flashed in my brain—my mom. If Luke was lost or hurt or anything he would call my mom back home in Chilliwack. Both of Luke's parents had already passed away, so my mom was near and dear to Luke's heart. But why wouldn't he have called me I wondered? Nonetheless, it was worth a shot, so I sacrificed a few precious phone minutes to call her.

"Hi mom," I said as quickly as I could, "it's Jill. Has Luke called you?"

"Oh hi Jill, just wait a second dear, something's burning on the stove," she said as she dropped the phone down.

"No! No!" I thought, "Don't leave me hanging."

Picking up the phone again she said, "Yeah, he called. Now what day was that? A couple of days ago, last week. Oh I can't remember."

"Where was he mom? It's very important you remember." I asked impatiently.

"Oh somewhere in the States. I can't recall," she said distracted by her pots burning, the doorbell or whatever.

Realizing this was useless information but costing me dearly in minutes I said, "Gotta go mom." I wanted to talk, get comfort and solace from her but there was no time. I hung up and tried to figure out how many minutes I had remaining—approximately six minutes. Oh God help me, I prayed.

What was I thinking calling my mom? She'd been in la la land ever since Arkel came into her life—or should I say back into her life! They had met when mom was just fourteen and he was nineteen. She was friends with his younger brother and never really noticed Arkel, yet he was enthralled with her. Mom was too shy to pick up on his advances and so nothing ever came of it. They both went their own way, moved to different cities, got married and had children. Sixty years later, Arkel went back to his home town to visit relatives where he came upon one of my uncles—my mom's brother. Upon inquiring about her, Arkel learned that Monique—my mom—actually lived not too far from him back in B.C. Once he returned home, he called her up and they began, what became a long distance phone affair. Both of their own marriages had ended many moons ago and they were like teenagers again. Arkel decided he wanted to finally meet up with Monique, after courting over the phone for several months.

The eventful day had finally arrived but unbelievably, mom woke up with a splitting migraine. My sister Cathy was visiting at the time and gave my ailing mom what she thought was a Tylenol three tablet. My mom had soon become very sleepy but Cathy continued to try and get my mom ready for her long awaited date with Arkel: helped her pick out the perfect outfit to wear, cleaned up the place, made lunch. Time was running out and mom had now fallen completely asleep. Arkel was to arrive within an hour! Cathy knew how much mom was looking forward to finally meeting Arkel after sixty years and wasn't about to disappoint either one of them so she dragged our sleeping mom into the bath, washed her hair, dragged her out again and then tried to dress her. My sister Cathy has terrible arthritis and I can't imagine her pulling and maneuvering this dead weight.

Finally mom was ready, but she was still asleep. So Cathy lumbered mom outside and sat her in the rocking chair on the front porch. Mom was slumped over and drooling now, but Cathy propped her up like a doll and then left her there to meet her knight in shining armor. Finally Arkel arrived! What a sight for him to behold, not what he was expecting or hoping for. Upon seeing Monique, he thought that she must have a drinking problem. He was sooo disappointed! He was trying to be cordial and make polite conversation with mom, when Cathy appeared. She was getting worried that mom was perhaps having a stroke, but neglected to say anything to Arkel as he continued trying to converse with mom. Cathy and Arkel then escorted mom to the kitchen table where they all sat down for lunch, but mom just had her head in the soup. Finally Cathy explained to Arkel the situation, for he was a retired paramedic and surely he would know if these were in fact stroke symptoms. But when he checked out the pill bottle, he realized that there were sleeping pills mixed in with Tylenol three tablets. Cathy hadn't thought to differentiate. Who would? After several cups of coffee, a walk or two and many hours of sleep later, mom resurfaced.

That was a couple of years ago now and mom and Arkel have been inseparable ever since. They got a new place together and are trying to pick up the pieces after sixty years apart. Needless to say, mom is in dreamland, where life is all good and sunny all the time. Not like the rain I'm in!

I felt expired and went to bed. I wish la la land was calling me. Maybe I should try some of my mom's Tylenols. Someone could then prop me up to face my life.

LUKE DAY 8

I awoke to a blanket of ravens and crows covering my tent—hundreds of them. Shooing them off, I stood up to stretch my stiff and aching body. I think the old geezer was getting tired of me camping in his back yard. He saw me pissing on his roses and that probably did it but no matter, I was ready to leave. I quickly dismantled my tent and began the arduous task of packing up. Rolling up my extra jeans and tees, I soon discovered to my dismay that everything was not going to fit. I knew I had picked up a few treasures at some of the booths in town yesterday: a Harley black sleeveless tee—just to rib my Harley buddies, a Sturgis baseball cap, a handmade brown leather belt with a large metal motorcycle for a buckle and some shirts for my girls back home. Somehow I acquired too many keepsakes. It no doubt had something to do with the three novels I had brought along as well. Why I continue to do that on every trip is beyond me. I guess I figure I'll have loads of extra time to chill out and read; catch up on all my bedside table books that I neglected throughout the year. Funnily enough though, I couldn't recall one trip when I actually read one of them.

    It reminded me of the time Jill and I had flown to Mexico with several reads in my suitcase. But Jill kept dragging me off to sail, windsurf or snorkel: some form of fun that involved the sea. But land lover that I am, I really just wanted to park my butt down on one of those comfy recliners under a palm tree and have someone serve me cool refreshments. But Jill would have none of that. She would remind me that we could read at home—for free, and that we didn't come all this way to sit all day. She had a point as we were there to explore and discover new experiences, possibly meet some new interesting locals. So as usual, we would conclude that trip with unread best sellers in tow.

I tried placing these hard covered books (why I could never wait till they came out in paperback was now surely questioned) over my rolls of clothing in my saddle bag and then kneeling, and then sitting on them, all to no avail. It was not working, I had too much stuff. I pondered my choices: I could buy another backpack and wear this extra load, or at least bungee it down on top of my kitchen trunk at the back of my bike; I could wear lots of layers and boil to death; I could just leave some stuff in the old geezer's yard; I could give things away; I could throw stuff out; I could pack it up and send some of these items home. The latter made the most sense. After all, I had done that before, recalling now the books I mailed back from Scotland on our European bike trip in 86' or the many souvenirs we picked up in PEI in 93' that we had arranged to get shipped back to our home in Chilliwack in order to lighten our load. But this wasn't about economizing fuel or space; this was about necessity.

So I emptied my kitchen trunk, both saddle bags, my tank bag with its multiple pockets of trinkets and lastly my camping gear bags and pack that were bungeed on top of everything else. I prioritized my load and proceeded to pack up the unnecessary items for their trip home. After retrieving a discarded box from the back alley in town, I dusted it out and began to layer a pair of blue jeans, two of my old but favorite tee shirts (I would keep my new one to wear—it might actually help me to fit in with all the Harley bikers around here), my runners (I'll just wear my riding boots all the time), some extra socks and underwear and of course all of my books. I was glad I had found a box large enough since I was sending more than I originally had planned to send. In fact, the box was so huge, I decided I might as well pack it full then I'd have more room for newly acquired stuff. How many clothes could I really wear anyway? Besides, lightening a load always pays off at the gas pump—cheapskate that I am. Satisfied with my selections, and chuckling at the size of the package, I hit the street in search of a post office. Past the partiers that continued to consume, over the empties that lay strewn everywhere, down some alleys that overlooked restaurant kitchens with their back doors revealing the piles of dishes that all these bikers left behind. It reminded me of when all the partying friends and family members are about to leave our Mayne Island cabin, laugh as they just get to walk away from all the mess—that we get stuck with! I smiled to myself realizing that I now get to just walk away from the remnants of such a party. No dishes, laundry, vacuuming and loading up of the truck to the neighborhood bottle recycling depot. No these poor folks in Sturgis were left with the massive cleanup of this event. I guess that is the cost of being the motorcycle mecca year after year.

    As I turned the corner, I spotted the post office across the street. Plunking down my parcel on the counter, I was met with rolling eyes from the woman behind the counter. Without saying a word, as this obviously had happened many a time before, she reluctantly handed me some string, a black felt pen, some tape and a roll of brown paper.

"Thank you," I nodded. "I'm not from these here parts. I don't have any of this here stuff with me," I awkwardly explained.

"Ya think!!" was her contorted reply as she walked away from me shaking her head.

I proceeded to wrap up my box, tied it up with the string and labeled it to my home address:

Luke Connor
45631 Silver Ave.
Chilliwack, B.C.
Canada

I thought about putting on a return address, but then figured against it. What would be the point? If for some reason this package didn't make it home, would I really want it to be sent back here to Sturgis. NO!

"Ah excuse me Miss," I meekly called trying to regain the postal woman's attention. "Could I please send this COD to my home in Canada? I don't have room for it all on my bike," I smiled. "I need to send it on home ahead of me," I explained.

With another rolling of the eyes, as if to say she didn't give one shit why I was sending stuff home, she grabbed my parcel and weighed it, and then threw it on a pile of other such parcels behind the counter.

I smiled my thanks and left. I was proud of my idea to send it COD as I was glad to keep whatever cash I had on hand, American or Canadian. Besides, it just means that package will wait at the Chilliwack Post Office until I retrieve it....whenever that is!

I made my way back to the yard beside the church, relieved to see no old geezers in sight. I easily packed up what remained of my things, with room to spare. What a novel idea that is! In record time, I had my bike all loaded up and ready to go. I didn't know where I was headed but the road was calling me—screaming at me to come. I just had to heed the call.

Something about riding into the wind, it's exhilarating beyond mere adjectives. You couldn't use enough words to describe it yet I had an overabundance of words: adventurous, spontaneous, winding roads, leaning into bends, knee scraping, bugs in your teeth, sun on your face, multiple revs, the swoosh of the wind, the bum numbing vibration of the engine, the woodsy smell of the trees, the salt of your own perspiration dripping down from under your melting helmet, the finger salute with other bikers, the racing and maneuvering between cars, the speeding past huge rigs and RVs, even the constant stopping for gas, and not to forget the crotch burning. Sure, motorcycling is synonymous with freedom, but it is so much more than that. It is a state of being. It could be a religion. Your worries melt away; your responsibilities disappear.

The ribbon of highway was stretched out in front of me and I went for it. Opening up the throttle, I cocked my head listening for revs, and then I shot down the road, looking for I don't know what........

JILL DAY 9

I was woken from my dreamless sleep with a phone call that seemed too early to be rational. It was barely light out, the girls were still asleep. "Hello," I answered sitting up in bed.

"Hello Mam, this is the South Dakota Police department calling."

I didn't want to know her voice so well. I didn't want that accent to be part of my life. I was thinking of Christine's English accent she played with and I wanted to hear that and all the frivolity that went with it. Mostly, I just wanted to hear Luke's voice, his familiar warm soothing voice. But instead I was barraged with this voice that I dreaded. It stood for death or perhaps life, but I doubted it more every day.

"Mam," she went on, "Do you know how much money your husband had on him when he left?"

"No!" Unsure of where she was going with this, "No I have no idea, but probably not very much. He would have used interact and Mastercard mostly. Why do you ask?" I asked in return.

"We're suspecting foul play at this point mam. Wondering if perhaps he'd been robbed and then something went wrong and things turned for the worse," she mused. "At any rate we're handing it over to homicide. We couldn't find his tent anywhere and like I said, we're suspecting something foul of the law. You know this would not be uncommon at this type of rally. Happens all the time."

All I could hear was "homicide"… I felt like throwing up. I stumbled to the kitchen to brew up some coffee. I needed to wake up. I chucked back my swill and dropped down onto the couch and as I looked up, I saw the word, LAUGH on the mantel. Large black, wooden letters propped up, were staring me down. I didn't feel like laughing at the moment, not that I could cry anymore either. I had this thing for decorating with words: EAT in my kitchen, LOVE in the bedroom and JOY in the entrance hallway. I was looking around the house for LIVE, or at the time even SURVIVE but couldn't find them anywhere! I was reminded of the time, on our wedding day actually, when Luke had placed the letters HE on the sole of his left shoe and LP on the sole of his right shoe. When we had knelt down for communion, during our wedding ceremony, our wedding guests burst out in unified glee, to see HELP sprawled across his feet. I had thought my dress had ripped and was therefore exposing my butt, while the poor minister wasn't sure why the crowds were so amused—surely not his message during something so serious as communion. But no, Luke had let out his final plea for HELP for all the world to see. After twenty years of marriage he still has not fessed up, but no matter. Who else would be asking for HELP? I wish I had those shoes now! I needed a help line, not that those stinking soles would suffice. Maybe if I had some flowers??

Determining to LIVE, I gathered up the girls for some paper mache craft making. We all needed to rise above this slump we were in. Spreading newspapers over the kitchen table, I went to the EAT room to mix up some flour and water paste and some slop bowls and towels, of course. I proceeded to show

Emily how to make a mask armature structure to build a face upon. I had many paper mache masks up on the walls that I had made in previous years, so I pointed to each to generate some creative potentials for Emily to emulate. She especially enjoyed my African Zulu warrior couple, although the female was all black with yellow eyes and somewhat terrifying to look at, the male had surprised eyes and a round mouth, with three chunky strands of hair standing straight up. She wanted to reproduce their daughter for them! So with newspaper strips dipped, she covered her skeletal face structure with lumps and bumps to simulate cheek bones, nose and fat, full lips. You never know, it might even be good enough for Emily to enter it in Mayne Island's Fall Fair. She had craft entries the last couple of years, but this was by far her best yet, surely meriting a blue ribbon. If not, she could always don her mask and be an African Warrior Princess on a float in the annual parade; that would be to her liking!

For my mask, I felt like creating an Iranian woman in full niqab. Something about a beautiful woman with large, black framed, luring eyes hiding behind a veil, intrigued me. She was angry, afraid, lonely, alienated and invisible and I could somehow relate. So I set out to duplicate the face that I had seen previously on a box of couscous in the supermarket. I found an old black cloth napkin I could use for a veil once the mask was completed and painted; this would take several days to build up the layers and let it dry fully in between.

Molly, however, being only a toddler was too young to participate in this mask making. I tried to show her how to smush together some newspaper and paste into a ball, but she wasn't interested; she just wanted to eat the rancid stuff. So as I kept admonishing her to take the goo out of her own mouth, Emily was building up her mask's mouth to unrealistic proportions. Hers was looking like an African queen with Botox. My mask, though, had no mouth—she had no say, no voice, no words—only a veil to conceal her femininity, or perhaps her identity. Emily had created a daughter, while I had created a clone. I no longer knew who I was without my man; this revelation surprised me, frightened me, and then angered me.

We cleaned up the sticky messes that we had made and set our unfinished faces beside LAUGH on the mantel to dry. We needed some perspective. Feeling suddenly playful, I then went into the kitchen and changed EAT to TEA, as I was reminded of Luke's love affair with tea, or as he would call it, "The Drink of Champions." I missed him!

Later that day Mike called, but before he could get in a mouthful of words, I stopped him and said, "I have approximately two or three minutes left—they've handed it over to homicide. Goodbye and don't call back." I'm sure I sounded rude and Mike was probably wondering why I was treating him so badly, he'd done nothing wrong. But honestly, I didn't care.

My poor girls had no idea what was going on. I never discussed anything of this with them. They were so young, they hadn't even clued in to the fact that their daddy hadn't been calling them every night as he had promised. I was glad for their innocence.

The remainder of the day went on in a blur. My life only seemed to exist for telephone calls, everything else was just filler. It was difficult to focus on one thing as my brain kept pin balling all over the place. HOMICIDE—MY GOD! I then found myself consumed with thoughts of the practical. How do I bring my husband home once they find his body? How does one get a body bag anyway? How do I tell the girls? How do I tell Luke's siblings or should I be calling then now to forewarn them. Oh yeah, can't—no minutes. I felt like life was meted out in minutes. That night I had a strange dream:

I had dreamt that when you are born, you're given a bank card with twenty five minutes of talking time on it. Every time you talk, minutes are automatically deleted from your card. Every month you are given twenty five new minutes. You go to the bank and withdraw however many minutes you'll think you'll need. The world was a very quiet place, everyone economized with their words—language was boiled down to verbs and nouns, but mostly verbs: "want", "eat", "like", "sleep". The bank however, was a meeting place, for you see, in there, words were free. It was a neutral place. So everyone gathered and chattered incessantly. It was so noisy and full of laughter and life that it became difficult to even complete your transactions there, before you re-entered the quiet world. And oh, if you overspent and talked more than the allotted time on your bank card—well you were watched from somewhere above and penalized with double time taken off your next month's statement. So very few people overspent. But then, you did see the odd or awed person being dragged off—words of defense spilling out of their mouths while onlookers marveled at the waste of words.

LUKE DAY 9

I woke myself up mumbling to myself. Couldn't decipher exactly what I was saying, just a string of nonsense words, so I threw them out of mind. I lay there for a while trying to replay last evening. Where was I exactly? All I could recall was riding way past tired until I spotted this private, half deserted campground in the middle of somewhere. After I checked myself in, some creepy guy with slithered back hair directed me toward this spot on the back lot—away from everyone else. I hadn't seen any other bikers around so I must have covered some serious distance from Sturgis, before unloading my body in this stinky site. Crawling out of my tent, I stumbled on its zipper, until my foot went right through the mesh.

"Bloody piece of junk, probably made in China!" I told the tent off, as I untangled my left foot. Standing up, I scouted the area for a toilet. All I could see were a few dilapidated old cabins that resembled worn fishing shacks, a couple of rusted out cars, an abandoned RV covered with a blue tarp and an old boat up on cinder blocks.

"Boy, I sure know how to pick the good spots," I poked fun at myself, echoing what Jill would probably say if she were with me.

As my sleep filled eyes scanned the area, I hadn't noticed any signs of life, not even some flowers—and this place could definitely use some life. I wonder why that creep at the front desk put me back here, as there appeared to be room at the front of the campground that skirted the highway. Probably intimidated by me being a biker and all. Anyway, the toilet was calling for me but I just couldn't see it, and a whiz in the bush just would not suffice this morning. An excursion of sorts was in order to find the stinker.

Bending down to retrieve my boots, I was met with an empty patch of dirt. Twirling around, I peered over my dome tent but couldn't locate them anywhere. That's strange, I thought, as I always parked them just outside my tent—no point breathing in that stench of sweat soaked leather all night. Poking my head in the tent, just in case I forgot to put them out for the night, I rummaged through my sleeping bag and Therma-rest, pushing clothes aside, lifting my tank bag—nowhere! How odd! I crawled back out and walked over to my bike in my socks—still no boots. I again surveyed the deserted back camping lot for anything that resembled my boots—my favorite black leather, well worn, knee high riding boots. Well they certainly could not have walked off on their own. Maybe they were pissed off at me, tired of my stinkin' feet, tired of being stepped on all day long, fed up with being put out for the night and they decided to rebel. The thought amused me as I continued to search for my lost friends. What would I do without you, I pondered.

Puzzled by their missing appearance, yet desperately in need of a dump, I gave up the hunt and traipsed around in socks till I finally found an old outhouse that was truly full of shit. Relieving myself as quickly as I could and having to keep the door open the whole while just so that I could breathe, I finally fell face forward out of that crap trap with my pants still around my knees. Scampering away on all fours, just to escape the stench, my knee got caught in my pants and I did a face plant in some wild flowers that grew along the ditch. What a relief! Even the dandelions were welcomed!

Making my way back to my tent, I again resumed seeking the safe retrieval of my beloved boots. Realizing at that point that they were not merely misplaced, that they had to be stolen, I began scavenging through other camper's belongings, looking for my other feet—my lost soles.

"Hey get the fuck out of my stuff!" some twenty year old skin head punk yelled at me through his ripped tent. I looked at him nonchalantly, then continued pushing his garbage aside, focused on finding what belonged to me. Once I realized that this guy had enough junk everywhere, but not my boots, I moved on. When he saw that I wasn't trying to steal from him, only locate something I'd lost, he chuckled. Did he know where they were? My now blackened socks were a dead giveaway as to what I was missing.

The next camp site was clean in comparison, didn't look like anyone was home, the tent had a padlock on it. Still no boots! One by one, I pushed my way through each camping spot, playing eye spy with my little eye, I'm looking for something black and made out of leather. An hour and a quarter later, I found my hands, or feet, still empty.

"Some culprit's hiding them in his tent," I explained to myself. This had to be the poorest campground I'd ever seen, as these were not mere recreational campers here, this was indeed a slum, where homeless people lived—this was actually their life. There were tarps everywhere, covering up outside kitchens, comprised of old, but working stoves and fridges with padlocks. These were not the outdoor kitchens of my neighborhood back home in Chilliwack, where the latest Canadian

Tire trendy stainless steel and flagstone rooms could be found cooking up some roasted lamb with mango chutney, no these were filled with cockroaches running through day old pots of Kraft dinner and half eaten cans of Spam. My boots would bring in a feast for these folks. Still, they were MY boots and I wanted them back.

Retracing my path, I eventually found myself face to face with what must have been the manager, Mr. Slickedback hair, standing in a doorway. He, unfortunately, was my only hope at this point. "Hi, I'm camped over there in the back lot and it appears that someone has walked off with my riding boots," I exclaimed pointing down at my now twig infested socks.

"Well what do you want me to do about it?" he replied, smirking while sizing me up and down.

"I want you to accompany me as we search through everyone's tents," I stated matter of factly, as if this was so obvious.

"Ha!" was his sarcastic come back. "That's not my job and besides if you're stupid enough to leave your valuables unattended that's your problem. See that sign?" He pointed to an old yellowed piece of paper tacked to the wall near the ceiling which claimed that the establishment was not responsible for lost or stolen items.

This was no establishment, and no these people were not the responsible types, this was true, but could he deny that my boots were indeed stolen. Surely not! Backed into a corner, without much choice, pleading would not work here, I threatened. "I guess that leaves me no option but to call the police then."

"Go right ahead," he laughed shaking his greasy head. "You think the police have time to come hold your hand and help you look for your boots? PLEASE!!"

"Well if I report them missing and describe this makeshift pawn shop you have running here, they might just think it's worth their while. You know, come see what other illegal activities they can uncover while they're here." I found myself saying with unfound courage.

With that, he jumped back through a yellow, smoke stained curtain and pulled out what must have been his wife, or old lady, as he referred to her as. She apparently overheard the whole conversation. Cigarette hanging out of her bubble gum pink swollen lips, bleached blond with dark vacant eyes and overly aged mottled skin, this woman held the power in their relationship. She leaned on the counter, supposedly to show me some cleavage; this woman was used to getting her way. "You don't need to go and do that," she offered through her crooked smile. "We'll help you find your boots, won't we Doug?" while back hand slapping Doug on the side of the face.

"Thank you," was my only reply. I just wanted my boots, not a fight, not a court case.

"Give us a few minutes and we'll see if we can find them for you." Doug Slickhead said, now amiable.

"I'm in camp spot number 27, when you find them," I shot back exiting the creaking door.

"Oh we know which spot you're in," they called out.

"Yeah, I'm sure you do!" Looking at my watch, 10:32, and wondering how long it would take them to find the culprit who stole them. They probably already knew.

I sauntered back to number 27 campsite and proceeded to pack up my things and take down my tent. Looked at my watch —11:07. Still no boots! HMMM!!! I sat on the picnic table that was badly in need of a screw or two, and waited. Finally, I saw the handsome couple making their way toward me.

"Henry over there doesn't have them. Tony doesn't either. Hank says he wouldn't want your stinkin boots and Walt, well he's in a drunken stupor and couldn't have taken them." Doug offers, pointing to where all of these locals pitch their homes and then scratching his oily hair.

Crossing her arms, and stomping out her smoke butt, Miss Big Hair looked perplexed as if she was confused and then annoyed that one of her trusted regulars had one on her. "We'll just have to tear through some of their tents," she said as she marched on, Doug close behind her.

Now here's a woman who means business, especially if she's inclined to believe she's been double crossed. So she led a now angry Doug and sock footed me, on an expedition. They wanted the guy, I wanted the boots. We were now in this together—what a hoot! It appears that Gwen, Miss Bubblicious herself, inherited this enterprise from her bootlegging father, who had quite the scam set up. Innocent campers would set up for the night, while the local hoodlums would scour for valuables in the night. The proceeds from the pawn shop, or from Gwen and Doug themselves if they were interested in the newly scoffed treasure, would be split fifty/fifty. The thought that someone stole the boots without reporting it to Gwen, had her in a tuff. She was determined to oust him forever from her kingdom. Unfortunately for me, I wandered into this crime nest innocently enough. I wanted to just leave—unscathed—and with my boots!

I followed them as they cut through the first tent, quickly realizing that they were committing a crime themselves while doing this. Then Doug picked up an old rusted pipe lying on the ground, obviously intending to clobber someone. I couldn't watch. I didn't want to be part of this. I just wanted my boots.

"I think I'll just wait by my bike," I said rather sheepishly, "let you guys do your job." I frantically turned around and tripped over some old unused lawn mower, as I high tailed it out of there. But this was not their job, I admitted to myself; I'm just being an accomplice to further crime. I did not like the predicament that I found myself in. I sat on the picnic table beside my loaded up bike and contemplated what I should do. If I left, I'd never see my boots again, but if I stayed I could land myself in the middle of something very ugly. I decided to leave.

Driving a motorcycle with only socks on your feet can be rather tricky, especially shifting gears, which is done with your feet. When you come to a stop light and have to stop, it is also very uncomfortable to balance without some thick leather under your toes. No matter! Driving along, I still did not really know where I was. It must be one of the Dakota's anyway. I had to find a store to buy some new boots, preferably a motorcycle shop and as luck would have it, some other bikers pulled up beside me at a stoplight.

"Nice boots!" one of them hollered my way, while chuckling and pointing out my white socks to his buddies.

"Oh thanks," I yelled back over the roar of our engines, while lifting my whites into the air. "You guys know where there's a bike shop round here?"

"Yeah, we're heading there, follow us," as the light turned green and they each torqued up their revs.

Dismounting our bikes at a Yamaha shop, we introduced ourselves. Ryan, Jeff and Kyle were young studs riding powerful Japanese bikes, with color coordinated leathers to match their colorful bikes.

"What happened to your boots?" Ryan just had to ask.

"Stolen....outside my tent last night," I answered to everyone, including my own disbelief. "Gotta buy myself some new ones I guess."

Kyle opened the door for us all and we stepped into the air conditioned oasis from the heat. Scanning the show room, I soon discovered that I don't like Yamaha boots. They either were too bright, too small or too tight around my huge calves. Japanese I ain't! Plunking myself down on a comfy black sofa by the door, I planned my next step. Do I purchase something that I hate and pay a pretty penny for it, just to get me by or do I ride on till I find another bike shop? Unsure of what to do, I stared pensively out the window and soon, my three new buddies had sat themselves down as well. It hadn't taken long before I unloaded on them what had befallen me.

Rubbing his chin, Jeff surmised that I should just call the cops. After all, that was fair and just and actually the most sensible and responsible thing to do. So with that, I borrowed the Yamaha Parts Department phone and reported my boots missing to the police. Twenty minutes later, the South Dakota Police pulled up in a cruiser in front of the Yamaha shop. Taking over the store's couch, we all sat and discussed what had happened. Writing everything down and not saying much, finally, the two cops stood up to leave.

"We'll see what we can find. We know the place well," the tall cop said nodding his head. "Where ya staying? We'll contact you when we've completed our investigation."

"Ah, I guess I'll check myself in there," I said pointing to the Motel conveniently located across the street.

As we all walked back to our respective cruisers, I waved to the police, "Thank you," and I meant it!

I checked myself in to my motel room and soaked in the tub and waited for the phone to ring. I found it humorous that the police would actually take up their time investigating some lost boots. There must be more going on here, I thought—a lot more! The police probably loved having an excuse to search that place, long having suspicions about what goes on there.

Several hours later, the phone finally rang. "Can you meet us down at the Police Station?" the voice asked. "We'd like to discuss some things with you."

"Did you find my boots?" I implored somewhat hopeful.

"Not yet, but we're still completing our investigation," the male officer's voice answered, sounding overly interested. He should have been bored—looking for boots!!

I hopped on my Kawi, with a fresh pair of black socks, hoping they might camouflage for black leather boots. I thought of tucking my jeans into my socks, but that was pushing it. I wasn't actually striving for the dorky look.

Finding the police station on the main drag, I parked and tip toed through their tulips looking for the entrance. In no time, the nice lady behind the front desk had me in a chair, with a cup of coffee in my hands. Two bulky, oversized police constables strode up to me, each dragging a chair behind them, and formed a triangle with myself. They plopped their hulky bodies down and stared intently at me as I sipped my java. Feeling nervous for what should have been mundane, I waited for these two to take the lead.

"Please state your name for the record, sir," the tall one with the tiny teeth asked.

"Lucas Connor," I said as a matter of fact.

"So, you find yourself in these here parts? For what purpose?" the gorilla with the grin asked.

"I'm just on my way back from Sturgis. I'm on my way back home actually,....eventually!" I quipped innocently enough.

They looked at each other and then back at me, or through me. "And why were you staying at the Happy Haven Campground last night?" they quizzed me.

Puzzled by where they were going with their questioning, you'd think they were investigating me. "I needed a place to stay—why else do people check themselves in to a campground?" I answered sarcastically, although as I said that I knew with that place there could be lots of unsavory reasons someone might stay there. With that thought, I started to laugh. "Oh you've got to be kidding me! You think I have something to do with that hell hole? I'm the one with the missing boots," I proclaimed, not yet fully irritated.

"Well we have spent the afternoon searching that campground for your boots and have come up empty handed. Gwen and Doug, the proprietors, fully cooperated in the investigation and led us through each campsite."

"Oh, I'm sure they cooperated alright. They want to find the goon who stole them just as much as you do, although for entirely different reasons. As for me, I just want my damn boots back!"

"We'll get to the boots, be patient sir. We need to know of your dealings with a Gwen and Doug Jones. What contact have you had with them, say in the last year?" the cop with the small bite asked.

I looked over toward the other cop, gorilla himself, hoping he'd see how ludicrous this was, hoping that he'd have more sense, although it is entirely impossible to take a grinning gorilla seriously. He just shot me that stupid grin—again!

"I haven't had any dealings with them. I just met them last night for the first time. I told you, I needed a place to stay. I was tired, it was dark and late and I just stumbled into that campground. I have nothing to do with their crime sprees," I said, tripping over my words and rolling my eyes.

"Wait here!" Mr. Big and Tall demanded and then they both got up and left down the hall, where I could see them standing close and whispering, shooting the odd glances my way. One of them got the receptionist to look something up on a computer, to which they stood there rubbing their faces and shuffling their feet. Finally they returned. None too soon, because I was past tired of all this nonsense.

"Mr. Lucas Connor....." Tall began before I interrupted.

"Just Luke," I mumbled.

"Pardon me, what did you say?" Tall asked, staring through me.

"Oh forget it! .... What? What now? Just tell me you found my bloody boots already!!" I shouted, fully regretting now that I had reported my boots missing.

"No we haven't found your boots. But you see, we're dealing with a string of missing boots. It seems every week a pair of boots has gone missing, reported stolen. We don't know who is responsible, or what the motive is, but we are determined to get to the bottom of this. We have several officers on this case." Gorilla offered, minus the grin now.

"All from the same campground?" I asked, myself now grinning.

"No, actually from that stretch of highway though, encompassing about ten miles. Yep, every week another pair gone. We're just trying to determine a profile of the victims, to see if there are any similarities, or if you are actually part of the problem. Wondering if you reported your boots missing on a lark—pullin' a joke to send us on a wild goose chase or something." Tall attempted to interrogate me.

"Well this is no joke, believe me and I am indeed the victim here," was all I could offer in my defense.

Staring hard into my face, watching for cracks, they finally backed off and slapped their knees and then got up. Surprisingly, they shook my hand. Their apologies indicated I was fresh out of luck in regards to my boots though.

"Wait, I can't keep riding in socks. Since you haven't recovered any of the other missing boots, I doubt you'll find mine. Would you happen to have any confiscated old footwear that I could have until I can replace my boots properly?" I asked, trying my luck. This all reminded me again of my missing helmet in Amsterdam, where the police gave me a confiscated helmet with a marijuana leaf on it to wear. This thought made me anxious however, as I recalled how long it took to find a helmet large enough and I already experienced Yamaha boots—YUK!

"Well let's see," Gorilla said, now grinning wildly again. He walked down the hall and motioned for me to follow. He led me to a room filled with shelves lining both walls with loads of boxes on each. He rummaged through some shelves until he found a box labeled, Men's Shoes. He pulled the box down and I jumped in to see. I couldn't believe they'd actually have a box of men's footwear—I mean how many people lose their shoes. Are these found on the streets, minus human content or are they taken off dead victims? I didn't care, I was tired of riding in socks and so any damn shoes would do, or at least I thought.

"How about these?" Gorilla threw me a pair of lime green fluffy slippers. "Or these?" A pair of Indian fringed moccasins landed near my feet. "You pick," he chuckled as he dumped the whole box upside down, with what must have been a hundred pairs of footwear: slippers, shoes, runners, sandals and even some boots.

"Hey, maybe some of those missing boots are in here?" I joked. None of them were leather biking boots however, more like winter boots, gum boots, hiking boots. But it was plausible that they were some of the missing.

"Na, we already checked," was his reply.

So I scrummaged through the pile, until I spotted an old worn pair of Nike runners that would suffice, but damn it, they were too small. Surprising since I only wear a size ten, not particularly large for men's feet. I kept looking, trying on several, until I found something that fit—kind of like Cinderella: too big, too small, too narrow, too ugly—oh wait, that was her step sisters.

I strolled out of the police department that day wearing some black leather dress shoes, laceless, with the tongues sticking out at me—mocking me! Half the department was watching, wailing, while I wandered past—always the wise guy! They were Brogues—ironically what I used to wear when I taught in a private school and all the kids would make fun of my formal old man shoes.

Outside, I mounted my bike with a smile. At least I didn't have on white socks. I pushed off the curb and headed back to my Motel. I watched an old John Wayne movie that night, envying his leather cowboy boots. Sprawling out over a King sized bed all to myself, I had a crazy dream that night. I dreamt that I was lying on the floor of some room and Nancy Sinatra was singing:

"These boots are made for walking, and that's what they're gonna do, one of these days these boots are gonna walk all over you you you...."

She was walking all over me, together with hundreds of pairs of boots—all kinds of boots.

Except these other boots were emptied of any souls, just empty soles marching over my dead body. I think I was dead in the dream because I sure didn't feel any pain. I lied there watching, numb, a spectator. As they exited my consciousness, the boots were singing:

"The boots go marching one by one hurrah, hurrah, the boots go marching one by one hurrah, hurrah, the boots go marching one by one, the little one stops to stick out his tongue and they all go down, to the earth.... to get out.... of the rain... boom boom boom rain!"

THREE YEARS EARLIER

Death came calling at the Foster household. Kevin Foster lived alone, three houses down from the Connor family on Silver Drive in Chilliwack. He was a strange old man, often seen lurking in his yard with his head down. It was rumored that he set out dishes of antifreeze for the neighborhood pets to consume, thereby killing them off. He was an unhappy soul. His wife had passed away many years before and he never did have children. He complained about everyone and everything to anyone who would listen. Sometimes no one was listening and you would see him whining to the wind as he was mowing his lawn. Often he would even appear to be arguing with himself. He didn't care what others thought of him; he was in his own world.

But this was his street. He had lived here many, many years, long before any of the other families had decided to call this street home. He made sure the school buses no longer delivered kids to their own homes, instead depositing them at the corner, lest the roads get worn from overuse. He once lobbied for more street lights however, so he took his self-ascribed role of street Lord, quite seriously.

They say he died of a stroke. No surprise as he was pushing eighty, and he was so full of anger. His head probably exploded on him—or imploded anyway! He was found in his front yard, with his arm pointing at something in the sky, when he just keeled over. The mailman found him that way and had called the police. Soon the yard was cordoned off and the neighborhood came out to see. Kevin was still lying there and everyone was looking up to see what he had been looking at—what he had been pointing to. Was it the weather, a plane or just the birds that had been nesting up in a tree? We will never know.

A public trustee came some time later and had arranged for his things to be brought to the auction house and his house put up for sale. No one knew if Kevin had any relatives.

Three years ago, three houses down, Death had come calling!

JILL DAY 10

The next morning, when I regrettably woke up, I found myself lying in my lonely bed, the sun barely awake itself, counting the number of words Emily and Molly were wasting in their verbal exchanges. Be frugal, be frugal I thought to myself. Don't waste those precious words. A sadness came over me and I opened my eyes. Another day in the quiet world I thought. How ironic, considering how noisy the sea was. It had been screaming at me all night long with its unrelenting waves smashing the rocks and I was tired of all the chatter gnawing at my brain as the waves were just echoing the chaos within. There was no escape. Violent tossing water smacks hard when thrown with such force by gale winds, demanding your attention as it assaults your silence—your attempts at sleep, or even mere thought. In similar fashion, words were being thrown at my soul, hitting me hard and demanding a response: lost, accident, injury, death, fear, alone. These words had such weight, such consequence, cracking my rocky heart as they crashed down upon me. I was drowning, yet not even trying to gasp for air; I was too numb. Hypothermia had frozen my heart. Rational thinking was stalled as if my brain could only move in slow motion. Clarity was replaced by mental haze.

At least I was somewhat calm. So I figured now would be a good time to see if we could get a ferry home. But I didn't want to waste precious cell phone minutes on the ferry reservation voice mail system, so off to town we went.

Even though the busy weekend traffic had left, I was still feeling anxious about whether or not there'd be room on the next ferry. As we traveled toward the pay phone, I wanted to put off the inevitable. I took the girls to see a fire truck at the fire hall, then we stopped in to the Tree House Clothing Boutique, for I don't know what, and finally, we dropped in at the Bakery for some ice cream cones. As we lounged outdoors, relishing every lick, I knew I was stalling. What was the worst they could say—we're all booked. I could always book for the next day, or the next, or the next. I was no longer rational.

"Let's go to Edith Point!" I announced to the girls, as we piled into the truck. They were still splashing down their double bubble gum and licorice tiger cones and so did not respond. At least it was no longer raining out.

I loved this hike; it was my favorite jaunt on the whole island in fact. It was actually private property—all thirty acres of it, but as luck would have it, the owners lived in Alberta and were very generous. They even put up signs: trail markers around their property so people could explore and not get lost. There was one wide trail leading down through the middle of the forested peninsula and then there were several narrow windy trails that led out towards the water: Campbell Bay on one side and Georgia Strait on the other side. That day we chose, or rather I chose to hike the loop while the girls just sauntered behind me. As we walked through the forest, Molly and Emily collected pine cones, arbutus bark, and many colored rocks until their pockets were bulging. I knew what I was doing—stalling—but I kept at it.

Once we reached the end-Edith Point-we plunged ourselves down on the mossy rocks and just listened to the waves crashing in. This was such a spectacular spot. The sky was various shades of blue, the wind was warm and gentle and the seagulls sung overhead. This place reminded me of my mom. To the right was Georgeson and Curlew Islands, behind them was Saturna Island, and straight ahead you could see Boundary Bay and White Rock in the far distance. What a panoramic view! The owners of this incredible property had built an architectural wonder of a house perched on the point. The only way in was over paths for a good half hour walk, so instead, the owners had barged in the materials needed to build this splendid home. They were seldom seen and I was glad for the solitude. We took the side paths going back, which edged along the water, first along the wild, windy and noisy Georgia Strait side, where waves smashed against the sandstone and then inward along Campbell Bay where it was quiet, still and warm. We watched the frisky seals play on a reef in the Bay and people swimming down on the beach.

 I thought back to the times when we would take our motor boat to this bay and go tubing all around. It was so hilariously funny. We thought it would be a great adventure for the girls, so we had purchased a two man tube, thinking that one of us could go with one of the girls and then switch it up. But once we had the boat and tube, I was too chicken to try, nor did I know how to drive the boat for Luke to go at it. Eventually I learned to drive and I even got the nerve to try tubing—what a blast! Of course Luke never slowed down when my thumb was pointing down, nor did he cut the engine when I motioned my hand cutting across my throat. He always did the opposite; he was just so playful. Thankfully, however, when one of the girls was on the tube with me, he followed all the rules. He could be responsible when he needed to be, but that was not his preferred mode of living.

Stepping over fallen arbutus branches, we meandered along the narrow trail until we could see the wide path merging with the one we were on. The girls were singing ABCD and arguing over LMNO; Molly was convinced that was one letter and Emily, the little teacher, was determined to set her straight. I stayed out of it. Suddenly, as we came around a bend, we encountered a dead deer, strewn along side of the path and with a unified gasp, we stopped to inspect it. Noticing the cliff overhead, it appeared the deer had pranced off the cliff, hit a tree and fell to his death with a broken neck. He was all mangled up, with his head twisted in an unnatural position. It was such a shame. His brown golden coat looked alive as ever since he couldn't have been dead for long. I was about to feel it to check to see if it was still warm and then I thought better of it. I wouldn't want the girls copying me. I always told them to leave dead things alone.

"Come on girls, just leave it," I said as I pulled them away.

"Maybe he's just sleeping," Emily reasoned.

"I wish he was....I wish he was," I whispered.

Back along the path, we could hear the screams and laughter from the beach below. It seemed like such a juxtaposition: life on one side, death on the other. The dirt path turned to gravel and then to paved concrete; we were almost at the truck. There was no more stalling, I admonished myself—find a pay phone.

Outside of the Trading Post General Store was the phone, but I needed coins. So I went in to cash a bill when my eye caught the shelves of liquor. I sure would like to get drunk, pass out and then find myself awoken from this stupor, only to learn that it was all just a nightmare. No, I still had some reason.

Putting a quarter into the pay phone, I dialed BCFERRY. To my surprise, and delight, they had room on the evening sailing to the mainland. We were going home! I darted back into the store and bought some pepperoni sticks to tide the girls over till I could make them some long overdue lunch.

We spent the afternoon getting ready for its end—when we'd be back home in Chilliwack. Cleaning, packing, loading the truck while still doing the regular meals, diapers, this and that. There always seemed to be more this and that than expected. I had almost forgotten the clothes still hanging on the arbutus tree clothesline, which we quickly bundled up and brought into the cabin still smelling of sea air. Next, I started to clean the oven and the fridge; I could tell in my preparations, that I wasn't planning on returning to Mayne Island anytime soon. I was being released from jail. Our ferry reservation for that day was the ticket I'd been waiting and longing for. I utilized my little live wires to stir me into an almost frantic pace and together, we three worked until we were ready to go, yet we had hours before the ferry was to depart.

Reading the girls a story to occupy our time and secretly taunt the god of words, I embellished the story more than usual. I loved wasting words for no reason other than rebellion. The girls didn't notice; they loved it all the same.

"Brrring...brrring!" Oh no I'm caught! I felt vulnerable picking up the phone.

"Hello this is Detective Smith of the South Dakota Police Department of Homicide speaking," came a deep burly voice. "I understand your husband has been missing and now his file has been passed over our way," he continued. "I'm recommending we begin an aerial search of the area with one of our helicopters. We'll be looking for a man, tent or motorcycle matching your husband's description. Please let us know if you hear from Luke in the meantime Mam." He had that same American accent but much more testosterone.

"Okay," I said glad that such resources were being spent on my husband. He was so worth the effort.

"You have three minutes remaining. This is B.C.Telus," intercepted that annoying operator again. That name said it all: Tell us. I'd love to tell them what I think of their service, or lack thereof!

Oh so I must have had more minutes than I thought. Three left. I felt rich, like I just got paid at the word bank. Realizing that I was still on the line to the detective, I shot back, "I'm going home today, but you can reach me on my landline at 604-858-9845."

"We'll keep you informed," he said clicking the phone down in my ear.

Luke must be dead. I'm sure of it. There was such a giant hole. He was so full of life. He was such a kind hearted and generous soul, something must have happened to prevent him from returning to us; he would never devise his own demise. I needed to stop referring to him in the past tense. "Have faith in him," I admonished myself.

Driving down that bumpy driveway I was running away from my demons. We were going home to Chilliwack. The ferry terminal was almost empty—just to mock me I'm sure. We loaded onto the Queen of Nanaimo with no problems, albeit they wanted us to park on the upper ramp, which meant I had to maneuver that four wheel monster around a tight curve.

"Daddy can do it," Emily reminded me.

"I know he can do it—your daddy can do lots of things, but I'm not daddy, okay?"

I shot back irritated for the comparison.

It was past Molly's bedtime and she was spent. Carrying her up two flights of stairs while holding Emily's hand, we finally managed to secure a spot by the coveted play area of the ship. This was vital to my survival. Here they could play on the small plastic horses or cars or watch a video while I read, interacted with other parents or just zoned out. The latter usually prevailed.

We looked so haggard, but then so did everyone on the evening ferries. Did I even brush my hair, I wondered, let alone makeup? Oh well, at least Molly's clothes are not desperately dirty and Emily is somewhat seasonal: she is wearing shorts with her winter boots today. I got a newspaper out of the recycling bin to read, but all the news was so depressing. I needed sunny news—mommy news! No wonder newspapers are grey, they should be yellow.

Peering out the window, I felt ourselves being pulled away. The shoreline was growing smaller and the sea was sucking us outward. It felt good! It was twilight and the pink hues filled the sky and spilled over onto the sea. It was my favorite time to travel on water, as the beauty easily transported your thoughts elsewhere. I tried to formulate some concrete plans of action for when I got home but was barraged with so many ideas, which I had to prioritize: call the police, my mom, Mike, Luke's family. I was sick of thinking about all this.

I stared out the salt stained window as we passed Helen Point, then Miner's Bay and before long, we had pulled into Galiano Island. Few passengers disembarked, but many more were added. I was relieved that we had such convenient seats. The girls were watching "Little Bear" on the TV overhead and I just gazed out at the welcoming sea, letting the waves swoosh over me. As we crossed the Strait towards Tsawwassen, the ocean waves picked up and the ferry swayed. No matter, I wanted to be lulled.

Hearing the announcement for disembarking, the girls and I gathered up our things and headed down to the truck. The hour and a half ferry ride had ended and it was now time to get off but I didn't want to get off. I had felt safe on that boat, like pronouncements of Death couldn't find me there. I'd have to be home, sitting next to my mommy before I'd allow myself to hear such awful words. Words of death were just that—awful words! Expensive words! Why doesn't the operator come on and say sorry—times up! You're not permitted to speak those words. And of course, if you can't say them, you can't speak them into existence. Therefore life prevails. Yeah! I like this scenario much better, I tell myself: la la land.

Driving home to Chilliwack, I felt my hopes and fears amplified. The girls were fast asleep in the back seat and I had my thoughts to myself. About an hour into my drive, I was getting rather sleepy so I turned on the radio to try and stay awake. It was one of those oldy goldy stations and they were playing "Staying Alive" by the Bee Gees. I had to laugh at the irony. It instantly brought me back to 1977, when I had just graduated from King George High School in Vancouver and got introduced to the bar scene at the height of disco fever. This song was the anthem of that decade. I was single, had my own apartment, worked two jobs and was saving up for college; I was so alive then....and reckless! Together with Sherrie, my high school best friend, we ditched our college plans however, and decided to discover who we were by traveling instead. It was all about "Staying Alive" at the time, living in the moment is what we would now call it. So we took our saved cash and hit the road in my 1974 Vega. That gutless thing barely made it through the steep mountains, but we eventually made it to Montreal, Chicago and Toronto. We slept many sleepless nights on the lumpy couches of old friends and distant relatives as we traveled night and day over several months. Arriving back in Vancouver in time to catch a pre-booked flight to Hawaii, we bummed around on the beaches of Maui before returning home broke, starved and stoned. Even after that trip, I still didn't know who I was. Living in Kits, trying on the hippy vegetarian thing was me for a time, followed by my three piece suited office girl faze, which gave way to the mountain co-op fleece woman in hiking boots. Eventually, however, I found spiritual harmony here on the west coast as I amalgamated my disco, hippy, professional and outdoorsy personalities together.

Fast forward several decades and I find myself lost again. It's like the equilibrium of my life is off kilter. It angered me that I had traded in my independence for marital dependence. I hated leaning on someone else to make my life work, but I loved Luke and I would have to be some sort of selfish bitch to not lament the hole he would leave in my life if he were gone. I felt such anger directed toward Luke for causing this pain, but I sure missed him! He was not perfect by any means—he could be demeaning or controlling and he definitely was manipulative. He left trails of messes where ever he went, but then expected others to pick up after his shortcomings. Being from West Van, he was entitled after all. We once taught at the same school, only to find myself doing his marking. That ended none too soon. At home boundaries were constantly being drawn and reinforced as his territory grew and mine diminished. Then something in me would rise up and I would scratch back some power. Yet still I loved this fallible creature, quirks, insecurities and all. I don't always know why I feel this way, but Luke still can make my heart sing after all these years. The glitter in our eyes remains and I still can grow weak in the knees when I think about him—most of the time!! In marriage, love grows more complicated with time. Sometimes we over analyze and try to make sense of the irrational or impractical or inefficient. But love doesn't always make sense; its borders reach well beyond the sensible and out toward the outrageous, the ludicrous, and sometimes the wildly insane.

Driving down the dark freeway, I saw the approaching neon signs of Chilliwack, not that I would need them to find my way. We had lived there almost fifteen years and it was home. Luke would have preferred to live somewhere else, anywhere else. Over the years, he had had some regrettable experiences with co-workers, which he would have found easier to move on from, had we literally moved away. But we had well-paying jobs, our girls were born there and the standard of living afforded us a comfortable life; we couldn't just walk away. So Luke resigned himself to live in a place where he never felt he belonged. He resisted becoming a country bumpkin and yearned for the urban fast track. But our community was growing and had reached about seventy thousand folks. We had a shopping mall, a few fine dining restaurants, a couple of movie theatres and a growing college seeking university status. We were on our way, I would try to convince Luke—to no avail. So he would take off on yearly motorcycle adventures to satisfy his need for speed, for thrills, for danger. He liked living on the edge. Ironic, since I felt like I had already fallen into the abyss.

As I turned down our humble street, Silver Drive, I tried to reassure myself that every cloud has a silver lining. It didn't work. The street seemed eerily dark and too quiet—like I had just entered Death's shadow. Pulling into our driveway, my eye caught the street sign adjacent to our house: Sesame Street. I didn't think of the cheery, children's TV program.... no, I thought of "Open sesame" as my garage door opened to swallow us up.

The house had its own smell, kind of like glue and celery. It was cool inside and the refrigerator was still humming. The many large windows in the vaulted living room still had their wooden blinds closed. The Heritage blue family room remained in the last decade and the green and pink kitchen reminded me of unfinished decorating dilemmas. Peering through the dimly lit house, I could see the flashing of the answering machine; was it signifying a beacon of hope or alarm? It would have to wait until I carried my sleeping bundles up to their respective beds.

Once everything and everyone was unloaded, I braced myself before pushing the play button to listen for the new messages. I was so hopeful...still! But no, just my mom, my sister and several telemarketers. Most people knew we were on Mayne, so I wasn't expecting many calls, but I did hope..... for one. I then pressed the 'Play Recorded Message' button just to hear Luke's voice. He was forever changing the message on the machine. One time it said: "This is big Luke and the little woman," in his best John Wayne impression. Another time it was: "This is Chinese laundry, you want laundry leave name," in his convincing Chinese accent, albeit so politically incorrect.

The worst one, however, was right after that building got blown up in Oklahoma and Luke decided, stupidly, to record a message, in his best southern drawl, which said: "Hi, this is Tim McFee and if you would like to learn how to build a bomb or rent a Ryder truck, then you just leave your name and number here and we'll get right back to you." Luke had wanted to hear this message replayed, but instead of just hitting the 'play message button', he somehow thought he had to dial 1911 to hear it back. It hadn't worked. But then the phone did ring, which was odd since it was almost midnight. Luke insisted we not answer it and instead let the caller hear our new message. They heard it alright, but then never left their own message. Oh well, we thought, and as it was late, Luke headed for the shower and I went off to bed. Within minutes there was a loud banging at the front door and the doorbell was ringing repeatedly. With Luke still in the shower, and the girls asleep, I quickly scrambled downstairs to quiet down the callers...whoever they could be. As I peeked out the window next to the front door, I had a flashlight shone into my face.

"It's the police. Open up!" They demanded.

With just my skimpy nighty on, I reluctantly opened the metal front door before they broke it down.

"Someone called 911!" they insisted, now standing in my front hall.

"No. No one called 911 here," I replied bewildered as ever. Stepping back and with knees shaking, I suddenly realized what had happened. "Oh wait a minute," I chuckled, "My husband left a crazy message and he had wanted to hear it back and so he dialed 11911 or something like that. Everything is fine....it was just a joke."

But they didn't think so. Shoving me out of the way, they proceeded to enter our home, all four of them. Roaming from room to room, with their hands over their holstered guns, they were searching for something or someone. Realizing that it had probably been them that had called and heard Luke's new message and then when we didn't answer the phone, they were obligated to come out and investigate, I was afraid for Luke. Would they take him for a bomb builder? But he was still in the shower. Climbing the stairs, they went into the girls' room and our bedroom, before I yelled up that my husband was in the shower. I fully expected them to barge in on him, but they didn't. Instead they came back downstairs and reassured me that everything seemed to be in order. And they left.

Thankfully Molly and Emily slept through the whole thing. As for Luke, well, he didn't believe me when I had told him what had just happened, he thought I was overreacting—as if I would make that whole thing up!! Lying in bed that night, I thought about what would have happened if I hadn't opened the front door. The police would have broken in, thinking that someone was in trouble. I, upon hearing the smashed in glass, would have called the police from the upstairs phone, thinking that someone was trying to break in. How ironic that would have been. All I could think was, Luke, you need to change that message.

Fast forward and I was again expecting to be entertained by what Luke's latest message could have contained, but I was let down only to hear my own voice. I had recorded the last message on the answering machine. It wasn't the least bit funny, only efficient, to the point and functional. Even his recordings didn't exist anymore!

It was time for sleep and before long I was stretched out in my own bed. Home sweet comfort—home. Restful haven from the storms of life. Death, nor storms: they're not permitted here either I thought. If only the police could have chased those boogey-men away! I would have gladly called 911 if it were possible for the police to rid my home or my mind of such dark invaders.

LUKE DAY 10

I awoke to the tinkle of rain outside my window, together with a laugh. Time to wear my rain suit with my dress shoes. I decided to treat myself so I picked up the phone for room service but only got some dumb answering machine message stating that they do not offer such service. What about service with a smile? No such luck! They should at least take lessons on how to compose a message—theirs sounded more like a morgue. I again glanced over at the phone, and sneered cynically. Wanting to call Jill, but then lamenting the darn phone companies and their inadequacies; what's the point? "ATT does not recognize the cellular network in Canada"—I had that line etched between my ears somewhere, burrowing through my brain like some earwig that laid eggs.

Just then the phone did ring. Startling me fully, I lunged at it mid ring.

"Hello, this is the South Dakota police department calling, officer McCullen here. Did you say your name was Lucas Connor......a Lucas B. Connor of Chilliwack, British Columbia, Canada?"

Recognizing McCullen's voice as that of Gorilla, I offered, "Oh hi, yup that's me!"

"Double checking that's all...double checking! Won't keep you then," came Gorilla McCullen sounding uncustomarily apologetic. "You might just want to stay in town though for another day or two. Let us try and wrap things up. We might just have some more questions for you."

Shrugging off that nonsensical phone call, I proceeded to pack my things and load my bike. They weren't going to find my boots so no point sticking around. Thankfully, this is a much quicker job when camping gear is not involved. Before long I was on the wet gray highway, filling up my thirsty new shoes. I headed west to Wyoming. As I rode that misty road, I pondered the poor souls who lost their soles. Why WAS someone taking off with stolen boots? Surely it was just one person, some sort of serial boot thief. Was it someone's form of a joke or mere retaliation? Was someone trying to distract the police by consuming their time with missing boots, and not being aware of some larger crime spree going on? Was the Happy Haven just a front for Gwen and Doug's boot thief ring? Was there some local Robin Hood giving all these boots to the homeless and shoeless? Were they just stolen for money... for drugs? But then why not take other valuable things as well? What's with the boots? These questions plagued me as I rode on through the rain, yearning for refuge from my persistent thoughts.

I went past a deserted lake with some fool tubing behind a motorboat in this rain. I passed deer hovering under some bushes, munching on berries beside the highway. Silver clouds hung over me as I rode through the mist. My speed was so consistent, that the bike engine reverberated like a sewing machine, producing a hypnotic numbing effect. My teeth began to chat in unison.

I pulled over for gas and hooked up my electric vest to my battery in an attempt to keep warmer. I found myself scanning the gas bar for Mike, Rod or Larry.....still! Of course they weren't there, just their memory. I did see three other stooges speed past: Jeff, Ryan and Kyle—my Yamaha buddies. Quickly paying the clerk for my fuel, I jumped over the rose bushes that surrounded the gas store and mounted my trusty friend. Inadvertently popping a wheelie, I slammed my dress shoes onto the pavement to stabilize my bucking bronco. Swerving over the asphalt, I sped along trying to catch up to them. Fat chance! They probably clock 140 clicks minimum.

I resumed my solo rain ride, feeling lonely. Warm fuzzy thoughts of Jill and the girls kept me company and I wished I could be with them. At least I was warmer now, all plugged in. I'm always leery wearing this in the rain, afraid of getting zapped or worse. But something about riding in the cold, damp wind, yet feeling cozy and warm; it makes you sleepy. Reminds me of all the times riding with Jill in the rain, especially on long trips, when we wore our electric vests and Jill would begin to doze off. She would get so comfortable back there, she would sway side to side, as sleep would pull her in. I worried that it would pull her right off. One trip I even attached her to me with bungee cords, then when she would doze off and start to lean to one side, I'd feel it, and push her back upright behind me. It was dangerous no doubt, yet preferable to freezing down to the core. Funny how that was only a problem in the rain; she never napped in hundred degree weather.

Oh there was that time I thought she was sleeping, all slumped over my shoulder. She actually had become dehydrated and passed out. I pulled over and pulled her off and then doused her with water while we waited for the ambulance to arrive. We had been riding along the California coastline, where it was fifty five degrees and freezing on a bike, then had turned inland and hit a hundred and twenty degree heat wave—all within two hours. Poor Jill! She always was more of a water than a sun person.

Riding through a string of small towns, I kept looking for bike shops, somewhere to buy some replacement boots. Not that I could replace my lost boots; they had accompanied me on many a road trip, they were all broken in and worn soft. But these dress shoes had to go!

This one particular town looked enchanting enough to browse, even in the rain, which had begun to lighten up a bit. There was no sign to welcome you when you entered, so I still didn't know where I was; this was becoming a familiar feeling. Slowing my speed to first gear, I noticed a small, charming outdoor market. There were booths set up with colorful umbrellas all in a row, selling enchiladas, jewelry, tie dyed clothing, handmade leather goods, various crafts and artworks. It seemed to go on and on, so I decided to stop and pick up some lunch and maybe get some souvenirs for the girls, maybe even find some boots—Ha! Ha!

As I strolled through this quaint little market it reminded me of the Mayne Island market and I wondered how Jill and the girls were doing. They would love it here. There was such a diversity of goods for sale and a few buskers keeping everyone entertained with their musical renditions of Neil Young or John Denver. There was even a whole area of used goods; a flea market consisting of tables of books, videos, toys, clothes and shoes. Actually, they were selling BOOTS! In disbelief, I waddled up to the table. Maybe luck was shining down on me after all. Upon closer examination however, this particular table was selling MY boots!! I could not believe what I was seeing. I picked them up, smelled them, turned them over, carefully inspecting them; I was sure of it—they were my boots.

I looked intently at the guy manning the table. It was not Doug or any familiar face I'd seen at the Happy Haven Campground. It was some young dope head, who looked stoned on pot, sucking on his cigarette, like it was just another joint. He was oblivious to me.

"Hey you," I screamed trying to wake him up to this world. "Where did you get these boots?"

I held them up in the air and started to wave them around.

He squinted his eyes and then stumbled to his feet when he saw that he had a customer. "You like them? They're nice hey?"

"They're mine!" I adamantly shot back. "Where did you get them?"

"I got them from a buddy over in SD," he said struggling to stay upright.

"South Dakota?" I clarified.

"Yeah yeah. My buddy gets me lots of boots. They have lots of nice boots in the Dakota's hey," the stone head slurred. "I'll give them to you for twenty bucks, okay? That's a good deal for you my friend."

As I examined all the boots he was selling, I realized that this was probably the boot thief or his accomplice anyway. There might be a reunion between souls and soles yet, I mused. Staring down this dope head, I pondered whether he was the culprit or not. I doubted it! He could barely stand, let alone raid sleeping tents.

"I'm not giving you anything, except shit!" I yelled his way, staring at all the lost boots, the missed boots and now the found boots.

"Hey hey Dude! You like my boots, right? Well then you can have them, man.....for fifteen bucks, okay?" he continued to slur and spit and mumble.

"Did you not hear me? These are my boots and I'm not paying for them. I'm taking them!" I grabbed them and shook them in the air just to make sure he got my point, and then I stomped off.

I hadn't got a few booths away, when I felt someone grab my arm...tightly. I swung myself around to see not the dope head, whom I half expected to react, but a security guard in full uniform, and loaded as is customary in the States. In Canada, I would have just shrugged off his arm and kept walking, aware of my rights. But somehow, seeing that gun in his holster intimidated me enough to comply.

"Excuse me," the guard explained, "You'll have to come with me." He escorted me through the aisles until we came upon his office, which was situated on top of a little cafe.

I could not believe the turn of luck. This guy thinks I've shop lifted MY BOOTS! "Let me explain," I said in my own defense.

"Save your explaining for the police, they'll be here shortly," this kindly, older Mexican man said as he sat down and took off his hat. "You might as well have a seat yourself. You might be here awhile."

"Not again," I muttered under my breath. I fell back into the hard chair and dropped my beloved boots onto the floor. I sighed and then fidgeted in my seat. "How about I just pay the guy then for the boots and be done with it?" I suggested to the security guard in an attempt to avoid another altercation with the police.

"Nope sorry. Can't be done. Too late!" the Mexican assured me how doomed I was.

So I gave up the fight and waited for what might, not should, befall me. I looked longingly at my boots on the floor and chuckled to myself thinking about how expensive they were, and not just monetarily.

Upon seeing me do this, the guard shot up and walked around his desk to my chair. "I'll be taking those." He motioned for me to hand him MY boots.

With reluctance, I handed them over, sniffing them as they passed by my nose. He carried the boots and threw them onto a table in another room, which contained, most probably a bunch of other confiscated items. Here we go again!

I heard the police, before I saw them. Their heavy boots clunking their way up the stairs. I was jealous!

Entering the room, they too took off their hats and then leaned against the wall near me. They were two ugly goons—looked like monkeys really. They were both short, fat and very hairy. They reminded me of Thing One and Thing Two in Dr. Seuss stories. Introductions were exchanged before they informed me that I was being charged with shop lifting some boots—DUH! "You'll have to come with us to police headquarters."

To my horror, they handcuffed me and read me my rights. I heard blah blah blah. Arm in arm we walked back down the stairs and into the waiting police car.

"What about my bike?" I implored.

"It'll have to wait here for you," Thing Two told me, probably full of shit.

"We'll get Gus here, the security guard to look after it for you until you return," Thing One tried to reassure me. It wasn't working.

Riding in the back of their cruiser I thought of the time our bike was stolen in Amsterdam and hoped that that would not be repeated here. "How long is this going to take?" I asked through the caged window that separated these two monkeys from myself.

"As long as it takes," Thing Two (the one that's full of crap) told me, smirking.

Thankfully, it was not far away, before we pulled up to a two floor red brick building with an American Flag flying out front. As they pulled me up and out, I resigned myself to being the victim of injustice—again! Thing One and Thing Two half dragged me into the station and plunked me down, criminal that I am. They then left me there and went off to concur in the hall, checked something on the computer and then returned to my face. "You say your name is Luke Connor from Sardis, B.C.?"

"Yes," I say bored at how tedious this all was.

They searched each other's faces intently and then turned to me. "It appears you're wanted in another jurisdiction – in South Dakota."

I stared blankly back and then laughed out loud. "Oh that was just a big mix up. I had reported my boots missing and they thought I had something to do with their disappearance. Like I was involved in some sort of boot legging, with boots instead of moon shine. Can you believe it? Apparently there was a string of missing boots and they suspected me of possibly being the mastermind behind the operation. Dumb shits thought I would steal my own boots I guess and then report them missing. Go figure!!"

"Did you say your name was Luke or Lucas Connor?" Thing One asked again.

"Same thing—both me." I smugly answered.

"Are you from Chilliwack or Sardis up in Canada?" Thing one demanded.

"Same thing!" I explained—Sardis is like a suburb of Chilliwack. I laughed knowing how ludicrous that sounded: hick little Chilliwack being accused of suburbia.

Thing One and Thing Two studied my face and then continued. "It doesn't really matter. You're wanted in another state. We're going to have to place you in our little cell over here for the night till we can arrange for the county sheriff to transport you back." The two monkeys removed my handcuffs and then escorted me to my cage.

Sitting on the floor next to me in this pissy, damp and dungy cell was a bald tattooed Frenchman. He was half asleep, all slouched over, but one scary looking dude none the less. I decided to keep my distance – didn't want to start a turf war. The cell could not have been more than ten by ten square feet, but thankfully Frenchman and I were left to divvy up the space ourselves.

Leaning against the concrete back wall of the cell, I contemplated the accusations against me. I was wanted! For what? Leaving town before Tall and Gorilla could complete their investigation about the missing boots? I knew I was innocent, why did I have to stick around? What did they come up with now to accuse me of? I couldn't believe my luck; they were actually going to send me back to South Dakota. With my brain further interrogating me, it was a surprise to have fallen asleep. I awoke to Frenchman kicking me in the groin.

"Wake up you idiot...wake up!" he screamed in his strong Quebecois accent. "Why you take my watch?"

Sitting upright and rubbing my eyes in utter confusion, followed by disbelief, I cowered under his shadow. "I never took anything from you. What are you talking about?"

"You shit....you took my watch when I sleep." He was now grabbing my belt loops and dragging me to a standing position.

"I don't know what you're talking about, I never took your watch. I didn't even come near you. Maybe someone else took it. I was sleeping too," I offered in my defense.

"You think I stupid, you little shit. I cut your throat. Eat you for breakfast with a pair of toast and two eggs side by each," he yelled in my face, glaring at me with dark mean eyes, leaving no doubt that he meant every word.

I freed my hands and pulled out my jean pocket, "See! Nothing!" I took off my jacket and emptied my pockets: a set of keys, some trident gum and some well used ear plugs fell out. "See! I have no watch of yours." I pulled my left arm forward and showed him my only watch. "See, just my old Timex." I was getting tired of being falsely accused, of defending myself.

Just then, one of the young guards came into the cell and pushed us apart. "Hey, hey, he might be guilty of skipping town and stealing some boots, but he doesn't deserve to die."

"Stealin boot, stealin watch he deserve to die!" Frenchman argued.

"I didn't steal any boots, they were my boots. And I didn't steal your watch either." I said emphatically, as I attempted to stand behind the guard, like he was the referee in a boxing ring. Frenchman would make a cream puff out of me, or as he said already, eat me for breakfast. I needed to get out of there. "I want a lawyer. This is ridiculous!"

The front door to the station clanged shut and we each got a waft of some cheap perfume. Frenchman's little tart came to pay his bail—he was leaving us. None too soon as far as I could tell. Walking past me, Frenchman shook his fist in the air to further threaten me. He then motioned the cutting of my throat and then eating it. This was one scary cannibal; straight out of "Silence of the Lambs."

I breathed a sigh of relief as the guard left with him and I fell in a heap onto the floor. I could see and hear the two police officers, two hairy shapes scratching themselves down the hall. They had just ignored the raucous in the cell and were too busy to care. Without Frenchman snoring or pissing me off, it grew very still and quiet. The mumbling monkeys could now be overheard.

"Why should we have to send him back? We have him on charges of shop lifting. They can have him when we're finished with him. Why do we have to always take the back seat to them? Just cuz they're a bigger county—they think they're all important. I say we take our sweet piss time," Thing One confided to Thing Two. "What do they want him for over there anyway?"

"He's wanted in connection with some missing boots, or something missing anyway," Thing Two answered.

I was fuming overhearing all this crap. To think they might just let me rot in here till they're finished with me. I had had enough. "Here you might need this." I said to the two hairballs as I threw them a roll of toilet paper.

Picking it up, Thing Two yelled back, "Hey it's you that's full of shit. We should have let Frenchman have his way with you for stealing his watch."

I couldn't believe it, he really does think I have Frenchy's watch. I rested my head between my knees and tried to control my anger, to no avail though as it was still controlling me. I slammed my fists on the concrete floor and then closed my eyes. I guess I might as well prepare myself to rot in here; who knows how long this will take.

JILL DAY 11

Surprisingly, we three slept in this morning, being in our comfy home beds, rather than the hard boards we call beds at the cabin. Not a ten thirty sleep-in like was possible in pre-kid days, no… a mere eight o'clock sleep-in, which was still a luxury, especially these days! After a breakfast of instant oatmeal, I decided a visit to Grandma's was in order. Packing up the truck with Molly's portable high chair, and some toys to keep her entertained at my mom's not very kid friendly house, together with a case of crayons and paper for Emily, we were all set to spend the day with my mommy. Along the river, around the mountain and across the valley floor we drove until we reached her house, on the other side of Chilliwack.

Stepping past her front flower garden and up her steps, I was so glad to be home; although we didn't live there, this was indeed my emotional home—my feelings were safe and secure within these walls.

My mom opened up her front door and embraced us warmly still in her nightgown. She smelled like soap. Her curly brown locks and French Canadian brown eyes danced.

"Hi mom," I said trying not to tear up. I hate that about myself.

"Hi hi hi!" she managed to say back between kisses and hugs.

"We've missed you mom," I said as we stepped inside, toward the wafts of coffee and the TV news blaring, the dryer drying clothes and breakfast sizzling in a pan. We lugged our things into the living room and the girls got straight to work—their work: play. I thankfully retreated into the kitchen, following my mother.

"So mom, what have you been up to?" I didn't ask what was really on my mind...not yet anyways.

"Oh, I've been busy moving things around in my garden lately. Everything grows so quickly and now it all just looks so overgrown. Especially those English Ivy and the Virginia Creepers—I can't keep on top of them. Do you want some for your garden Jill?" my mom had asked me beseechingly, wanting to rid herself of some greenery, as she would never throw it out. She was too nurturing.

"No mom, I don't want any more plants because I will be in the same spot you're in, given a few more years. I just don't want the work mom."

"But ground cover eliminates the weeds and reduces your work dear," she said gazing at me quizzically, for she knew I already knew that.

I was having a difficult time following her conversation and muttered, "Whatever mom."

She poured me a cup of coffee and started dishing me out some eggs to which I happily accepted. "Are the girls hungry for some too?" she asked, reminding me that I did have kids in the other room.

"No they ate breakfast already, but thanks mom. Hey, have you heard from Luke recently?" I finally had to ask.

"Well yes, he phoned me from the States not too long ago, but I told you about that already when you called the other day. I haven't heard from him since then in case you're wondering.

Oh Jill have you not heard from him yet? I'm so sorry." She stared at me in disbelief.

"No mom, I don't know where he is." I thought of unloading all the information I knew regarding the police and the search, but I didn't want to worry my mom. She was getting on in age, she was diabetic and had high blood pressure; she didn't need this stress in her life. Although I wasn't sure if this news could even be given entrance to her la la land existence. I decided against it nonetheless. I ate my eggs in sad silence.

"So mom, show me your garden," I said, putting my dishes in the sink. The girls overheard, dropped their playthings and followed mom and I outside, where we traipsed through her tiger lilies and her geraniums, azaleas, rhododendrons and rose bushes. Life was beautiful and fragrant again. Mom had grabbed some garden shears and snipped us a bouquet in no time, while Emily and Molly kept pointing to more. Flowers are such a wonderful distraction to all that is ugly in life, I thought, and they can convey so much. It reminded me of Anne Greenaway, an author and illustrator who matched flowers to their meanings. Certain flowers stood for jealousy, others for disdain and some for pride, apathy or boredom. During the Victorian era, when it wasn't proper to speak your feelings, you could express yourself with flowers. You could mix and match and express a multitude of feelings in one bouquet. I laughed to imagine telling a foe off with flowers. Although I was delighted whenever Luke presented me with red roses, which represented romance, for Valentine's Day or on our anniversary, I was always touched when he gave me yellow roses, which stood for friendship, since it meant so much to me to be considered his best friend.

Scooping up flower petals, I had gathered enough to dry out and make into fragrant potpourri, for my underwear drawer and linen closets. It was all just so feminine, which for some reason I wasn't particularly feeling lately. Following the scent of lavender, I tip toed through delicate lilies overhanging the garden pavement stones. I was in heaven! These sweet odors were overpowering any stench of death in my mind. I didn't want to leave, but eventually the sun's rays were too hot to stay. I contemplated pulling some weeds for my mom, for they were threatening to overtake her flower beds, but I wasn't up to it. I already was constantly weeding my own mind for negative weedy thoughts that threatened to overtake it!

After a very pleasant day with my mom, I realized I could not be reached by the South Dakota Police Department while I was there. I, unfortunately, needed to go home. With a truck full of fragrant flowers, we fled furiously home before they all wilted in the heat. It didn't seem to matter that we were also wilting.

Thank God for air conditioned homes, where we, along with the flowers, were instantly revitalized. We all lied down on the kitchen floor to feel the cool beneath our sweaty, sticky skin. After some refreshing lemonade, I checked the answering machine for messages. None! It was time for me to make some phone calls; I had unlimited minutes at my disposal—I might even waste some!

Not my sister Cathy, nor the wives of Luke's riding buddies had heard any news of his whereabouts either. The guys apparently were still looking—searching for him. I again contemplated calling Luke's family, his siblings, to ask if they had heard from him. But my queries would only hint at my alarm and the whole story would then have to be spilled. They were all so sensible and even keeled that I was sure they would think I was not being rational. Either that or I would feel their blame for not calling them earlier. Nonetheless, I didn't want to burden them unnecessarily, so I left it at that.

While deep in thought, I looked up to see my two girls standing sheepishly in the doorway. They had that look—they were up to something. Not something necessarily bad, as they were giggling. Letting my gaze turn to the here and now, I focused intently waiting for their guts to be spilled, or their plan to be unveiled.

"Mommy, we have something to show you," little Molly exclaimed with utter glee. She could hardly contain herself, jumping in time to her words.

"We took it from Grandma's," Emily blurted out, looking quite mischievous.

Oh no, they stole something from my mother, their only remaining grandmother's house, I pondered in disbelief.

Accurately reading the disdain on my face, Emily quickly reassured me, "It's not something from inside her house mom. We got it from her garden."

Wondering if they had snuck more flowers, but then dismissing that idea as I would have seen them, I became quite curious. "Just tell me already!"

Slowly walking toward me, Molly was carefully balancing as to not stumble with her precious find cupped in her hand. "We found a caterpillar—look mommy!"

Craning my neck to see, I realized this was life to my little girl. She was holding this creepy crawly little thing like it was her most cherished possession. I marveled at the care she was lovingly bestowing on this creature. "Oh" I let out relieved that

that was all it was, yet trying to muster up all the attention I could give.

"Let's go get it a leaf to munch on Molly. Come on!" Emily squealed running for the door, with her little sister in tow, cautiously plodding along lest she drop her treasure.

They were barely outside when I heard it. "Oh no! Oh no! Aaaaagh! Look what you did!" I could only imagine what had happened. I knew I would be in for an earful.

"She killed it mommy, Emily killed my caterpillar." Molly sobbed, slowly walking towards me for a cuddle. She crawled into my lap and deposited snot all over my shoulder, as she continued to wail into my ear.

Sauntering into the room, replete with a reddened face, and looking downcast, Emily confessed. "She dropped it and I stepped on it by accident."

Her guilt and remorse were obvious. It had been an honest mistake. Trying to turn the situation around, I said, "I know, let's have a funeral for your poor little caterpillar then. We can find a small box for a casket and we'll bury it in the backyard. How's that Molly? Would you like to do that?"

Molly looked up at me with her tearful doe eyes and nodded her head. She slowly squiggled out of my lap and headed back to the crime scene. While Emily had trotted off to find a suitable casket, Molly came traipsing back in dismay. "Mommy, I could only find part of him," she said revealing what remained of her caterpillar.

Before we knew it, Emily had returned with a small cardboard matchbox stuffed with neatly folded toilet paper inside it. Molly somberly laid the caterpillar inside and then Emily slid the lid closed while watching her sister's face. Emily felt bad and we were both trying to be respectful and yet somehow get through this without Molly bursting into tears. So I gingerly retrieved the casket from Emily and made my way out to the backyard. The sun was going down as we dug a hole in the garden, next to the bridal veil spirea. We placed the box in the soil and using our hands, we covered and patted its burial plot. I broke off some twigs from a neighboring tree and made a makeshift cross and placed it on the grave. As the girls watched me, they followed my lead, unsure of what to do at funerals. So we stood there all quiet, hands folded and looking down at the spot where Molly's dead friend now rested.

"Emily would you like to say a prayer. That's what they do at funerals," I said offering Emily a way to redeem herself in her sister's eyes.

Emily grabbed the opportunity, albeit with some uncertainty. "Now I lay me down to sleep. I pray the Lord my soul to keep. If I should die before I wake, I pray thee Lord my soul does take."

She prayed the only prayer she knew and I loved it, and so apparently did Molly as she reached for her sister's hand in gratitude.

"Amen" I said as I collected a handful of dandelions and threw them on the grave. Molly watched me do this and then grabbed a bunch of forget-me-nots and tossed them onto the pile of dirt. Emily looked unsure of herself, pondering perhaps whether the bug was worth the effort. I then took the girls by the hand and led them back into the house. I wasn't sure of how resilient the girls would be after experiencing death. Should I capitalize on the moment and read them a story about the circle of life? But I did not wish to visit that philosophical discussion, so I changed the subject instead.

"Time for a snack," I exclaimed almost running for the kitchen. Pulling out a box of crackers, "What do you want on them?" I rummaged through the fridge for some jam and cheese whiz.

"Jam! Jam!" Molly blurted out, as she climbed onto one of the island stools.

Turning around to look at Emily, I waited for her response, but none was given.

"What do you want on your crackers Emily?" I asked again.

"I just want them bare naked," she spoke gazing at the floor.

I handed my guilt ridden daughter three plain crackers and didn't push her need to deprive herself. It was her way of administering penance – her take on justice.

"It wasn't your fault," I said to Emily, trying to alleviate her load. But she just ate without saying a word.

That night, when I put the girls to bed, Emily in the top bunk, and Molly in her crib, I sang them a song:

"You are my sunshine, my only sunshine

You make me happy when skies are gray

You'll never know dear how much I love you

Please don't take my sunshine away

The other night dear, while I lay sleeping

I dreamt I held you in my arms

But when I woke dear, I was mistaken

So I held my head and I cried."

I tiptoed out of their room, leaving only the night light on to guide them through the night. I knew Luke would have wanted to be here for this moment—but he wasn't. He missed out on this hushed moment in time, when life stood still.

I had hardly got down the stairs when Molly beckoned me.

"Mommy I'm scared of all my animals," she whimpered.

Scanning her room, the only animals I could detect were her numerous stuffies, scattered around her room on shelves, ledges, dressers and on the floor. Surely she wasn't afraid of these harmless creatures who had offered her many nights of comfort.

"Those ones Mommy," she pointed to her stuffed lion named Sheila and her black lab named Midnight. "Tie them up Mommy so they can't get me."

In disbelief, I began to leash Midnight and tie him to Molly's bed frame, before I realized she had far too many stuffed animals for me to tie them all up.

"How about I just take them all out of your room for the night?" I suggested, to which Molly gratefully agreed. So I loaded them into the laundry basket after I dumped its load of unfinished laundry onto the hall carpet, and dragged the terrorizing stuffies away. It was odd that tonight they were no longer her friends, but were instead agents of fear. Poor Molly!

It was getting late and I tried to watch an old movie, which had Clark Gable in it, but even he wasn't enough to hold my attention. I just couldn't focus on the story line.....too preoccupied I guess! I stumbled upon some love story where the hero died and his love had to pick up the pieces of her heart, her life, and put them back together. Kind of like Humpty Dumpty, only all the king's horses and all the King's men couldn't put him back together again. How would she do it? How could I do it?

Up in bed, I charted my feelings in my journal, where I usually turn to vent my emotions. But all I wrote were questions—so many questions! What was the worst: he's dead!! The implications of that were horrendous however. Not only would my heart be shattered, but that of my children as well. Our lives would be forever altered. I would lose my best friend, my lover, my co-provider, my handy man, my fellow traveller, my professional colleague, not to mention the father of my children. If Luke was dead, a large part of me would die too. Our lives were so intertwined, how would I untangle myself? I couldn't always tell where Luke ended and I began—we were truly one. I was scared! I missed him! I needed him! I loved him! Yet I was so angry with myself for feeling this way and I wasn't sure why. Maybe I resented feeling so vulnerable. Maybe I disliked being confronted with my fears, or my dependence. Maybe I loved too deeply, a kind of addiction perhaps. Was this whole episode revealing my foibles – my character flaws that I just could not stand to face? Sure I was mad at Luke for taking off from the guys and not calling, but I think I was actually more angry at myself for all the crap in my darkened heart that was being brought to the surface. He was forcing me, through the threat of his loss, to deal with my shit. I didn't like what I was seeing. I did not want to deal with it. I needed a healthy perspective for I was sure lacking one of my own.

Sometimes, when I'm looking for answers, and all else fails, sleep is usually a good remedy. So to sleep I went—or at least I tried. Maybe my dreams would provide some answers.

LUKE DAY 11

There were some flies buzzing around my head in this old cell as I awoke to the smell of piss. I couldn't tell what time of day it was as there were no windows and my watch ironically stopped working. I thought of my mother in law, who, for every contest she entered or every raffle ticket she bought, she seemed to always win another watch. She had several of them now. It all reminded me of an old Guess Who song, "No Time Left For You." I hated that song.

I was expecting some breakfast, perhaps a pair of toast with two eggs, side by each, minus my bacon. I would have been happy if the monkeys had thrown a banana into my cage. But no, instead I heard the iron door open and a pair of hairy guys were hovering over me. "We gotta move you."

I guess they were talking to me but before I could utter a word, a protest, a plea, they had dragged me off to another cell. Not sure why, but at least this cell was cleaner, newer and it had a bed and bonus—a window! It looked more like a temporary holding room or an interrogation room than a jail cell. I later heard Frenchman screaming at someone else. I guess his bail didn't hold up. I was glad to be moved as I wouldn't be holding up with him either, and the guards probably didn't want to referee any more boxing matches between us two, which is why they moved me no doubt!

"I need to use the washroom," I hollered to anyone who would listen. Thing One and Two were arguing down the hall over who would do all the paper work, probably on me, with my loooooong record, I mused to myself sarcastically.

A skinny, young guard appeared, one I hadn't seen before. He was very nervous looking, couldn't be more than eighteen, I thought. He fumbled with the keys and then opened my cell door, after which he escorted me to the bathroom. Standing outside the door, he warned: "Don't try anything stupid."

As I closed the door behind me, I just wanted to take a crap. The room was tiny, but clean. No bathtub, just a toilet and a sink.....and a window. I thought of climbing out, but I'd never fit. I took my time behind closed walls, relishing the privacy, when suddenly there was a loud clanging of iron on iron. I could hear people fighting and screaming. It sounded like bodies were being thrown. I opened the bathroom door to peek out and there saw the main cell, my old cell with Frenchman fighting with one of the guards. My skinny guard was in there trying to break it up and then the two hairy things were drawing their pistols through the iron bars. All their backs were to me. I was trying to decide if I should watch this entertainment or finish my dump, when a third option presented itself. The back door was open down the hall, next to the police officer's station. It was hot outside and they had propped it open with some books. I decided to take my chances. I pulled up my pants and looked down at my dress shoes, still sticking their tongues out at me—daring me! So I slipped through the bathroom door and then pressed the door knob in to lock behind me. Sheepishly, I slinked down the hall and out the back door, stumbling on the steps.

Running frantically down the street, I was both terrified and exhilarated at the same time. Lucky for me the outdoor market where my bike was parked was only a few blocks away. I wondered if I could prove Guess Who wrong; maybe I would have time on my side. Zipping up my jacket as I sprinted down back alleys, I spotted my bike tucked in behind a dumpster, with my helmet unbelievably still clipped on. Even my tank bag and camping gear were still intact. I owe that Mexican gentle man some words of thanks. Slinging my leg over my Kawi, while throwing my helmet on, I jammed in the key, let out a handful of revs, and I was off. I didn't know how much time I'd have. I zoomed through the side streets, hoping that no kids or balls or pets would appear, until I saw that I was parallel to the highway. I opened up the throttle and sped for the border. I knew that if I could just make it to the next state I would be out of their jurisdiction and they would end their chase. I figured it couldn't be that far and I was determined to beat this rap. Montana here I come!

I really wanted to go home. I also really wished I had proper riding boots, but that was out of the question now. I could not use my debit card or charge cards and chance leaving a paper trail for them to find me. No I had to be smarter than that!

Screaming down the highway, I chuckled to myself, picturing that skinny guard knocking on the bathroom door and trying to coax me out, after all the kerfuffle had died down. I wonder how long he banged on that door, before they had to break it down to find they had nothing but a pile of shit! Thing One and Thing Two would have felt right at home.

Careening down Highway ninety, I could see the Montana state line up ahead. I crossed without a cruiser in sight. They were probably still arguing back there like Laurel and Hardy.

I lifted my dress shoes up in the air and smiled back as their tongues were now pressed in by the wind. Look who's laughing now, I admonished my cheeky shoes.

    I rode until dark, making my way through Montana. I found a farmer's field to pitch my tent, in order to conserve whatever cash I had. Stepping over a ditch and what looked like a skeleton of some sort of critter, I kicked some stones out of the way and set up camp. If I was lucky, I would have no geezer staring me down in the morning, perhaps only a yowling rooster or some cocky dogs scrapping over dead meat.

TWO YEARS EARLIER

Death came calling at the Cooper household. Mark and Donna Cooper lived two doors down from the Connor family on Silver Drive in Chilliwack. Donna's aged, bed ridden mom lived with them as well. Mark was the gregarious, salesman of the street. He sold appliances for a living, but would try to sell anything. They often had garage sales; Donna wanted to get rid of junk, but Mark just liked selling stuff. He was good at it too. We would find ourselves all buying things we didn't need because he was so convincing and charming.

He arranged all our block parties and knew everyone's business. If you wanted to get an update on street gossip, you asked Mark. It always amazed me how he had a knack for gathering information on people. His personality drew you in, yet you kept your distance lest he spread the dirt on you. Not that he would invent rumors, it was just that some things you preferred to be kept private. Nothing was private to Mark! He would discuss openly all of his mother-in-law's ailments, until poor thing, she would admonish him for his indiscretions. He pretended that he didn't have skeletons in his closet; he didn't keep a closet—his life was on full parade at his weekly yard sale.

Apparently his heart was for sale too, as he gave it away for rock bottom prices, to any cutie that came his way. His little black book of appliance repair clients held a different kind of clientele too. He had a string of pretty females lined up like his pearly whites. His house calls were just that! Service on the house, and with a smile. Poor Donna was so busy tending to her ailing mother, she hadn't noticed the lack of income coming in. Sure he did have some legitimate business calls, to make some money and cover his butt, but those weren't his preferred business mode. He knew how to turn refrigerators into hot plates; and he could dry tumble with the best of them. His washing machine slogan was: Let Me Wash Your Cares Away. He had a line for every lady. So it was no surprise when his goose got cooked. He got caught in the act by one of his client's husbands, who strangled him with one of his own electrical cords. If it hadn't been for Donna, the whole street would have laughed in unison, when we heard how he died. Silver Drive became fairly quiet after that; no more block parties or weekly garage sales or daily gossip updates. We missed our Mark!

Donna eventually got over it, we think, and had decided to stay on with her mom, who was too old to move anyway. She opened up his garage one day and put a FREE sign out on their driveway; she wanted to rid herself of all his appliance parts and the memories they delivered. Neighbors showed up to pick through the remains of his livelihood, more out of curiosity than anything else. Mark's life had been extinguished and there wasn't anything left over.

Two years ago, two houses down, Death had come calling!

JILL DAY 12

The next morning, plunked down on the couch with Molly and Emily, listening to the laugh track on a.m. programming I felt numb. Some vortex sucking me down into the abyss. This is crazy I thought, trying to reassure myself. I need some levity to cope, to counter this crap going on in my life. I tried so hard to laugh with my kids at the funny antics of Clifford, the big red dog on TV but I couldn't muster up the joy. Only pain in my hollow shell. Where was I to go? What was I to do to escape this.....or survive through it? I wanted to run—to hide. I wanted off this ride. I needed an emergency exit. I needed an out—a fire escape. Insanity was tempting me. Ouch!!

I thought of calling Maria, one of my closest friends who lived in Vancouver. She was a bridesmaid at our wedding and we had remained pals for decades. She was a great listener and a strong shoulder to lean on, exactly what I needed. But it was daytime and she would be at work. I pondered my other supports: Shelley or Debby—both long time friends but they also were at work. Their kind words of wisdom and perhaps a fresh perspective would have been most welcome, but in all honesty, I didn't really feel like talking to anyone. I found it difficult to follow a conversation as I just could not focus. I could see mouths moving but I couldn't hear the words.

Suddenly I was startled and jumped to the ringing phone. "Hello," the American accent drawled, "This is the South

Dakota Police Department-Homicide calling. Could you please tell us of your husband's spending habits? Does he usually pay for traveling expenses with cash, credit card or interact?" a female officer quizzed me.

I paused—land lines afford such luxuries. My thoughts scrambled to answer but there were many variables to consider. When traveling by car, Luke likes to use Mastercard to keep track of all the gas, but on a motorbike the amounts were so small, he wouldn't want to charge each transaction. On the other hand when we had traveled on the motorcycle in Europe several years ago, Luke insisted on using credit cards to avoid the exorbitant exchange rates that gas stations charge. So I wasn't sure. Maybe he decided to use interact. What did I know?

"Probably cash," I finally droned out.

"Oh that's not good. No paper trail," the detective snapped back. "At least if he used a credit card or something you could call and find out when and where his last transaction was."

A ray of hope sprung into my spirit. "Well I'm not sure what he's used but I think I'll try that. I'll call Mastercard and see what they say," I said half dazed, nudged slightly out of my numbness.

Wondering why she hadn't made that call herself if she, or her department for that matter, were supposed to be investigating this, I resolved in my mind I'd be the one to make that call.

Seeing that the girls were still engrossed with their cartoons I decided to get on it immediately. Lugging the heavy yellow pages to the table I found the number and dialed.

"Mastercard, how may I help you?" the friendly receptionist asked.

"Yes, I need to know when and where a card was last used," I said sounding as professional as I could.

"Certainly, and what is your Mastercard number?" she asked.

"It's actually my husband's card that I'm inquiring about," I shot back.

"Oh, I'm sorry. We can't give out that information on someone else's card," she explained.

"But you don't understand," I interjected. "He's missing and I just want to know if he's alive. He went on a trip with some friends and disappeared and has since been reported missing. We don't know if he's been murdered or what and I just want a sign," my words tearfully tumbled out. "Tell you what," I continued, "You don't even have to tell me where or when the card was last used, just tell me 'if' it was used. I just want him to be alive....somewhere." I let out, trying to control my sobs.

Next thing I know she's consoling me. "I'm so sorry!" and "That's awful!"

I wasn't expecting compassion, just information.

"Here I'll let you talk to my manager," she said passing the phone on.

I didn't know if that was a positive sign that they were about to break the rules for me, or bad news—the manager was better at brushing people off. So I recounted my story to him and took my chances.

"Well," he said cautiously, "I can tell you the card was indeed used."

Realizing that this information was actually useless without knowing "when" it was last used, I pushed. "Could you possibly give me a date on that? On his last transaction?"

"August 4th," he replied suspiciously.

"He's alive!" I exclaimed, laughing through my tears. "Thank you so much," I gushed ready to hang up, when suddenly, unfortunately, I realized I still had nothing. What if he was mugged and someone was charging stuff up on his card. Or if he was murdered and then someone robbed him and is charging things. Quickly I surmised that a thief would be charging up lots of things, expensive things and frequently too. Not Luke! He'd be using the card meagerly. He's too thrifty to spend extravagantly. So I pushed further, "Could you just tell me if what was last charged was a small or large amount?"

"Oh alright, the last transaction shows eleven dollars at Arco," he conceded.

I paused and before I could reply he added, "Arco is a gas station here in the States."

That was it! My joy was complete. No thief charges eleven dollars, that's got to be my husband. The rock in my stomach started to turn into stones. Things were breaking.

Dancing around the kitchen I started to make tuna sandwiches for lunch. See everything is going to be just fine Jill, I mused. Why did you ever doubt? My energy had started to rebound, so I decided to capitalize on it. I wanted life to look normal again.

"Girls, we're going to go to Mommy's school today. I need to get some things." I alerted them to start getting ready, as I made my way into the family room picking up socks, stuffed animals, felt pens and other signs of life strewn about.

"Why Mommy, why are we going there in the summer?" Emily had to ask.

It was true, Luke nor I ever visited our classrooms in the summer months until it was time to get set up for

September—but that could be left till the last week, or even possibly the last few days if we could stretch out our vacation mode without getting anxious about the new school year. But this summer was different! We weren't in vacation mode, nor work mode; we had even taken survival mode to a whole new literal level.

"I thought we could do some clay art today. Daddy bought a box of clay for us, that has been sitting here all summer, but I left the tools at school. I had meant to bring them home with me in June, but I must have forgotten," I explained.

"Yeah for clay!" was all Emily could say as she jumped up and down. Crafts, any crafts, got her so excited.

Seeing that "Sesame Street" had just ended, it was a safe time to whiz Molly off the sofa without too much complaint. I needed not worry anyways, as Emily bounded into the room, chatting away to her sister about our excursion. Before long, we were loaded into the truck and heading down the freeway towards East Chilliwack Elementary school. We pulled into the empty parking lot and parked in the fire lane beside the front door.

"Girls, you have to stick very close to me now. I have to shut off the alarm," I said quite seriously, since I had on more than one occasion set off the alarm unintentionally. You had thirty seconds to disarm and you had to stay within the parameters of the motion sensors—if you took too long or stepped out of the permitted corridor, or as I had once done, put my bag down in the wrong place, you would set off the silent alarm. It was very nerve wracking to have to explain yourself to the security guards or the police, who would appear within minutes, and I was not wanting a repeat of that. Consequently, I was anxious and sweat was creeping up over my face. This always was a reminder as to why I stayed away from school on weekends or in the summer months. I hated alarms!

Thankfully, we managed to gain entry without incident that day. We made our way down the darkened hallway, past all the closed doors and vacant rooms, past the empty bulletin boards and deserted library. The building was cool and smelled of cleaners and floor wax. The janitors had finished for the summer and now the school was just waiting for September and the return of life and all its noise and energy and vibrancy. Fumbling with my keys, I opened my classroom door and flicked on the lights. The girls instantly ran to my window seats, which contained drawers of lego and connector blocks and puzzles stored away for rainy day recess play. They knew those drawers well, for they contained toys for which they were allowed to touch. Molly and especially Emily, had learned which bins of school supplies and learning materials and papers were out of bounds to them. So as they happily engaged themselves, I sauntered around my room. So many fulfilling memories had taken place in that classroom, rewards of a satisfying career. My eyes scanned the twenty desks all piled up on one side of the room and the stacks of chairs. The walls of whiteboards that had replaced my missed chalkboards. The many windows that overlooked the courtyard garden on one side and the huge vaulted open indoor area on the other side. My wooden desk, all freshly scrubbed. I loved this work, although teaching primary often seemed more like play than work. I knew who I was there!

Remembering what we had come for, I opened up my art cupboard and located the clay tools: a box containing wire, wooden rollers and an assortment of metal pronged instruments for imprinting designs.

"I found it girls. I have the clay tools." I said, slowly rising to my feet. "Clean up your things now."

In no time, my classroom was returned to its former dormant state. We skipped back down the halls, toward the front doors and the dreaded alarm box. Thankfully, I reset the alarm without breaking into a sweat. Piling into the truck, the girls were giddy with anticipation at the prospect of making something out of clay. This only happened once or twice a year, and Emily understood just how special it was.

Back at home, I cleared off the kitchen table and covered it with newspapers. Using the wire, I sliced off a slab of red clay for each of the girls. As they left to don some of Luke's old shirts, I set out the tools and bowls of water to dip their small fingers into. Emily was only too happy to show Molly how to mould with clay. She cupped her hands around her little sister's and proceeded to make a pinch pot, over soaking the clay... and the table...and themselves. Molly was determined to do it on her own, so Emily set out rolling coils to which she would score and add slip, layering up the coils to make her own pot, which was much more elaborate than her sister's.

As the two of them were engrossed in this messy, but delightful past time, my thoughts were drawn elsewhere. The phone conversation that I had had earlier with the credit card company kept repeating itself in my mind, like the play button had gotten stuck on the answering machine, causing me to relive the message over and over again. Only each new hearing seemed to diminish my hope, instead of adding to it. My joy began to wane into just that—doubt. I had so many questions. Why hadn't Luke called me or anyone for that matter, if he was still alive? Why couldn't the guys or police find him? Was he trying to run away? Maybe a Sturgis biker did have his wallet and had been charging all kinds of things, and the gasoline transaction just happened to be the last one. With his wallet stolen, he wouldn't have his calling card and thus, no calls home. This actually made the most sense, but I didn't want to go there with that thinking, I'd been living in that dark hole and possibility thinking was my only way out. I wasn't going to give it up. So I kept on hoping on hope. After all, tomorrow Luke would call: August 7th, his birthday—of course he'd call. Absolutely!!

LUKE DAY 12

"Happy Birthday to me, Happy Birthday to me, Happy Birthday dear Luke, Happy Birthday to me," I sang myself awake. With the rooster and dogs serenading me, I woke up happy this morning. I wished I could call home, but ATT wasn't in a birthday mood, which I long ago realized and gave up on. Wait till Jill hears about my trip, she won't believe me, I'm sure. She's probably bored stiff by now. Well it is my day to celebrate—what should I do?

I was so exhausted and drained from this whole mess, I decided to park myself in a pub and watch motor cycle races on the large TV all day. I wasn't sure if I wanted to splurge my coveted cash in this way, but I decided to anyway. I would throw some Canadian funds their way. I stumbled across an old saloon just off the highway that looked like something you'd see in an old western flick. It even had the wooden rails out front for you to tie your horse to, before you kicked up a few spurs and waddled in. Parking my trusty Kawi out front, I sauntered in to get pissed. I drank away the hours until the owner suggested I just camp out back when he saw I was not fit for riding anywhere. Responsible guy he was!! More than I could say for myself!!

My attempts at setting up a tent, in the dark, fully inebriated, were hilarious. All I remember was that I kept poking myself with tent poles in the night. These should have been fed through the sleeve and hammered into the ground. But they were instead jabbing my hammered self.

Why do we say we "fall" asleep? I didn't fall into anything. I staggered perhaps, or crashed, but in truth, I was already down dead. You couldn't move me if you tried. I slept fitfully, but was near comatose as it was. I dreamt that Death had come calling that night, but nobody was home!

JILL DAY 13

Luke's birthday came and went. He's dead—absolutely!

LUKE DAY 13

Z z z z z z z z   Z z z z z z z z z z z
- ——————————————————!!!!!!

ONE YEAR EARLIER

Death came calling at the Stewart household. Joan and Carl Stewart lived next door to the Connor family on Silver Drive in Chilliwack.

"Your yard is looking beautiful, as usual," Jill had remarked to Joan one day. She was a great neighbor but living next to her yard made other yards look pathetic, even at their best. Her front yard flower garden changed with the seasons and was well orchestrated for color, for beauty, for life. Jill and Luke Connor's, on the other hand was always encroached upon by weeds. No matter what herbicide, fertilizer or lawn seed they used, or weeds individually yanked out, their lawn always seemed to be choked by dandelions or chickweed or pampas grass. No wonder Jill was glad when Joan changed the subject. Anything rather than their yard would suffice to distract Jill's embarrassment.

"You know Carl had been sick for some time," Joan offered hesitating, looking down at her shovel stuck into a mound of top soil. "Well...I lost him a couple of weeks ago," she languished.

SILENCE

Jill wasn't quite expecting their conversation to take that turn. "I'm so sorry," Jill had finally blurted out. No wonder Jill hadn't seen Joan working in her yard for some time.

"Was it his stomach that finally got him in the end?" Jill had asked stupidly. She wasn't trying to be nosy but didn't know what to say in her nervousness.

"That and a bunch of other things," Joan had replied, more at ease now. "The doctors aren't really sure what caused his death exactly as he had so many things go wrong with him in the end."

Jill was amazed at how well Joan was handling all of this. She knew she'd be a mess.

"You know, ever since his car accident, then his being in a wheelchair, and then the quick decline of his health, I felt like I lost him long ago," explained Joan in what sounded like relief. "I think it was all for the best," she continued. "He didn't much enjoy his life anymore."

Joan needed to vent, not only to convince Jill, but perhaps also to justify her own feelings. She had let go. Maybe she wanted permission to leave the guilt behind as well. But Jill wasn't about to blame her for her lack of tears; Joan seemed ready to celebrate his life, not mourn his loss.

Jill had started to feel really antsy but knew she needed to say something, not words to comfort but words to acknowledge.

"Well it sounds like you're ready to get on with your life," Jill finally blurted out, not sure if that was the wise thing or appropriate thing to say.

"Yeah," Joan shot back, mustering a smile, "now I can stay out in my garden all day long and not worry about coming in to fix Carl a meal or something."

Jill hadn't known how to respond to that. She just stood there.

Sensing Jill's discomfort at her own bad choice of words, Joan smiled broadly and said, "Oh, did you see? Donna has put her house up for sale."

Relieved to change the subject, Jill quipped back, "Yeah, I saw her sign go up the other day." Donna lived on the other side of Joan and had recently put her ailing mom into a full time care facility. She had become too much to look after.

"You knew that Mark her husband had passed away a year ago and I guess she just felt she no longer needed this big house with the upkeep it involved." Joan was determined to fill Jill in on street news. It appeared as though Joan had taken over Mark's role as the busy body.

"Oh," reluctantly fell out of Jill's mouth. She hadn't known any of this, but she didn't want to reveal her ignorance of street gossip either. The truth is—Jill really wasn't paying any attention.

Suddenly, Joan looked at Jill, laughed out loud and tossed out, "Hey, with Mark passing away last July and Carl dying this summer, I guess it will be Luke's turn next year."

LOL

"Yeah right, Ha! Ha!" Jill had chuckled, astonished yet enjoying Joan's morose sense of humor.

At that, Jill had waved so long and walked back to revisit her dandelions. Recounting all the deaths on their street, year after year, house after house, she paused. "What an eerie thought," she had murmured to herself, as she knelt down onto damp, limp grass.

The fall went by in an uneventful manner. Death hadn't visited their street lately, albeit he left signs, such as the scythe that the Connor's found on their doorstep November

First. Some little trick or treater must have dropped this plastic accessory to his costume the night before. Or the night Jill woke up in terror from a gripping nightmare only to find a black cat staring down on her from their skylight. Jill had occasionally recalled that conversation with Joan and pictured Death knocking on their doors, one by one. Such nonsense!! If he came to their door, Luke would probably stand there engaging him in conversation, until Jill would come and slam the door in his face.

JILL DAY 14

Waking up from a dazed daydream, I found myself squatting on my kitchen floor. Several seasons had passed since my neighbor Joan had spoken those predictive words of death's march on our street, which now no longer seemed like nonsense. It was August. I was in Chilliwack. This was supposed to be home—reprieve, but the anxiety was still there.

I hadn't noticed any beauty that day-not in my home, which was truly lovely, not in my two wonderful and attractive daughters, not in the natural beauty that apparently abounds in Beautiful B.C. I saw only gray. I could hear the phone ringing sometime in the day, I think it was afternoon. The ringing was gnawing in my brain.

"Hello," I droned into the receiver.

"Hi Jill. It's Ruth Hamilton," said the voice. "How are you doing? Are you holding up okay? Are the girls handling this okay?" she asked in quick succession.

Her tone was a mixture of concern and a carryover from her husband, Mike's frustration. I think I replied with a grunt.

"Mike called again last night," she went on "and says the guys haven't given up looking."

I had nothing to say.

"You know Jill, the whole of our church is praying for Luke's safe return," she offered. "They're praying for you and the girls as well, so hang in there."

"Thanks Ruth. I'll try, but the girls don't know anything yet. Funny thing is, they don't seem to notice their father's absence," I said surprising myself with this revelation.

"Perhaps it might do you good to get out of the house. You know...a change of scenery and all that. Why don't you join some of us women tonight? We're going downtown to help out in the local soup kitchen. Seeing others' pain sometimes helps to get our minds off our own." Ruth offered in a preachy sort of way.

I was insulted that she would try to reduce my feelings to shambles. Although I probably could relate to the helplessness of the homeless and my pain was sufficient that drugs and alcohol were a temptation to escape this gnawing in my chest, I just couldn't stomach being around the walking dead—bodies with souls lost to meth or crack. Their hollow eyes offered me nothing and I was bankrupt of anything to offer them. I had no shoulder to lean on—mine was weak and crumbling under its own weight. I couldn't listen to their problems as I was blasted with my own inner screams. And I certainly didn't feel like chopping up carrots and peeling potatoes for others—I wanted to crawl underground and join the rooted vegetables myself. I was already a zombie going through the motions of life yet devoid of all feeling; I was numb to the core. Besides, it would remind me of my own sister, lost on downtown Vancouver's east side, swallowed by a life of drugs and pain. I had enough guilt and remorse over hiding her from my heart's reach. I couldn't afford this field trip, this jaunt into that which I avoided myself, so I declined Ruth's offer, guilt laden.

"Well best to let you go then, keep the lines clear. Let me know if I can do anything," she said, glossing over my objection.

"Thanks again Ruth...for your concern," I said before hanging up.

Oh my, I thought to myself, a whole church congregation praying. Can it move those mountains that separate Luke from us? I half-heartedly hope so! Won't Luke be so embarrassed when he finds out all the fuss he's stirring up, I smile to myself. Way to go Luke!! I smile again. Part of me doesn't acknowledge this nightmare. Maybe this whole thing is a joke.

I remember watching a documentary once on TV where the guy didn't like his life and took off, framed or set up his supposed death, then established a new identity and a new life. Luke wouldn't, I thought. I knew he struggled with his loss of motorcycling freedom since we started a family. Sometimes he resented my concern for his safety. He was after all almost forty before becoming a dad. Maybe this was all just too much for him.

I felt so drained and exhausted from this ordeal that had entirely consumed my life. I didn't want to think anymore. Why? How? Where? These words had become too expensive for my soul.

Yet that night, with the girls safely tucked into bed, I proceeded to torture myself some more. Sprawled on the kitchen floor was a huge atlas opened up to the Northern States of the U.S. Running my fingers over the pages, I cried out, "Where is he? Where is he?" I shouted in anger. I don't think anyone was home upstairs, so I shifted my attention to the basement-where darkness prevails. For some reason I kept thinking of Joan's words: "Next year will be your husband's turn," meaning his turn to die, kind of morbid now when I think about it. How we laughed about death back then, as if the grim reaper could be sneered at. We obviously didn't take it seriously, the fact that the men on our street had been dying house by house. But how could you take that seriously? How would anyone in their right mind take that seriously? It had to all be just coincidence. Yet here I was struggling to free my husband from Death's grip, and I certainly wasn't laughing now. No, Death demanded attention. He called when it suited his timetable not yours. However inconvenient, however unfair, we succumbed, relented to his beckoning. But I couldn't surrender without some resistance, some fight. So I prayed, renouncing the spirit of death....to no avail. I would gain no release. This power seemed so much beyond me. There was possibly history being lived out.

Pondering my geographical location, I wondered about our crazy street and all the deaths that occurred here, almost systematically. Could those taken souls, which were now so missed, all be part of a payment, or a retribution perhaps? What had possibly happened a century before on this strip of land? I wondered about the native drums I often heard on Saturday nights from a Long House Pow Wow down the road. Maybe there was some kind of territorial spirit reclaiming the land. Was this just revenge, and Luke just so happened to be in the way? Were the gods needing appeasement?

I thought back to a happier time several years earlier when Luke and I had been camping with Tim and Christine on the tip of Galiano Island. Awakened in the middle of the night, I felt such a dark presence in my tent. Climbing out quietly, as to not wake Luke, I sought some peace down on the rocks. Listening to waves crash on the shore was like a native tongue lashing out at me to leave: "You don't belong here. Get out! Get out!" it seemed to scream. I was certain what we had to do the next day, yet I was bewildered how Luke could sleep through the whole thing. Why wasn't he being tormented, chased away by such demons. Trying to drown out the voices, I finally hid in sleep.

The next morning Tim came out of his tent, "Did you guys feel that last night?" he asked stumbling to his feet.

I knew exactly what he meant. "You too," I responded still trembling. "I could hardly sleep. What was this area used for before it was a campground?" I asked trying to make sense of my night.

"I think this was a native burial ground before the forestry services took it over," replied Tim in an "AH HA" moment.

Shaking their heads, Christine and Luke had felt none of it. They had slept peacefully and couldn't make sense of what Tim and I had been rambling on about. But this was serious business. Tim and I sat down together on the rocks while they made breakfast.

"So, what are we going to do?" I asked Tim, already knowing the answer.

"I guess we should just leave. We're not wanted here," Tim replied.

Anger awoke in me, "But why should we have to leave? " I shot back.

"Ah, I don't know," Tim said squirming, while scratching his head. "These aren't the kind of spirits you play with. We're not in a life and death situation, no need to test them. I say we just leave in peace."

I knew he was right. There was no other choice, but convincing the other two wasn't going to be easy. Standing up and breathing in the wonders of this incredible spot, we then turned and walked toward the camp cooks.

"Are you kidding us?" Luke said standing now. "This is so beautiful here—I mean look at this place. Have we ever camped on a site so breath-taking and natural as this?"

Christine concurred as she continued to make cowboy coffee over the cook stove.

Luke was right. There was indeed unforgettable vistas here. Yet Tim was right too. We had to leave. And that we did!

That camping experience ranks up there as the best, yet that spiritual encounter had to be one of the most unsettling, unnerving. There were so many questions this temporal world just couldn't attempt to answer.

Here I was, years later wondering, questioning, could this be that same spirit: territorial, demanding, uncompromising?? What had this street once been? Had these homes been built on Native ancestral burial grounds? Were we tramping on their sacred ground? Had this land been taken without consent—stolen?

I couldn't figure out why death was at our heels. Yet there was no mistaking it—this feeling of night perpetually upon us. It was like Death was constantly there, demanding payment and there was no way to avoid it, no way to appease this foreboding presence.

Glancing over toward the mantle, I caught sight of a family heirloom. Fumbling through this huge, thick ancient Bible that had been passed down through Luke's family, I found myself reading the twenty third psalm. I was seeking solace, searching for a way out—an escape hatch. As I read aloud, I pondered the words: "The Lord is my shepherd, I shall not want." Well I certainly wanted things now. I wanted my husband back.

I wanted the ache in my stomach to leave. I wanted my life back. "He leads me to green pastures, beside still waters." But I was being engulfed by stormy rough seas, definitely devoid of any serenity. "He restores my soul." My soul though, was in dire need of restoration, it had become totally depleted. "Though I walk through the valley of the shadow of death, I will fear no evil, for thou art with me." Ha! I was consumed with fear as I trudged through my death valley. "Thy rod and thy staff comfort me." Where was my comfort, I wanted to know? "Thou prepares a table in the presence of thine enemies." This statement, however, resonated with me, for I knew only too well my enemies of fear, death, gloom, despondency and anxiety that took up residence at my table, daily gnawing at my spirit. "My cup runneth over." I wanted so desperately to be overflowing with joyful wine, but instead was drowning in oily despair. "Surely goodness and mercy will follow me all the days of my life." Oh, to be chaperoned in life by goodness and mercy seemed like such a dream, whereas I felt like I was being stalked by death, in hungry pursuit of my absent husband. "I will dwell in the house of the Lord forever, Amen." I never did get this line. Surely God wasn't expecting us to live at church, after all, weren't we the temples of the Holy Spirit? Didn't God live in us? Maybe he was saying that we need to live, really LIVE within our spirit. I, however, was not feeling particularly alive....anywhere!

Finishing that psalm, I hadn't found any comfort, only more reminders of how short I fell. I started to flip through other pages, searching instead for words to soothe. I stumbled upon Exodus, the second book of the Old Testament. I was reading about the Passover, how the first born in every house was visited by the angel of death. Those poor mothers, in their desperation would put blood on their doorposts, and death would then, "pass over" their house and go onto the next family in line.

Well, the similarities struck me so. Here was this book written so very long ago, for another culture in a land far away, yet the words came to life. They applied to me and my situation. I read them again and again. I wondered if the blood made the angel of death think that death had already visited that house and that there was then no need to go in and destroy. Yet Death could not be tricked, I was sure.

As I pondered this truth, I relived a nightmare I once had. I was in a war and soldiers and captains of high rank were driving around in their army jeeps shooting at anything that moved. There I stood in the midst of my civilian clothed friends, who were all shot one by one. In terror, I also fell to the ground, their blood stained bodies collapsing all around and over me. I attempted to get up, when I noticed that the jeep was signaling to return.

"Wait, wait," a soldier yelled, standing in the jeep. "Someone over there moved. Go back! Go back!"

Realizing what was to befall me, I called out to God in my dream. "Cover me with your blood." To my amazement, blood then covered my face, legs and arms. I was drowning in it. When the jeep returned, the soldiers looked around and all they could see were bodies strewn everywhere all covered in blood, blanketed by death. I was included in that lot, as I lay there motionless in shock.

"Oh never mind," I heard one of the soldiers say. "I thought we had missed one. Never mind, go on." And away they drove.

As I awoke from that night terror I acknowledged the power of blood; it represented life itself, not just death, which it usually signified.

I reflected back upon that dream and wondered if I had found a solution to my pain, a way out for Luke, a deflection for his life. Could it be possible that the Passover would work in modern times? It was definitely worth pondering.

I went to sleep that night not sure if I had found a key. Nonetheless, hope was tickling me.

LUKE DAY 14

I awoke to a collapsed tent on top of me. Apparently I had not erected the thing properly according to the directions. I had attempted to take short cuts, thereby missing the step where you attach the poles together. I, instead, jammed the short little pole pieces into all the wrong crevices, stretching the nylon fabric in ways it was not meant to be pulled and prodded, totally against its will. As a result, my tent had retaliated and collapsed on top of me. No matter! I relished the protective cocoon.

I saw a sign indicating the Idaho state line was two hundred and six miles ahead and I reminisced about how silly Mike, Rod, Larry and I had been with our western accents and Howdy Doody talk as we crossed this way at the beginning of our trip. That seemed so long ago. So much had transpired since then. I felt like I had changed, but not necessarily grown from all my experiences. I viewed the world through a more cynical lens now. Being falsely accused jades the soul, steals at your innocence. I winced more now, I judged, I mistrusted everyone. My joy had been robbed and I wasn't sure what I was to glean from this episode in my life. Perhaps hindsight would be a good teacher—better than me!

I seemed to pass many a bike shop now that I couldn't take the risk involved with charging up some boots. I was stuck with these old brogues, until I crossed over into Canada anyway.

But I had several other pairs of riding boots at home waiting for me in Chilliwack, so I might as well accept that fact that these shoes were along for the ride. I glanced down at my feet as I rode, noticing the tongues of my shoes again poking out at me. We were stuck with each other!

Catching the brake lights of the old Volvo in front of me, I slowed to a stop. A flagman up front was holding up his red octagon, yielding to dump trucks carrying more tons of gravel. Oh great—construction! I sat and waited in the heat slowly stripping my layers, until I was down to a tee shirt. Just when I was starting to feel like I was about to deconstruct, the flagman held up the SLOW yellow sign. And that was what we did for the next ten miles: slow!

When winding roads tease you with their leans, slow means riding upright. When the wind washes over you, cooling your core, slow means you sweat. Slow means you breathe in the exhaust fumes of the rigs in front, dragging their heavy butts up the hill in first gear, leaving trails of blue smoke for you to inhale. Slow means you ride in first gear, relying more heavily on your footwear to maintain your balance through all the starts and stops; the soles of these shoes, now wearing mighty thin. Slow kills the riding experience to a motorcyclist, which explains why, once the traffic gets moving again, we bikers over-accelerate, reacting to all that pent up adrenaline. Like shots out of a cannon, we appear out of nowhere, snaking through the vehicles, trying to escape their restrictions. Bikers just want to be free! We don't like being hemmed in by deadlines, curfews and obligations. Commitments cramp our style!

People in well concealed cars might sneer at us rambunctious bikers as we pass, wondering why someone would choose to expose themselves to all the natural elements. But to a biker, we ride in spite of the rain, the heat, the wind, the bugs, the traffic; we rebel against anything that would resemble constraint. Air conditioning and cruise control are just too tame for beasts. The more raw the riding experience, the better. We can take that puny uncomfortable little seat. We thrive on complaining about our sore butts. We take pride in our Iron Butt races. We can handle the non-stop vibration that jiggles your bladder making you pee every ten minutes. We tolerate, and even brag about the mammoth bugs that we ingest. Aching lower backs and arthritic knees are just part of the journey to make us strong—make us men. We can take it!!

Just as I was thinking this, a rig driver threw out his burning cigarette, hitting the lip of my fairing and bouncing down to my crotch. "Oh crap!" I swerved as I tried to swat the butt away, but my thick leather riding gloves prevented the dexterity needed to accomplish that job. I tried to stand on my pegs, allowing the wind to push it on through beneath me, but instead the butt reverberated on my seat, bouncing along till it leaned to the right and at last, fell into my shoe. Flicking my right leg into the air, I knew this would not extract the burning bullet lodged now under my arch and stinging like a mad bee. Shifting down, I let the rig pass as I retreated to the slow lane behind him, and then onto the shoulder, where I came to an abrupt stop. Jumping off my bike, I kicked off my shoe and watched the still burning cigarette butt propel through the air, landing in the dry ditch. "Bloody hell! What was he thinking throwing that out the window at me? He doesn't own the highway." I yelled at the now long gone rig. Of course we know who really owns those roads!

After climbing down into the ditch to locate my missing shoe, I found the little flicker of fire and extinguished it with contempt. I should phone those numbers you see on the back of Semi trucks, inviting you to report unsafe driving practices, and claim assault causing bodily harm. Or isn't it illegal to start a forest fire? Jerk!!

I mowed down the pavement till I passed the guilty rig at a weigh station, in a long, long line of Semi trucks. I laughed at the justice!

The road was now growing windier and I was one giddy soul! I was searching for the straight line through the S curves, when I found myself too close to the shoulder of the highway. The asphalt had split and separated, leaving a large unforeseen rut, to which I, unfortunately found myself wobbling through, to the point of bending my front fender as well as my front tire rim. Slowly coming to a complete stop at the end of this five foot long ravine, I assessed the damage. Dragging my injured animal off to the side of the road, I wondered if I could nurse it back to health. Nope! My bike needed a hospital; it would require a generous donation of body parts. Luckily its organs were still intact, just some major twisting of its limbs. It could be revived, with a little help. I was just glad that I didn't need reviving; things could have been a lot worse if I had not been able to maintain control of my beast.

I tried to spin the front wheel manually, but it caught on the bent front fender. Unloading my camping gear and lifting my seat, I uncovered my small patchwork of portable tools that I carried in a cloth satchel. Retrieving a screw driver, I unscrewed my twisted fender, which then permitted my front tire to at least turn, albeit in a contorted manner. Surveying a map, I decided to limp along, fender bungeed onto my tent bag, until I hit the next town, thankfully only a few miles away.

Riding in first gear, with my hazard lights on, I attempted to steer straight, when my tire wanted to drag me off to the right. Every vehicle that I had passed that day, was now passing me. It is indeed a humbling experience for a biker to be passed by a motor home, let alone huge rigs, cars pulling their holiday trailers, or worse: Greyhound busses. I had to swallow hard and keep my head down....and focused.

Wobbling into town, the one and only gas station was closed. Run down and derelict the gas pumps looked like they were out of the fifties. Like Fonzy should step out any moment, with his white socks and dress shoes and black leather jacket, combing his slicked back hair. Gazing down at my attire, I kinda belonged! As I pulled off my helmet and combed my own sweaty hair, I wished I could sing "Happy Days." That wasn't what was coming to my mind though, I looked more like "Wild Rider"—all crazed out!

Arms crossed and staring at my bike, my transporter, I knew that I needed a mechanic shop to bend my bike rim back, sure that I wasn't going to find a new rim in this small town. As I stood there sizing up the damage, I could feel someone's eyes sizing ME up. Spinning around, I saw an old convertible Buick filled with scantily clad teenagers, hooting and hollering at me. Seeing that I was probably old enough to be their father, their focus shifted.

"Nice bike!" one of the girls sang out.

"Yeah!" I waved them off. Picturing Emily in a decade or two made me realize that that time would come before I knew it. This reflection made me miss her. I surprised myself at how little I actually thought of home. I guess I was living my adventure alright! And more!! Guilt set in, until I reminded myself that I was bound for home, shouldn't be too long now, I reasoned.

A throaty roar then came from behind me as a fellow biker pulled up to this deserted gas bar. "You lost?" He yelled out from his Harley.

"No.... broken down!" I replied exasperated with myself.

I watched as his thick tattooed arms steered his bike around to get a better look. He stared a while then shot out his cowboy boots and walked his bike around mine, examining the extent of brokenness. Finally, he parked and strode over. Kneeling down he scanned my front tire and then stared pensively toward the sky.

"You're going to need a new rim, this one here is bent bad," he said diagnosing the problem. "No shops around here though to buy a new one."

He wasn't telling me anything that I didn't already know. "Yeah, it looks that way. I think I'm doomed!" I said, relenting to my own dismal prognosis.

Studying the damage some more, this middle aged man took off his helmet and scratched his curly blond locks. He was somewhat pimply faced, overweight and much shorter than me. Folding his parrot tattooed arms over his black leather vest and black tee shirt, he stood quiet for some time. "You know, I have a shop out back if you want to come and bang this thing out, you're welcome to," he offered kindly.

Staring at this walking invitation, I accepted, and before I knew it, I was back on my feeble bike following George home. He lived about two miles down the road, off the main drag and down a gravel road lined with small homes and barking dogs. These were all older homes on acreages with mature full trees hovering over each yard. I pulled up behind him and then stopped as he opened his garage door of his shop. Walking my bike in, I couldn't help laughing at George's face as his eyes were stuck on my dress shoes. I dismounted and shook George's hand. "Thanks a lot man. I really appreciate you letting me use your place here." I offered genuinely grateful for his generosity.

"Hey, no problem," he shot back with a warm, friendly smile. "Us bikers gotta stick together."

I thought George was going to just leave me to my own fixing, but instead he pulled up an old plastic lawn chair and sat himself down. I wasn't expecting an audience, but then again, I guess he did not want to leave me, a complete stranger, with all of his valuable tools either. I started to unload my bike, when I began to look around. What I would do for a shop like this!! It must have been a thousand square feet of man cave. There were tools covering all the walls, several tool chests and work benches. He had a few other bikes, in pieces, up on blocks—projects in process, no doubt. There was a large laundry sink next to a small beer fridge. On the other side there was a working wood stove with boxes of kindling next to it, beside which was a recliner, all worn and ripped up and comfortable. I was in heaven! Walking around the place, George even had a bathroom in there. But best of all, he had a paint booth way in the back. There was even a wench to lift out engines. All he needed was a bed and he'd be set for life, I thought.

"Wow!" I let out slowly as my eyes feasted on everything around me. I had never seen such a shop as this. "Are you married?" I just had to ask, as I couldn't imagine any wife consenting to the cost of this playhouse.

"I was, but she left me. I just spend all my money and time in this place now," George confided.

"Doesn't seem like too bad a deal to me," I said insensitively.

George shirked off that response and started to clear off his largest work bench, which was in the middle of the room. He picked up a hammer and pointed to the vice. "We can try and bend this back, but first let's get that wheel off."

He was going to stay and help me: a friend! How lucky was I! We spent the evening hours, pounding away at the thing. There was even more damage than I originally found. It was quite humorous to watch George be so resourceful and use Harley parts to fix a broken down Kawasaki. He even had to manufacture a small metal clamp to hold my fender in place. This was one talented guy!

We ordered in some pizzas and he pulled out some beer and then we just sat and admired our handiwork. It was getting late and he offered a couch for me to sleep on, to which I gratefully accepted.

Finishing off our ales, George had to ask, "So what are you doing in these here parts anyway?"

"I'm just on the back end of a trip to Sturgis." I replied looking down at the floor and my feet, wondering how much to divulge.

"One of these days, I'm going to make it there myself," George admitted wistfully.

"Yeah, it's been quite the trip," I said, not really wanted to say much more.

"So what kind of work do you do George? ....When you're not in here?" I asked to change the subject.

"Oh this ain't work in here, this is play!" he corrected me.

Feeling stupid, I agreed.

"No, by day I'm an officer with the Montana Police department," he said, checking my response.

I'm sure he could see my chin drop visibly to the floor. When I bent over to pick it up, I slapped my mocking shoe tongues, back into place. Now what do I do? Glad for one thing, I hadn't confided any information that could be used against me in a court of law. Hiding behind my eyeballs, I scampered to say something, lest I reveal my cover.

"Oh that must be interesting work," always a safe thing to say.

"Not really! Not here anyways. Idaho is quiet most of the time and this county is downright sleepy. Not that I'm complaining, I just miss the excitement of say....South Dakota where I used to work. That is before I got transferred here."

The pause was growing too long, and not to draw attention to it, I needed to respond—but with what? Oh, have you talked to any of your former colleagues lately? Or how about, do you still engage in any file sharing with them? Or worse, have they told you about any files that got away on them lately? I mean, why horse around, let's get right to the point? Hang me now!!

My imagination was getting away from me, I needed to reign it in. "Why did you get transferred here anyway?" I just had to ask, stupid me!

"Oh, it's a long story, which I'd rather not get into." He let me off the hook.

Breaking up the subject with a pee, I hurried to my feet and left the room. It was deja vu in the can, spotting the small window up high over the toilet. I was again feeling uncomfortable and I was looking for an out. I should just tell him I've changed my mind about bunking on his couch, and that I'd rather just go find myself a motel somewhere. But that would draw too much attention to myself, after I've already accepted his couch, and I'm sure being a cop, he's already detected my uneasiness. How can I escape my predicament?

Some old Beatle tune could be heard, to which George answered his cell phone. I could hear the mumblings through the wall, but not make out the words of his conversation. Flushing out his statements, I opened the bathroom door to find George now reclined in his old lazy boy and laughing, almost hysterically. I started to panic. Now was my chance.

"Hey man," I interrupted his phone call, "These bones are in serious need of a bed. I think I'll check in to the local Motel. But thanks for everything, man!" I said, trying to let my words pour out of my mouth smoothly as I made my way for the door.

Putting his hand over the receiver, George looked up and responded with: "Oh, okay then. No problem! Ride Safe!" And with a salute, he then continued laughing into the phone.

Hoping that my Kawi would pass the road test after we put the re-bent wheel and fender back on, I hopped on it, while still in his shop and rode out through the open garage door. I could see George waving me off through my side mirror as I spit up some stones.

I by-passed that town's line of roadside motels and skipped a few more towns after that. I felt like I was about to shit my drawers; like I just escaped being sent to the principal's office, like I just narrowly escaped detection. I wasn't sure how much of these thoughts were real or just my imagination. I couldn't even remember giving George my name for Pete's sake, which is odd, how I could have omitted that—not like me at all! I mused at the silly roads my brain was taking me down, playing with each thought for a while, before shrugging them all off. Having felt like I finally rode through my fears, it was time to stop for the night. I was drained!

I had no cash left for a motel, or a campsite and I sure was not about to charge anything—especially not now! Driving along a forested stretch, I pulled over into the dark cover of tall cedars. Tucking my bike out of sight of the highway, I set up my tent in the blackness of night, with only the moon to guide my tent poles into their correct sleeves. I should be able to accomplish this, I chided myself.

I lit up a cigar and kept checking over my shoulder. I wanted to be the predator but I couldn't help feeling like prey.

Before I knew it, I was snoring in my finely erected dome, snug as a bug like all the creatures that surrounded me.

That night I had a strange nightmare. I dreamt that we were at our Chilliwack home and hosting a dinner party with my family. My sisters were busy helping Jill prepare the food in the kitchen and the house was noisy and full. Compounding the load of work was the fact that snakes were creeping in through window cracks and guests had to step over them in the front doorway. Everyone was going on with their tasks, just kicking them out of the way or picking them up and throwing them outside. It became overwhelming though, as they couldn't keep up with all the snakes trying to gain entrance to our home.

Finally Jill screamed out in frustration, "Luke where are you? We need your help!"

Bewildered by my lack of response, she scrambled around the rooms looking for me, until she came across me in our bedroom. She stood at the doorway and stared in horror and disbelief. There I was in our bed, sleeping and covered completely with hundreds of slithering snakes.

JILL DAY 15

The next day was very quiet – too quiet. The phone didn't ring, my daughters didn't fight. I dug out the wagon from the garage and plopped Molly and Emily into it; a walk would do us good. With the girls in tow, I walked up and down our street, past the Stewart's house, the Cooper's, the Foster's, the Smith's, the Frank's and the Bancroft's. I just stared at their houses, looking for answers, picturing the men, the fathers, that used to reside there, thinking about how each of their family's lives had been forever altered. I felt as empty as each of those houses. We slowly made our way to Sardis Park, an oasis in the neighborhood. It had a large pond, or small lake really, inhabited by many ducks, swans and plenty of Canadian geese. The landscaping was lush and colorful and so well-tended. There were swings and an assortment of playground equipment for the girls to scamper over. On this particular visit there weren't many visitors strolling around the pathways that ran the perimeter of the pond, we pretty much had the park to ourselves. On some occasions that might make me feel a little uneasy—a little unsafe. But not today! I welcomed the solitude and the peace. This place, in all its beauty and tranquility was so alive—in stark contrast to my soul. Drinking in the wonder was like tonic. Molly and Emily chased the geese as I tried to tiptoe around all the droppings that littered the grounds. One particular goose was getting quite aggressive and trying to peck at Molly's bottom, so the chase turned on her. She did not like this one bit and quickly clamored back into her stroller. We proceeded to stroll around the pond and I relished the wind blowing the low hanging weeping willows across my face. I had something in common with those trees. As we rounded the bend we came across a young boy fishing on the edge of the pond with his grandpa. It hadn't appeared they caught any trout yet. I had once heard that the city stocks this pond with fish for youngsters and seniors to fish. Watching those two seemed so idyllic, like something out of a Norman Rockwell painting. I had never known a grandpa, mine had both passed before I was born. Even Molly asked once, "Mommy, what's a Grandpa?" She too had never experienced that relationship.

We returned to the park entrance gate, when Emily reminded me, "Mommy we forgot to feed the birds." She pulled out the bag of old bread ends that we had brought with us and grabbed one freezer burned slice. She ripped it into some very large pieces and began throwing them to the swarms of geese that had gathered around.

"Emily, you have to break them into smaller pieces or you'll choke the birds." I said as one was already straining to get a chunk down its throat. All three of us began to tear and throw, tear and throw. But we couldn't do it fast enough for the birds' liking. They began to close in on us and squawk loudly. Sensing Molly's fear, I lifted her onto a picnic table, where she was relieved to be out of their reach. Soon the swans had joined us, and as they were as tall as Emily, she too was feeling threatened. She joined her sister on top of the picnic table. Once I saw more swans wading out of the water and approaching us I knew it was time to high tail it out of there, for they were being especially aggressive, not even waiting for the bread to leave our fingers. They would try to snatch it right out of our hands. It struck me how, even though they were only dried up stale bread crumbs, all the birds were desperate and starving. I guess I felt desperate and starving for any snippets of hope I could snatch too. Maybe my tears could swell those crumbs and fill my hollow shell. It was time to go back home, to our own empty house.

    Pushing the stroller into the driveway, I realized that I had left the garage door open. As Molly climbed out of her stroller, my eyes gazed at the contents of the garage. This was indeed Luke's space. Other than the shelf of gardening tools, I couldn't see anything that I used. Everything was a reminder of Luke! I found myself pushing stuff aside on his work bench, opening cupboards, looking through bins—but what was I looking for? Was it akin to sleeping with his pajamas, or his pillow? Or perhaps using his favorite mug, or sitting on his favorite chair. No, those latter two were done out of spite. Now I just wanted to touch things Luke had touched, to smell things that reminded me of him. And he did reek of oil and gasoline more than I would have liked. To him, those scents were more fragrant than the most expensive cologne. But the garage held more than Luke's things and his memory—it contained possible clues to his whereabouts. I scanned the walls, read every scrap of paper in the garbage can, looked through the Lordco bag for a recent purchase, until not sure what I should look for, gave up the search. Nothing pointed me in the right direction. No answers were found.

    I decided to try his journal. Running through the house and up to the bedside table, I was disheartened to find his journal not there. He no doubt had it with him as he liked to write his morning pages daily. Too bad, as that would surely have offered some clues as to whereabouts if he had indeed planned all this. But what if he had left it behind, would I have actually have read it? That was such a personal possession, like unlocking someone's heart. I was of the belief that you had to be invited in to that special place, given the odd peek into its precious treasures; you couldn't invade uninvited. That would be breaking a solemn trust. But wouldn't the present circumstances permit this entry? I wasn't sure!

I continued my search throughout all the rooms, looking, searching for clues. I stumbled upon a pile of mail in the entrance hall that had been accumulating from the mail slot, yet surely neglected. Probably just a pile of bills anyway, I thought. I kicked them off to the side as I didn't have the energy to deal with their contents, when I noticed a post office card sticking out. It was addressed to Luke Connor. Apparently there was a package awaiting him at the post office. I wondered what that could be. I pondered who could be sending him something: probably just some bike part he ordered from some American company as he so often did. Yet I remained curious. Should I go and retrieve it? But it wasn't addressed to me; that would surely be a violation of his privacy. They probably wouldn't give it to me anyways, seeing that it is not addressed to me. I resigned myself to leave it in the pile, deemed as junk mail. It was just that after all: junk. It offered me nothing!

I continued to search the house for clues. It became too depressing to continue, however, so I abandoned that idea. After some pesto pasta for lunch, the girls and I were all ready for a nap. After putting the girls down in their room, I laid on my bed pondering what to do. I just didn't know the next step; I didn't know what to think even. I again thought of that post office card sitting down by the front door. I decided I had nothing to lose. I would take the girls downtown and try to obtain Luke's package, in the hopes that it gave me some clue, any useful information. With that thought, I drifted off to sleep.

Suddenly, the doorbell woke me from my slumber. Wondering who it could be, I sauntered down the stairs, but no one was there. As I made my way back upstairs, I noticed the girls' bedroom door ajar. Looking in I only saw Emily, still fast asleep, but no Molly! I ran back downstairs and starting searching for her under furniture, in closets, in the back yard. That's strange! I called her over and over as I continued to look for her. By this time I was getting frantic. Where would a toddler go? Then I remembered the doorbell ringing shortly before and wondered if perhaps that had been her ringing it. But how or why would she be outside? Opening up the front door, there was still no one there. As I was about to close the door, I heard someone talking—and it was a kid's voice—Molly's voice actually.

Leaping outside I spotted Molly with only her undershirt and pull up diaper on, squatting cheerfully in the middle of the road. As I raced down the driveway toward her, I could hear her talking to herself. She had my wallet and was pulling out the contents; identification cards were spilled out over the pavement and tens and twenties were trickling in the wind towards the neighbor's house. The worst part however was that she wasn't in the driveway or even next to the curb, but sprawled in the middle of the street, like some sitting duck ripe for a fast moving vehicle to run down unnoticed. And she was all alone! I could not believe what my eyes were screaming. I was angry, scared but mostly grateful. I scooped her up in one huge embrace. I couldn't stop kissing her. She had apparently awoken before Emily or I had and escaped through the garage, which I had left open a second time. Such carelessness I could not afford. When I had asked Molly who had rung the doorbell, her answer startled me.

"It was just the lady next door Mommy. I asked her to come for tea."

No wonder she was ringing my bell! I was surprised someone from Social Services wasn't accompanying her. Scooping up my baby, I carried her up to check on Emily, not wanting a double whammy. Thankfully, she was still asleep in her bed. Waking with a smile, as she always did, she rubbed her eyes and made her way over for a hug. I sure loved my girls!

With the post office beckoning us, I piled the girls in the truck and headed for town. Placing the card on the counter, I mustered up a smile and politely asked, "Could I please pick up this parcel for my husband. He's out of town and asked that I get it for him," I lied.

The post office clerk, being the half dazed teenager that she was, just looked at me, examined the card and shot back, "Do you have any identification?"

"Sure, I'll get it," I said in delighted disbelief at my luck. Fumbling with my wallet, I quickly placed my driver's licence on the counter before this teenager thought better of it and checked the post office policy, or just changed her mind. She looked like one of those types who lived on whim, probably changing her clothes, hair style and nail polish a gazillion times a day.

Walking to the back room with my ID still in her hand, I was sure I was busted. Instead she came out with a parcel, Luke's parcel. "Here you go," she muttered as she slowly handed me the package. "You'll have to sign for it."

Grabbing it quickly, and scribbling my name, I headed for the doorway, before I realized I had left Molly sitting on the counter. I shot back around to retrieve my relieved daughter and, taking Emily by the hand, headed back for the door.

"Excuse me," my now favorite teen called out, "You forgot your driver's licence."

Again returning to the counter, now fully embarrassed, I took my card, nodded in thanks, and left.

Should I open it now, I wondered as we made our way to the truck, or wait till we get home? I thought the latter would be a wiser decision. We sped along full of anticipation and curiosity. I was trying to caution my expectations, warning myself that curiosity killed many a cat, but that did not dampen my hope.

Once home, Molly scampered off to some plaything, while Emily followed me to the kitchen table.

"What is it mommy? Who's it from?" Emily asked in eager succession.

"I don't know what it is, but we'll soon find out." I said looking through the junk drawer for some scissors. "And I don't know who sent it," I quizzically said, noticing no return address.

I flipped the box over and there was nothing written on the other side either. That's puzzling, I thought.

With Emily hovering over me, I snipped the string and opened up the parcel. Upon seeing Luke's worn, and somewhat smelly things, I gasped. I was expecting some brand new biker toy, like saddlebag liners or some obscure, impersonal item that is difficult to buy here. Instead I am seeing something very personal. I slowly sifted through Luke's clothes, sniffing his favorite tie dye tee shirt that he purchased on Salt Spring Island many holidays ago. Holding up his old holy socks and over worn undies, Emily chuckled. Pulling out the books, I too had a laugh at one of the titles: The Idiot. A Russian classic that was a gift from Norm, Luke's brother, a joke gift no doubt, for Luke was anything but an idiot. Lately, however, I wasn't so sure!

As I rummaged through the remainder of items, my confusion grew. Who sent these and why? Were these all reasons to celebrate? Was each item evidence that Luke was still alive? Had he sent these? This appeared plausible, since I remember doing so on previous biking excursions, when we needed to lighten our load. My excitement grew, as I fell into my chair in questionable shock. Could it be? But if Luke was still alive, why would he send things home and not include a note for me.....and come to think about it, why not just call. I still don't get it. And he would not have sent home so much stuff, this looked like most of his packing list. Nonetheless, optimism was bubbling up within me. But I remained unconvinced; there were way too many things for that to ring true. When I finally uncovered his running shoes, my joy subsided until it diminished altogether. Was this just the remains of his life? Did some morgue send me these, as all that could be retrieved from some crash he might have had? Was this the contents of some saddlebag that had got flung to the side of the road in a head on?

I sadly picked up the box, as if it was all that remained of my husband, and I hugged it close. I clutched the corners of the box as I drooped my head and heart over its contents.

"What's wrong mommy?" Emily asked now consoling me, rubbing my back.

She was too young to understand the implications and just stood there, following my lead, until she too started to weep.

Could she possibly know the meaning of this box? I doubt it! She was just full of mercy for her mom.

Grabbing Emily's hand, I pulled her close, letting my tears run down her face, blending with hers. "These were daddy's things," I explained unnecessarily. I didn't have the stomach to explain things further. With both Emily and Luke's box on my lap, I began to rock back and forth.

"Hush little baby,....... don't say a word, ...momma's going to buy you........ a mockingbird", I found myself singing expressionless. "And if that mockingbird won't sing.......momma's going to buy you a diamond ring.......and if that diamond ring gets broke,....momma's going to buy you a billy goat..........and if that billy goat won't pull........momma's going to buy you a cart and bull.......and if that cart and bull falls over.......momma's going to buy you a dog named Rover.........and if that dog named Rover won't bark.........momma's going to buy you a horse and cart.....and if that horse and cart fall down.........you'll still be the sweetest baby in town."

I reflected upon the words of this lullaby and wondered how this momma always knew what to do; for every "if" she had a solution. I sure didn't have any!! Instead I just held Emily close and we rocked in silence.

* * *

Later that evening, out of desperation, I eventually mustered up the courage to pray. I decided to apply what I had read in Exodus, after all, time was ticking and Death owned the clock. In a state of spiritual ritual, I stirred up all the faith I could. "Lord" I implored as if he were deaf, maybe he was tired of hearing from me, "Lord, I plead the blood of Christ on this house. I pray that the spirit of Death would pass over this house as he did in the days of old. You did it in the book of Exodus and I believe you could do it here, now for me and my family. Please spare Luke's life I pray in Jesus' name. Amen."

I then picked up a sharp knife and proceeded to cut myself. Slicing my finger, I squeezed out the blood into a small custard dish. Like a zombie, I then went outside and smeared some over the front door frame and then around back, where I reached high to smear some on the back door as well. And for extra assurance, I put a dab on as many windows as my blood would allow. I felt foolish, yet desperate.

I was exhausted and emotionally spent and dragged myself back inside where sleep surrounded me, covered me like a blanket. A red blanket! Peaceful sleep!

LUKE DAY 15

I woke up excited, because I thought I should head north toward Glacier National Park, instead of heading west into Idaho State. I had always wanted to tour that park. This was indeed insane because all the holiday travelers, who incorrectly thought that they owned the road, were all traveling in that direction as well. Every camper, trailer, RV and his dog were going to the Park. But I wanted to go too! So I joined the throngs, and I resigned myself to a day of weaving and winding, racing and SLOW riding. Not sure why?? This pace is pure torture for a motorcyclist, but it does make you stop often to sniff out the weeds in life.

Like this one pit stop, where I met some fellow bikers, with blue vinyl suitcases and old worn hiking boots bungeed onto the back of their bikes. Their mismatched riding gear and wrinkled, second hand clothing matched their dread locks beneath their helmets. They were on their way up to Nelson, BC: the hippy haven that had replaced the Kitsilano locale years before. They were strung out on something, but had a genuineness about them all the same. They weren't in for the ride as much as the destination. They probably just found the cheapest way to get there, minus hitch hiking of course.

Ironically, they knew where they were going; I, on the other hand, was wandering around aimlessly. Not sure exactly where

I should be. But I did feel a pull for the park, so that was my destination for the day.

Riding toward the looming mountains, I felt small and insignificant, just what I was wanting. I wished to be invisible—not seen or found. I certainly did not want the police to find me, but I don't think I had wanted my wife to really find me on this trip either. And I was actually relieved, if I was honest with myself, that Mike, Rod and Larry did not find me. I don't think I wanted God to even find me. I just wanted invisibility. Attention required a response and I didn't want to be held responsible or accountable for a response to the police, my wife, my friends, God or even life. What should I do? How should I be? What should I say? How should I live? I could not handle all the "shoulds" in my life. I was too tired to think of all the rational responses that required a brain. I did not want the proper answers or the correct answers and I didn't know Luke's answers at the moment. So, like the saying goes, when you don't want to answer—avoid the question. So this trip was all about that: avoidance. I was stalling for time..... for surely this road trip would afford me the time I needed to consolidate my feelings, untangle my thoughts, decipher my emotions and come to terms with myself: to look at my inner aspirations as honestly as I could. I just needed time to think!

It reminded me of a poem I once read, a prayer really, where the poet asked God: Show me thyself. But the ugliness and flaws that God revealed were too much to bare, until the man finally pleaded for God to take it away from his face, he could not stand to gaze upon his own shortcomings any longer. Finally God replied, then gaze upon my beauty instead and then you will become lost in me, and in time you will realize how much I love you and don't even see your ugliness. Perspective was everything!

I felt such peace that day riding into my soul. Something had been missing...besides my boots! Perhaps I was looking for the missing pieces of my life, but l think I found some of them on this trip. I found parts of myself!

I met several other characters that day, who like me, were searching to find themselves. Like Brian, who flirted with every girl he saw, searching for his masculinity; or Brenda the shopaholic, searching for new identities to don; or Richard who tripped over his own big words, searching for his intelligence; or Tom, who dressed like a teenager, searching for his long lost youth. Everywhere I looked, people were searching. Everyone appeared shattered, missing parts of themselves that they desperately needed in order to feel complete. Sometimes we find these missing attributes in others and so hitch up with someone to make us feel complete. Usually we make friends with those who possess the very qualities we lack, in the hopes that some will rub off on us. Sometimes we might drug or drink ourselves numb to avoid the truth; it is painful to honestly confront ourselves. But mostly, we tend to run or we hide! What we really need is grace for ourselves. PURE GRACE! If they could bottle it, I would drink plenty. I would share it with all my friends, and I would give it to strangers. The world would be a better place for it; we could get on with living and loving, instead of always searching. Just think of all the energy that could be diverted into proactive living, instead of merely reacting to life. But yet, that was one of the beautiful things about the human condition. You could take something imperfect, and see the magnificence of it! See the beauty, not despite the imperfection, but in the imperfection. Oh for the grace to not only accept, but to truly cherish our weaknesses; they do, after all, make us who we are!

This made me think of Jill and how she tends to worry about everything. Yet that is who she is. Gotta love her for it! And I do love her! And I miss her!

Riding along I sniffed the sweet mountain air, the scent of cedar trees and then the fragrance of wild flowers flourishing in the mountain meadows. The beauty was sucking me in. Without resistance, nor avoidance, I succumbed. Breathing in the wonder of it all, I felt my senses relishing such delightful feasts. The air was warm and welcoming and my taste buds were anticipating some fresh spring water bubbling up from the brook that ran like a ribbon alongside the road. Stopping to replenish my water bottle, I splashed some liquid life onto my face and instantly revitalized myself. I just couldn't get enough and so, without hesitating, I lied down in the cold mountain brook, soaking myself down in full riding gear. Even my dress shoes were thankful for the dip, as I was thankful for them; their wagging tongues no longer bothering me, but now becoming my road weary friends. Making water angels, I chuckled as I heard the water ripples emanating out from me. Fully drenched, I clamored up over the rocks, shook myself off like a dog on a hot summer day, and then mounted my Kawi. That was one wet, wild ride!

Entering the Park, I was surprised to see such little traffic. It was past the dinner hour though and I guess the campers and trailers had all settled down for the night already. So I rode, in freedom, truly owning the road that August evening, enjoying every moment. Eventually, seeing that I was still so wet, leather and denim taking forever to dry in the wind as they tend to do, I decided to stay in a hotel. I contemplated camping, but

I really wanted a dry room and a hot bath. Besides, this would require the use of a credit card as well, and if I had to take a chance, I might as well book myself a room.

Spotting a Motel Six on the eastern side of the park, I pulled in to the parking lot. Examining the contents of my wallet, for any loose strays, hoping for some American or even Canadian bills to be lodged in between my identification cards, or photos, I came up empty handed. I did, however, spot an old American Express card that I never used. In fact, I forget entirely that I even had it. I suspect that it had been years since I last used it. I never did apply for it, they just sent me one in the mail one day, which on the spur of the moment, I called up and had it activated. So whether or not it would still work, years later, I wasn't sure, but I was willing to try. At least the paper trail on this particular card wouldn't be so obvious, perhaps even overlooked.

Marching in to the lobby, still wet, but at least not dripping, I plunked my American Express down on the counter and asked for a single room. To my delight they had a vacancy, but even more worth celebrating was that my card was accepted. Yippee!! I sauntered up to the second floor and soaked in the tub for several hours. I even ordered Chinese food to be delivered to my room. I felt so rich… in more ways than I previously knew. I had a good time celebrating with myself in my room that night, followed by much too many hours of restorative sleep.

JILL DAY 16

Peace was following me all day, not misery, not sadness, not even confusion…..just the purity of peace. I had a renewed sense that Luke was okay. But where was he, where was he?

Not really expecting an answer, I went about my day with some kind of calm assurance. I just kept getting this picture of Glacier National Park. It was a clear, confident answer. Okay, I thought, puzzled. Wanting it to be divine intervention, I found myself afraid of my own sanity. Was I imagining this? Did God in the sky really care?

Suddenly, the phone rang very loudly as I was sitting right next to it. Reality was yanking me from the heavens.

"Would you accept a collect call from Luke Connor?" I heard the operator ask.

"Pardon me?" I responded in utter disbelief.

"Would you accept a collect call from Luke?" the operator repeated rather sternly.

"Yes! Yes!" was my panted reply. No way, I thought. Is this a joke? Could it be? My heart was pounding like nails.

"Hi Jill," came Luke's soft gentle voice. The voice I've come to know and love for nearly twenty years of marriage. The voice that sets me back to our dating years when we spent many an evening on the phone, where his voice would woo me, would romanticize me. His voice always brought me back to our first love.

Stunned, I couldn't speak. My bank account of words had just run out.

"Jill, are you there?" Luke asked.

"Luke?" I spoke in slow motion. "Luke? Where are you?" I had to ask to see if he was still of this world, as if he'd say, "Well actually I'm an apparition!"

"I'm just outside Glacier National Park," he answered.

Too spooked to respond, I froze.

"Jill, are you there? Are you okay?" He pressed for words from a woman who had never known a loss of them, at least when she was awake.

"Yeah, I'm here," I volunteered as I grabbed for a chair to settle my wobbly legs.

"I just pulled in and boy am I tired," Luke admitted, totally oblivious to the ordeal I've been put through.

"Did you find the guys or should I say, did they find you?" I asked, anxiously seeking for answers.

"No! No I haven't seen them," he replied, in what I sensed was a very exhausted voice.

"Do you have any idea what's been going on since you went missing?" I questioned him.

"Missing? Missing? They took off on me!" he shot back.

"Whatever! Anyways you've been reported missing. The South Dakota Police Department have been looking for you. The homicide department is investigating your apparent possible death. You need to call them right away and call off the search." I said, gulping for breaths between every few words.

"You've got to be kidding me??" Luke asked, mustering up a laugh.

"No, I'm not. I'm dead serious!" I quipped. "They've conducted aerial searches looking for your body. I think they said they were planning another one tomorrow. You need to call them immediately. Are you camping or staying in a hotel?" I quizzed him almost frantic.

"I'm staying in the Hotel Six Eastern Ring," he answered from a multitude of thoughts. "No wait! I was at that hotel last night. I just checked in to the Western Ring Hotel Six."

"Well, you need to call the S.D. Police from your hotel room then," I suggested.

"Now? It's late!" Luke snapped.

"No! Right now! Call them right now." I emphasized, aware that he had no idea of the magnitude this thing had taken on.

Changing my tone, "I'm so glad you're okay," I whispered.

With a chuckle, "Oh Jill! You know me. I'm a big boy. I'm fine!" he reassured me.

"You have no idea Luke what's been going on, do you?" I asked rhetorically. "By the way...why didn't you ever call? You said you'd call every night. The girls were very upset. They waited for your call every night," I lied.

"You know I tried," he went on to explain what to me could only be excuses. "The calling card wouldn't work. ATT wouldn't connect me. I think they were on strike or something. Only management operating the lines. Anyways, it didn't matter how many times I tried, I just couldn't get through."

You've got to be kidding, I thought to myself. What a bunch of B.S. But it wasn't the time to fight. It was time to celebrate.

"Well, we'll talk about it when you get home," I said, in what would be in my mind, the understatement of the year.

"I'm on my way home now. I'll probably make it by tomorrow night if I boot it," Luke offered as some sort of restorative justice.

"Well don't do that," I laughed. "Don't kill yourself trying to get home in a hurry." What an ironic twist that would be, I mused.

"I'll call you tomorrow night then, if I just can't make it," Luke remarked.

"Yeah, where have I heard that before?" I chuckled.

"Sigh! No I mean it," he retorted.

"Sleep well. I love you," I whispered into the receiver before hanging up.

I sat there for a long while. Then slowly, slowly, joy overcame me. I was bubbling! I cried! I laughed! I danced! I shouted! I sang! I jumped! It felt like my sense of reality was being twisted, contorted, confusing my sense of what was up and where was down. It is like standing on a moving floor! I tried to gain my bearings. I tried to distinguish between reality and a nightmare. The tectonic plates were shifting and I wasn't sure if the volcano was about to erupt or if I would merely fall through the cracks. Such a strange sensation! We build our world on what we think life to be and then when the rug is pulled beneath us, when we are free falling, we question when we have hit the floor. Can we trust that this really is solid ground or is it mere illusion? I waited for the world to stop spinning… for my brain to stop grasping for sense… to ease into acceptance. I finally let go of my grip on my chair's arm.

I ran upstairs to wake the girls up. "Guess what?" I said sitting on Emily's bed. "Daddy's coming home—maybe tomorrow."

"I know," she replied in a sleepy yet angelic manner.

"Oh!" I responded quite puzzled. How could she know that? Since she wasn't surprised by my news, I felt no need to explain further, and left. Molly could wait. I didn't want to soothe her back to sleep afterwards.

Hallelujah! I rejoiced within myself as I bounded down the stairs. I felt so relieved. My life was hopefully going to return to normal. The pit in my stomach hadn't left but it was changing. I still had so many questions, but the interrogation would come later; the anger could be chipped away at. There was time now. Words were restored in abundance and boy was I going to cash in. It was my due.

Funny thing how joy can be so complicated though. For even while I'm happy, I'm still miffed with Luke and myself. Why do I need my man to feel complete? I hate to feel so dependent on another human being for my happiness. Recalling how utterly helpless and hollow I felt without Luke in my life made me realize how much I loved him, but also how vulnerable I was. I wanted to be stronger than that—to rise above the anger that was bubbling beneath my joy.

The phone rang again. It was late now.

"Hi, it's Mike," came a voice of resignation.

"Oh Hi Mike," I said in a cheery voice.

"Jill, I just wanted to let you know that we've been in touch with the police daily and have spent many days looking in campsites and even ditches for Luke. We just don't know what else we can do," he said in a very sombre voice. "We're coming home."

I paused, realizing he doesn't know. The juxtaposition of perspectives seemed almost comical, yet I needed to be sensitive to Mike's plight, for this was the first time I noticed his pain. Drowning in my own, I neglected to feel what those guys must have felt searching for Luke. How awful for them.

"Mike," I interjected his thoughts, "Mike—Luke's okay."

After hesitating for a moment, he quipped, "What? What do you mean?"

"He just called me a while ago. He's just outside of Glacier National Park." I said with a smile on my face.

"Did he happen to say where he's staying? We're actually not too far from there right now," he mentioned quite excitedly.

"Yeah, he's at the Hotel Six," I said, amazed that these guys are really going to get together after all.

"We're on our way," he quickly said. "We'll find him."

"Great!" I enthused. "See you all when you get back home."

Feeling quite contented, I hung up the phone and went to bed. Ironically, sleep couldn't find me, even though I was no longer hiding. But sleep could wait. I had lots to daydream about now. Lying on my bed, reflecting, I was again startled by the phone. It was really, very late and therefore the ring brought alarm.

"Hello," I muttered into the bedside phone.

"Hi Jill. It's Mike again. I'm sorry it's so late, but we're at the Hotel Six by Glacier National Park and there's no Luke Connor registered here. Are you sure this is the Hotel he said he was staying at?" he asked in a concerned, but exasperated voice.

"Yes I'm quite sure," I responded. The truth is I was now questioning whether I had been talking to a ghost. The blur between reality and nightmare was returning.

"Why wouldn't he give you the correct name of his hotel?" he quizzed me.

"I don't know. Maybe there's more than one Hotel Six," I suggested dumbfounded by the returning confusion.

"No, we've driven up and down this strip several times. All the hotels are right here," he defended himself.

"What's going on?" I asked with such a mixture of emotion. I let it all slip through my fingers. Resolution was an illusion. "Mike, I don't know what to think anymore," I said with a sigh. "Sorry to send you guys on a wild goose chase."

"Well, we're going to stay here for the night. We'll call you tomorrow and see if your hubby has called again," Mike hung up with frustration.

Why was Luke not wanting to be found? I questioned myself. There must be a good explanation for all of this. Yes—for every bit of it. With that, sleep found me quickly.

LUKE DAY 16

Lying on the bed, staring up at the ugly ceiling, I recalled all the details of my conversation with Jill. She said I had been reported missing? Missing? Not missing boots...that I had reported, but me—actually reported as being Missing. Confusion set in. I sat on the bed and pondered things. Who would have reported me missing? Jill? The guys? But I didn't go missing—they deserted me. Could that be why Wyoming Police said I was wanted by the South Dakota Police Department? Not because I took off after reporting my boots missing, but because I was actually missing? I had to laugh at it all. Could it be? I looked down at my dress shoes, with their tongues sticking out to the sides and they seemed to be laughing right along with me. I no longer wanted to rip them out, to silence them. Instead, I wanted to give them voice, to hear them back me up. After all, if shoes could talk, if you could walk a mile in my shoes, etc., etc. My shoes know what happened. The whole thing was so humorous and ridiculous. I fell asleep laughing!

Waking up at three in the morning in a queen sized bed, I rolled over to snuggle with Jill....but she wasn't there. I had dreamt about her and I guess my subconscious had mistaken that for reality, because here I am searching for her in the bed. No matter, I chuckled to myself, I'll be home soon and can cuddle up to Jill for real, I told myself all giddy like a school boy with a crush.

JILL DAY 17

I waited all day for the phone to ring— a familiar feeling by now. I was hoping Luke would call before Mike. Luckily he did.

"Would you accept a collect call from Luke Connor?" the operator asked.

"Yes Yes!" I quickly interrupted her.

"Hi Jill. It's Luke here," he said in that wonderful voice of his.

"Hi!" I said mustering up as much love and cheer as I could in case he was having doubts about coming home.

"You know what?" he started to excuse himself again. "I'm not going to make it home today after all. I'm just too tired and hungry. I probably have another five hours of riding. I think I'll just call it a night and head home tomorrow."

"Where did you stay last night?" was all I could think of asking.

"What do you mean?" he asked detecting my suspicion.

"Mike called last night. I told him where you were and they went to the Hotel Six outside of Glacier National Park and you weren't there. So where were you?" I asked in a demanding fashion.

"Hang on," Luke defensively said, "Hang on! I was at the Hotel Six, just west of Glacier National Park."

"Well I don't know what happened here Luke, but we're all growing quite exasperated with you." I tried to reason.

"Oh brother! Cut me some slack, will you?" Luke shot back.

I have to admit for someone who's intelligent, with their feet on the ground, he was starting to sound flaky with all his lame accounts.

"Whatever," I countered. "We'll see you tomorrow then." I scuttled away from the phone shaking my head.

When Mike called a couple hours later he had acknowledged the other Hotel Six on the other side of the Park that he hadn't discovered until driving through the park. He was now on the East side, Luke was on the west. There was going to be some mud slinging yet.

"You know what Jill? Mike hesitated, changing his plans on the spot, "Since Luke is okay and on his way home, we're not even going to try and catch up to him. We still have a few days of holidays and we might as well have some fun now. We're going to break away and head back north to the Rockies for a while. We'll catch up with Luke in Chilliwack when we get back. See ya later."

"Okay Mike. Bye!" I said feeling guilty that they hadn't had time to enjoy their holiday but rather spent their time looking for Luke, who no doubt had a fabulous time.

LUKE DAY 17

As I felt my still slightly damp clothing, I decided to wear only a sweatshirt, instead of my clammy leather jacket. I found another pair of jeans, that I thought I had sent home, but was gladly mistaken. Loading up my bike, with a spring in my step, I felt myself closer to home. I rode out of Glacier National Park that day feeling contented.

    Heading west for the Idaho State line, I was going to cross that elusive line this time around. I was going home. I rode through the northern tip of Idaho by noon, clipping off that State in record time. Entering Spokane, Washington, I felt the pull of British Columbia, and home, drawing me forward. I kept at it, riding west till I was dizzy with sleep. I became so tired that I was beginning to see things on the highway that I suspect were not really there. It appeared as though raccoons, birds, snakes, rabbits and all sorts of oversized bugs were scampering across the road as I averted them, going record speeds. I felt like I was playing some video game and winding my way through all these obstacles on the road, gathering up points for every object I could avoid. I was good at avoiding things, so very quickly I had acquired the winning score, with my name and number of points flashing across the screen. As I kerplunked over a large rock, reality beckoned me to acknowledge that there were no obstacles crossing the road, only my own imaginations, hallucinations revealing a weary traveller in desperate need of rest. Pulling over for a cup of java to wake myself up, I gulped at least three cups of thick sludge that was probably left over from this morning, or at least lunch brew anyway. As the caffeine pumped through my veins, I felt the jolt necessary to continue on.

I really wanted to make it home....today. But for some reason, I was just so exhausted. Through bleary eyes, I sped and then slowed down to a hum. When several cars passed me, I realized I wasn't really paying attention....I needed to focus on the road. I felt like plugging my electric vest wires straight from my battery to my veins—a higher voltage than coffee was necessary to keep me plugging along.

Halfway through Washington State, I had had enough torture for one day. Time to call it quits for the riding day. I was still hours from home and I relented to the nagging thought that I was not going to make it in one day. I told Jill I would be home tomorrow and I really wanted to prove to her that I meant it, to redeem myself in her eyes as she no doubt considers my word as mud. I wanted to be a man of my word, but yet here I was letting her down and myself down again. I felt guilty. I felt like crap. I started to beat myself up....again.

GRACE Luke! Be gracious with yourself. My new mantra was offering me a way out, a reprieve from my own tyranny. I took it!

Checking myself in to a quaint little Bed and Breakfast, I gave myself permission to relax. It looked like a stone mansion from the outside, but it was warmed up with flowers everywhere. Big red and white geraniums were planted in planter boxes outside every window. And the sign was handwritten in calligraphy: Old English Inn B&B. Inside, it was palatial and awe inspiring, with antiques and warm, richly colored paintings adorning the walls. There were large vases with fresh flowers in every room. All the doors were left open, so I peeked through doorways and down halls, until I just couldn't help myself, I snooped through several rooms of the place.

"Can I help you?" a voice finally bellowed out of the dark recesses of a room, laden with Persian carpets and valuable furniture.

"Oh, I'm sorry, I didn't see you there. I was wanting a room for the night. Do you have anything available?" I asked, still looking around.

As the person glided toward me, a figure emerged from the dark. "Yes, we do. I have the perfect room for you. Follow me." A lean sickly older man, dressed in a smoking robe of golds and black velvet, led me to a room on the second floor.

"It has an extra long bed to accommodate you." He said, scanning his eyes up and down me. "You should be most comfortable here, I would think." Walking over to the door again, he pointed down the hall. "There is the washroom, with a full bath for you to enjoy," he said, offering music to my ears. I loved my baths!

"This would be perfect. Thank you!" I said with a smile, already thinking of a warm soak.

"And breakfast is served downstairs in the parlour between seven and ten," he said as he was already walking back down the stairs.

Closing the door behind him, I could not believe my luck, and all for forty dollars. I had never stayed in such a beautifully decorated and furnished room. Jill would just love it here. It always amazed me how English and Scottish homes were always so plain and unadorned on the outside, but filled with treasures on the inside. When Jill and I had toured through the British Isles several years back, we had encountered that time after time. She would look at me lovingly and then comment on how we English are like that; our exteriors conceal the depth of character that resides within. I liked to think that too!

After unloading my bike, I couldn't help but notice how quiet the place was. I hadn't seen anyone anywhere. I was on my way to the washroom, when I saw an open door, with a meticulously furnished room within, which led to another room beyond that, which led to yet another room, a nursery of sorts. Every room was vacant, so I snuck all around the second floor, marveling at the decor. I pretended I was royalty, or that my rich grandmother lived there. I belonged, I told myself. I got so brazen, that I even wandered downstairs to the main floor and snooped in every corner, opening doors and sliding down halls, until a voice shot me in the back.

"Excuse me! Where do you think you're going?"

Turning around, I again saw the old man of the manor, now glaring at me. "I...I was just admiring your lovely home," I said embarrassed by my sense of entitlement.

"Well, these are my private quarters, and certainly are off limits to you," he said, now rising to his feet to escort me back to where I belonged.

"Oh, I'm sorry. Your house is just so incredibly beautiful. I've never seen anything like this. Where do you find all these antiques?" I asked genuinely intrigued.

Flattered by my remarks, he gushed, "I like to attend antique shows, but mostly, because I'm a renowned collector in the area, all the antique houses hunt these fine pieces down for me."

"Well, I'm sure impressed," I let out, nodding my head.

"Take a good look then," he said opening doors for me, "Be my guest."

"Really?" I blushed. "Thank you!" I proceeded to tour this magnificent building, where every room, including those of his private quarters, was dressed and accessorized beyond belief. He was indeed a collector of beautiful things, unlike myself, who was a collector of ugly, old, broken down things. I also liked to collect experiences, or memories perhaps, but mostly on this trip anyway, a collector of mishaps. I decided that day that I too wanted to collect beauty: beauty not necessarily in things, but beauty in thought, in people, in nature, but mainly in myself.

Soaking up those thoughts in a warm bath later that evening, I unfortunately got careless and before I knew it, was moving too quickly in a bath too full of water. Like a whale maneuvering in a tank much too small, I inadvertently began to splash water onto the floor.

"Hey, hey!" I heard a stick pounding the floor beneath the tub. "Quit sploshing water about! You are soaking up the floor boards and it is now leaking through my light fixtures! What are you doing up there?" He yelled in angry disbelief.

Embarrassed, I replied, "Oh, sorry!" I tried to not move, but I kept sliding down this claw foot tub. I wished I hadn't filled it so full. I again splashed water over the sides and I could again here the old man uttering profanities and grunting out his anger. I decided I better get out of the tub. This was not an easy thing, as any movement created tidal waves of water, which no doubt made its way directly and without delay to where he sat stationed below. I tried to move gingerly, grabbing both sides of the tub and then clutching for dear life as I placed one foot on the tile floor, which had become slippery with warm soapy water. Suddenly, as fate would have it, lifting my other leg up and over the rim of the tub, I lost traction and slipped on the achingly hard tiled floor. It reminded me of a scene straight out of a Jacky Gleason show.

"What are you doing now?" the voice and the stick returned.

"Sorry, I fell!" was my only recourse. Grabbing every towel in sight, I bent on all naked fours to wipe the floor dry. Then, with no clean towels left with which to dry myself off, I wrapped myself in one of the soaked ones and ran to my room. Thankfully, there were no other guests around to spot this sprinting sea serpent, who was now trying to slither into oblivion. There might have been some ghosts though, thoroughly entertained by human mishaps.

Taking one of the extra blankets off the shelf, I ensnarled myself in it, wriggling and cocooning myself in its warmth. I laid myself down on my long bed and placed a call to Jill. I had to confess to her that I wouldn't be able to make it home just yet. Surely she would hear my exhaustion.

I then unwrapped a blueberry muffin that I had picked up earlier and a bag of sour cream and onion potato chips and munched away at nothing.

Afterward, I turned on the telly. It was best to keep quiet now and not cause any more fuss or this old man's going to throw me out. I thought of venturing out for a pint and something more substantial to eat at a nearby pub, but I thought better of it. Instead, I amused myself with memories of Grantham, England, where we veered many moons before, which similarly contained beauty within its plain walls. I recollected its prestige for having won the contest for MOST BORING PLACE IN ENGLAND. I pondered how a contest such as that would ever get started. And who would want to win? Such an honor to boast about for sure! Instead I bored myself with boring television, for which I dread. Such a complete waste of time! At least it is good for boring yourself to sleep. Zzzzzzz.......

JILL DAY 18

I WAITED!

LUKE DAY 18

I floated downstairs to the wafting aroma of bacon and eggs. The old man had conjured up a traditional English breakfast, complete with fried tomato and fried bread. How the English survive such a daily meal, is beyond anyone's arteries to understand. But it was tasty and satisfying to feast on fat. No frolicking with fruitloops here.

Gazing at the old analogue clock on the wall, I knew I had to get going, in order to make Chilliwack. I had also learned to leave time for mishaps, as they seemed to be a daily occurrence with me.

My jacket and jeans were now fully dry, so I happily slipped into them—my riding gear of choice. Bungeeing my tent bag on for the last time on this trip, as I would surely be home by day's end, I happily piled on my saddlebags, tank bag and knapsack. I was going home.

Hitting the highway by ten, I headed northwest toward Chilliwack. I could easily make it by nightfall, I reassured myself. No sooner had I thought this, when I was attacked by my stomach. Huge pangs of pain slit through like a knife, waiting to perforate my intestines. Impossible to ignore, I jerked my bike to the right and pulled over onto the shoulder. What now?

Keeling over in agony, way beyond mere pain, I held my guts close. Walking, rather staggering in circles, I clenched my teeth and wiped my brow. Falling to my knees, the sky began to dance and twirl, clouds changing partners in free style dance. Eating dirt, I groaned and dug my fist further into my abdomen. With face fully planted in pebbles, I tried to breathe through the burning, cutting ache in my gut. My stomach was betraying me big time. Was this just heartburn from eating that English fatty breakfast? I doubt it! I had never experienced anything like this before. I wreathed and squiggled and contorted my body around trying to avoid the anguish, to no avail. I could not escape it. I tried to just accept it, but I couldn't do that either. I tried to understand what could possibly be causing it, but couldn't. This was beyond my understanding.

Staggering to my feet, an old woman's kind face came into focus.

"What seems to be the problem here dearie?" she asked out of concern.

"I'm not sure," I replied through gritted teeth.

"Well, I'se think you'd better make your way to the doctor then," came her kind advice. "Better yet, I'se think ye need a hospital, son."

"No, I don't have travel insurance." I said, leaning against a tree. "I can't afford to get sick here. I'm almost home." I tried to sound coherent through panted breath. "I'll wait till I reach Canada."

"Suit yourself then!" she answered waving me off, under the mistaken belief that my pain was not that bad.

But it was pure agony. I tried to be patient with myself and just allow myself to hurt. That lasted a few minutes. I then tried to ignore it, but avoidance was not working. Luckily I was near a gas station and store, so I dragged myself in and purchased some Tums and a bottle of water. That helped....a wee bit. Finally I just lay on the ground in a fetal position, beside my bike and accepted my pain. It lasted for about an hour and then thankfully, I had regained my body; the stabbing knives subsided.

I limped back onto my bike, not sure if I could trust my health. I decided to just try and get home. My new mantra became: Home or Bust. More like Home or Busted Gut, I egged myself on, trying to distract myself with humor. As I rode, I started to count my mishaps on this particular trip, and there were many. My goal was to outrun, outwit the shadows trying to befall me, a survivor of sorts. But I wasn't being very successful. I knew that my earlier suffering was more than just heartburn, but I was determined to flee unharmed across into Canada. I'd let the doctors there dissect me for what was wrong. It could wait....it had to wait!

As I continued my journey northwest, I grew hungry, tired and sore but I would not allow myself to succumb to those needs, lest the pain re-emerge. Stopping only to drink water, pee and gas up, I pressed on till dusk. Home was so close, I could hear Jill's voice. I could smell little Emily's hair and I could hear Molly screaming at her sister. Yes, home was calling me. I wanted to answer. I was ready to answer.

Holding steady at one hundred and twenty clicks an hour, I passed through towns one after another, in a blur of pavement, buildings and trees. The border was relatively quiet and the line-up was swift.

"Where do you live sir?" came the custom's officer nasal voice.

"Chilliwack, BC." was my happy reply.

"How long have you been out of the country?" she asked peering at me through dark, shifting eyes.

"Oh, about a couple of weeks, I guess," I surmised, not really certain how many exact days had passed.

"Are you bringing anything back with you sir?" she asked so routinely.

"Just myself....that's all I've got!" my weary voice answered.

"Okay then, may I please see your identification?" her words droned on, ad nauseam.

Standing up to retrieve my wallet from my back pocket, I pulled out my driver's licence and then handed her my passport from my tank bag. I knew I did not need to show both, but I wanted to be sure. I wanted to give no excuse for another mishap to occur.

Scanning over my documents, she again stared intently at my eyes, I guess waiting to see if I would look away, indicating I had something to hide, or stare right back at her, indicating innocence. But I was running away from the police and therefore did have something to hide. Concealment must have been smeared across my face because she asked me to pull over.

Dismounting my parked bike, a young stud of a custom officer came over to search my bike. He asked for the key to my kitchen trunk, opened and inspected its contents. He then asked me to open each saddlebag, whereupon he fished through my stinky clothes, apparently looking for something. Unzipping my tank bag he pushed my rain suit aside and pulled out a peach.

"Ah ha!" he said confident that he actually found something of interest.

Shocked, not so much that he found something that I even forgot I had, something as innocent as a piece of fruit, but rather startled to believe that that was the extent of their concern. No mention of the South Dakota police department or the Wyoming police for that matter, only alarm at discovering a forbidden fruit.

"Where did you get this?" he implored, holding up my bruised peach.

"Oh, I don't remember, some little roadside stand a few days ago I think." I answered innocently enough.

"Well you can't bring this into Canada. It is unlawful to carry agricultural products, purchased in the US, into Canada. That is how we transfer insects and the like," he explained, well versed in what to say in such cases.

"Okay fine, you can have it then," I said pushing his hand containing the peach toward his chest.

He instantly jumped back, dropped the peach onto the ground and held both hands in the air. "I cannot accept this."

"Well then where's a garbage can? I'll throw it out." I said now holding this naughty peach myself.

"You can't do that sir. This is Canadian Customs. You are now on Canadian soil and you cannot just throw that in a trash can here," he shot back in all earnestness.

"You've got to be kidding me. Well, then what would you like me to do with this here peach?" I asked trying to refrain from laughing. I wanted to tell him where he could put the stupid peach, but I stopped myself.

"You'll have to drive back to where you purchased it sir and deposit it there." He was serious.

I just stared at him in utter disbelief. "Let me get this straight. You expect me to drive back the way I just came, for two days until I reach the fruit stand where I bought this damn thing?"

"Uh, yes!" he stood his ground.

"I'm not going to do that!!" I started to lose my cool. "How about I just eat the damn thing already?"

"You'll have to do that in the US, not here then. So get back on your bike and head back through American Customs and then park and eat away," he quipped, pointing to the booths across the way.

Examining this bruised, dropped and now dirty, squished up piece of fruit, I suddenly changed my mind. I did not want to consume that, especially risking a flare up of my earlier stomach ache. "You know what, I don't want to eat this thing after all. So what other options do I have?"

"Well you can turn around and get in line for the US Custom's booth, like I told you. But then you need to park, go inside that building there," he said, pointing to the brown brick building in front of all those waiting car lineups. "Tell the officer there that you'd like to deposit this peach in the agricultural bin. He'll show you where it is."

Being a bit of a shit disturber I asked, "What makes you think that I'd actually do that? Maybe I'll get over there and then just throw it in the garbage can outside that building."

"When you throw this peach here in the agricultural bin, the kind officer will verify that you've done this by completing a form. You will then have to bring me this form when you cross back into Canada," he said in a condescending way, now fully irritated with me.

Glancing over his shoulder, I counted approximately twenty cars in line for the US Customs. "You expect me to wait in that long line just to do this?" I asked just to clarify the absurdity of it all.

"Yes, you'll have to wait in line to get up to the parking spot."

In total exasperation, I hopped onto my bike, rode around through Canada and then into the line-up for the US Custom's parking lot. After thirty five minutes of SLOW riding, I slammed my bike into the parking stall and carried my peach into the DECLARATIONS building. Once inside, I stopped myself short, as I encountered another line of patrons waiting in seats along a wall.

"Are you kidding me?" I yelled out, now fully laughing. "I just want to throw this peach away," I said to the female custom's officer behind the desk. Surely logic would prevail.

Instead, she waved me off. "Take a number please."

Imploring the help of all the long suffering patrons, I looked at them and asked, "Is she really kidding me?"

Several of them jumped up, trying to hush me up, "No, no, she's serious. Sit down, sit down here and wait. Trust us, she'll make things hell for you if you don't."

Feeling like I was in Outer Limits or some Gong show, I gazed around, fully expecting the Big Reveal. Instead, I was pulled to a seat, where I sat and waited silently. Finally my number came up and I sauntered to the counter.

"Yes, I'd like to throw away this peach please," I said in a mocking tone.

But this hag of an officer, who must be married to the other one or related anyway, did not bite. The humor was totally lost on her. Though she did not bite at my words; she bit at everything else. Her nails were chewed right down and the skin around her nails had been gnawed to the bone, leaving little stubs. But this day, it wasn't her fingers jammed into her mouth, rather her hair. Locks of it being sucked on and played with by her tongue. Watching her, the whole thing seemed rather cannibalistic, like she ate the crumbs of her existence for a snack, but one would never know when she would turn fully on herself, when a meal was required, and she'd take a chunk out of her arm or something. Or worse yet, take a chunk out of you.

"You'll have to complete this form then," she said shoving the paper into my face. As I filled it out she got on the phone and spoke with the Canadian Custom's officer. I could tell that was who she was talking to, for she turned around, while still on the phone and waved to him over in his booth. He waved back. She then hung up, took my form, held out her hand for my forbidden peach and then rolled her eyes at me. Holding it up in the air, she then pressed her foot down on a lever to open a can—the agricultural bin – where she dropped it, in a rather exaggerated fashion. She wanted to make a point: This is how we do things—properly!!

Shaking my head in disgust, I tried to exit but was called back.

"You'll need to take this form with you to verify that you actually did deposit your agricultural produce into this bin here," she said scribbling something on another form and then handing it to me.

I really wanted to correct her and tell her that actually I did not deposit it in the bin—she did! But then I thought better of it. I didn't want to be her next appetizer. So I left. When I returned back through the Canadian Custom's booth, I handed the form back to the same officer, without saying a word. Not one word. No smirks, no sarcastic reply, nothing!

He smiled my way and then said, "Much better, thank you!" and snatched the required form from my extended hand.

As I began to motor away, I just couldn't help myself though. I yelled out, "Well the guy behind me has a whole trunk full of fruit." I don't know why I said that as I certainly did not know if he had any fruit or not. But the look on that officer's face, relishing the thought of giving some other poor soul a hard time, while licking his lips and wringing his hands, was well worth it. I hope he's truly disappointed!

Thankfully, my ride through Abbotsford and onto Chilliwack was without incident. No police or custom officers haranguing me, no bike problems, no health scares, nothing, no mishaps whatsoever. I rode home in peace.

Good thing, because I had a feeling a storm was already brewing there.

JILL DAY 19

"Daddy's home, Daddy's home!" Molly and Emily chanted in unison as they stumbled upon him sleeping, fully clothed on the couch. It couldn't have been any later than 6:30 in the morning, and I was still fast asleep upstairs. He must have arrived home very late and didn't want to disturb us all, either that or he was just too darn exhausted to change his clothes. And he knew better than to try and climb into bed with me in his bug encrusted attire. Sitting up, he enveloped both girls in a long squeeze.

"My geels, my little geels!" Luke gushed.

Now fully awake, Luke stood up and walked to the door. With two little confused onlookers, he started up his bike and rode it toward the garage. I guess he hadn't wanted to wake me the night before, as the garage door opener had a tendency to shake the floor beneath our bed.

Hearing the putt putt of his motorcycle's engine, I too was awakened as we three ran out to watch Luke swerve along our driveway. The girls were jumping up and down with excitement. I thought he was going to hit them with his bike, as he wobbled to steer between them. I was glad to have my husband and best friend back and I could tell by my girls' squeals that they were very thrilled to have their daddy back as well.

Getting off his motorcycle and sauntering slowly towards me, he looked like a wreck. Probably had terrible sleeps the whole time knowing Luke, who truly loves his own bed. And motorcycle hair is way beyond merely having a bad hair day.

"Is this really you?" I asked, pinching him to make sure he wasn't just a mere shadow of his former self. Embracing him, I shuddered at what might have been. "Nice shoes!" I chuckled, looking down at Luke's feet.

"Don't even ask!" was his only reply, as he held me close.

LUKE DAY 19

I had not decided yet how much truth to reveal to Jill. Some things are better left unsaid. Did she really need to know about the police? After all I was not guilty of anything, it was all just so much misunderstanding. The boots were mine, I did not steal them. Sure, I didn't wait around for the police to complete their investigation, but that does not make me guilty. And okay, I did escape detention, but that was their mess to sort out, I didn't need to be in the middle of it.

It's all like one bad nightmare that I wanted to avoid, yet I knew I had to confront these demons, or they would forever haunt me. So I made a call to the police department in two states to set things straight. It turns out that the doper dude who was trying to sell my boots, confessed to the police. He was the Happy Haven's latest recruit. Thankfully, those charges were dropped. When I apologized for not sticking around, they said it was no problem really, more of a courtesy, their request. As for being missing myself, they were only too happy to close that case. I apparently had been found!!

Got my doctor involved with my nagging abdominal pain. Seems I passed some gall stones along the way: fair, fat and forty apparently seems to do the trick. I'll have to schedule surgery soon, after I try avoiding it for a while.

My Kawi is up on blocks and a new fender and wheel are on order. Gotta look after my baby, since she took such good care of me. Parked next to her, are my new friends: an old pair of brogues dress shoes, with flapping tongues and no laces to confine them. I think I'll keep them!

I thought of giving Mike, Rod and Larry a call. Ah...maybe not! They can call me. I still had to work on that issue in my life: being wrongfully accused. I hadn't taken off on them, they deserted me. But I do now know that it is the accuser's problem, not mine! This I know!

Still feeling guilty however, I took out some special parcels from my saddlebags: presents for my girls. Waddling, sheepishly into the family room I presented my peace offerings. I pulled out three black tee shirts: Motorcycle Baby, Biker Chick and Hot Biker Momma.

Following their mother's lead, all three groaned, "Oh Daddy!"

I felt right at home—at last!

JILL DAY 20

It amazed me how quickly life returned to its normal rhythm. Girls fighting, TV blaring, routines and schedules; life was no longer on hold.

"Do you take milk in your coffee?" Luke asked, as he poured me my morning zip.

"Oh Luke, you never change do you?" I was glad to have my same old, same old back. He always asked that stupid question, to which he surely knew the answer. He did not want to become too familiar with me, he claimed.

"Yes please, with milk," I smiled back as I noticed the large bouquet of "I'm sorry" flowers sitting there waiting to be noticed. Gorgeous yellow, red and white roses, claiming friendship, love and innocence.

Handing me my favorite mug filled with His coffee, not mine, he sighed and dropped down on his usual spot—in the love seat by the window with the ottoman pulled up, piles of newspapers by his side, although there weren't many this morning. He hadn't been back long enough to acquire his usual stockpile yet.

"So, how have things been around here?" Luke asked.

He really was out of touch with my reality. "Well let's just say bizarre might come close to describing life since you left," I answered back with a sideways glance.

"Why do you say that?" he asked so innocently I had to laugh.

"Let's see, you go missing, Mike reports it to the police, everyone searches for you in campgrounds, ditches, etc. to no avail," I continued exasperated. "They conduct aerial searches, hand your case over to homicide who suspects foul play and the whole time you are entirely unaware that something might be considered amiss, that Mike and your riding buddies or your family back home might be a bit worried over your whereabouts." The lecture had begun!

"You amaze me Luke, truly you do," I blurted out, with nary a breath. Reddened face and hands trembling I went on, convinced that the whole truth and nothing but the truth would be revealed, if only I persisted. "I don't understand why you didn't call," I asked, in a rather accusing tone. It was hard not to be sarcastic when the solution could not have been more obvious.

"Don't you think I tried," he shot back defensively.

"I don't know, did you?" I continued to shoot those arrows.

"What? Do you think I did all this on purpose? Come on Jill. You are really over-reaching now," Luke said in his condescending voice that he sometimes liked to use when he's avoiding precision in his defense.

"I don't understand how you can offer me nothing to justify your actions. Don't you feel you owe it to us to produce some explanation?" I said trying to control my anger. The last thing I wanted to do right then was to shut him down. But I didn't like the idea of making him feel emotionally safe to spill his guts either. He owed me.

"First off, I didn't go missing, those guys took off on me," Luke offered. "I did not know you were all worried about me back home. I'm a big boy. I've ridden a lot. I can take care of myself. I know that and I guess I thought you knew that as well. Jill, I just didn't think you'd worry about me. If I did I guess I would have tried some other means to contact you. It's really no big deal. I'm fine aren't I?" Luke reasoned.

I just stared at him blankly.

"I had met so many interesting and wild characters. I decided early on Jill that I might as well make the best of a bad situation. So I let myself have a great time." Luke continued. "I went to Sturgis, then Mt Rushmore and the Black Hills and I saw some vintage drag races. After that I just rode around, met different riders from different parts of the States and Canada.

Sometimes I rode by myself and at other times I rode along with new friends that I met along my travels. I got sick of camping and stayed at some Bed and Breakfasts and met some wonderful hosts and other bikers from all over. Although I did ride into a rut and bent my fender and wheel, and I was keeling over in pain one day as well. Sure, I had more than my share of misadventures too. But it was the trip of a lifetime; I learned so much about myself." Luke tried to give me what I would want to hear.

"After those initial unsuccessful attempts at calling you, I just accepted the fact that I wasn't going to get through, and before long I wasn't thinking of home. I was enjoying the moment.....mostly." Luke explained, frustrated and somewhat disappointed that he had to defend his actions.

Molly was sitting on the floor by the front door listening to Luke's tirade, while she attempted to apply gum to some strange looking shoes, ones she had never seen before: big, black, filthy brogues! I guess she wanted to stop the tongues from flapping!

Realizing that it was all just a stupid phone problem did anger me but I had seen that Luke's heart was still good. In the excitement of his journey, he neglected to be persistent with the phones. Instead of questioning why he wasn't getting through and problem solving his way out of his mess, he just accepted it and went on his merry way. It hadn't donned on him that you can't make a collect call to a prepaid calling card phone—especially if there's not enough time or money left on the card to receive an expensive international call.

Although it did appear he had some misfortune along the way, which I was actually glad for, the balance of justice was still not meted out fairly. Misery does like company after all.

Funny how life plays out sometimes. There was no point in harboring bitterness or resentment towards Luke, the phone companies, Luke's riding buddies or anyone for that matter. It was an innocent mistake that Luke made, yet for me it resulted in diminished innocence. Staring death in the face tends to blacken the soul. I still had more questions than answers.

On a practical note, I definitely knew we needed a cell phone plan with unlimited international calling, and a computer with Wifi at the cabin wouldn't hurt either.

Stretching over to the love seat where Luke was seated, I reached out to hug my husband. I wanted to forgive him. I wasn't sure how long that would actually take to completely forgive, but I was willing to make it work. With tenderness, his full kind lips met mine. I was home. Not only was my Luke alive, I had my life back too. I was weary dealing with my dismantled existence and with the slow and agonized dismantling of my spirit. Love is indeed a gift, whereas death is a thief, perceived or real!

Interrupting our cuddle was Molly standing in the doorway with a fistful of leashes tied to her numerous stuffed animals, and one hand on her hip. "Mommy I want these back in my room tonight. Only you have to keep them all leashed up to my bed or they'll party so loud they'll keep me up all night!" Molly rolled her eyes in exasperation.

Luke and I laughed at our little girl who had such an active imagination. She had reconciled with her stuffy friends, who no longer ushered fear into her night life. It was time for them all to party! It was time for us all! I smiled in my belly.

Just then Emily came running into the room. "I have a gift for you mommy." She handed me a basketful of words printed on small bits of paper. "I made them myself." She had been practicing spelling words, yet the sense of abundance I felt, was truly overwhelming. All these words sitting in my lap in a stock pile….I loved it! Such extravagance, I thought.

The sun was shining warmly that day, casting a beautiful golden light on the street. Watching Luke now playing with his daughters through the living room window, I felt drawn by the shadows outside. Venturing to my garden by the street, I looked up to find myself bathed in this warm glow. It reminded me of Amsterdam many years before where I had marveled at the sun's light. It was that pre-sunset glow all day long. Yet here it was—on my street. I reveled in it. It was so luxurious to be loved by man and nature.

Slowly, I looked up to see my next door neighbor, Joan strutting towards me. Standing up to greet her, she leaned in, arms crossed, ready to confide some street gossip.

Oh goody, I thought. No longer consumed with my pain, I eagerly opened my ears for some juicy neighborhood news.

"Did you hear all the commotion the other night?" Joan whispered, pointing to the McNeer's house that stood next door, on the other side of our house from Joan's.

"No, I didn't hear anything", I said shaking my head, surprised since I live right next door, with our bedroom window facing the McNeer's house.

"Well there were two ambulances that showed up, sirens blaring. Apparently Stan McNeer died of a heart attack Saturday night." Joan explained.

"Did you say Saturday?" I asked slowly in disbelief.

"Yeah, it was in the middle of the night. I guess if it's your turn to go, you might as well go in your sleep," Joan reckoned.

I stood there motionless realizing that I had prayed that Passover prayer also on Saturday night; I prayed for the spirit of death to pass over our house. It had done just that! Poor old Stan, a doctor of philosophy, would not have stood a chance against Dr. Death himself. Reasoning wasn't enough to appease that spirit's appetite. I just hadn't thought about the ramifications of my prayer. Could it all be just coincidence?

"What's wrong?" Joan asked. "You look like you have seen a ghost."

I slowly turned my head towards her and hauntingly replied, "I have!"

THIS YEAR

Death came calling at the Connor household, but no one answered. It was their turn, however, so death persisted. He waited, he stalked, he stole, he injured, he captured, but then he missed. With his appetite, requiring to be fed, to be appeased, his obsession for yet another life caused him to divert his gaze. If only for a moment, his blood thirst distracted him long enough to be tricked. Whereupon seeing the remnants of destruction—blood itself, Death passed over, only to devour the next household in line. Such a shame!!

This same year, Death did come calling. He will be calling soon in a neighborhood near you!

JILL'S EPILOGUE

Soon afterwards, I convinced my husband to move to another neighborhood, away from the street of nightmares. I had read in the papers, the following year that Karen's husband, Neal was in the hospital, hanging on from what appeared to be a fight for his life with pancreatic cancer. I don't know if he made it. They lived on the other side of the McNeer's.

Periodically I find myself driving down that same old familiar road, always in the light of day. I stop; I ponder events past. Then I look down the road towards the future, and I wonder...... What will become?

As for lost souls, I guess they do come home.......

> LITTLE BOO PEEP
> HAS LOST HER SHEEP
> AND DOESN'T KNOW WHERE TO FIND THEM
> LEAVE THEM ALONE AND THEY'LL COME HOME
> WAGGING THEIR TAIL BEHIND THEM

The little shit!!